# Goodbye, Ruby Tuesday

### By Michelle Swisher

"Love is the flower you've got to let grow. A loving heart is the truest wisdom."

~ Charles Dickens ~

1

This book is dedicated to my grandma, Rosalie O'Connor, whose beautiful heart continues to beat inside of mine.

4

# SALT OF THE EARTH
♥♥♥♥♥♥♥♥♥♥♥♥♥♥♥♥♥♥♥♥♥♥♥♥♥♥♥♥♥♥♥♥♥♥♥♥♥♥♥♥

No one can concentrate on the last day of school; it's not just me, but my English teacher, Mr. Tichik, is not giving up on lecturing the love and loss of *Romeo and Juliet* even though he knows no one is listening. True love can end tragically. Got it!

I look around room 209 of Warren G. Harding Middle School and I see a few sleeping heads, some note passing, and a lot of doodling on notebooks. The soft sound of a distant snore, mixed together with the drumming of fingers on desks, competes with the loud tapping of feet against the hardwood floor. I concentrate on a song being quietly hummed two seats behind me, and as I try to identify it, Mr. Tichik indomitably continues on.

For the second time in just two-and-a-half minutes I glance up at the analog clock that hides in the corner, and I'm positive that the minute hand has not budged.

English is my favorite subject and Mr. Tichik, my favorite teacher, but it's clear we have all lost interest in young love and the great William Shakespeare. After all, summer vacation starts in just fifteen minutes.

*You Can't Always Get What You Want* –that's the song being hummed two seats behind me.

I wipe my forehead from sweat and then fan my face with my English folder. The Weatherman's forecast this morning calling for "a blistering 100-degree day in Detroit," has given him his first correct prediction of the year. I grab my hair that is matted to the back of my neck, strategically pile it on top of my head, and

5

then fidget in my seat to try and catch a breeze from any one of the open windows in the classroom. The absence of air conditioning in my antiquated school has been another distraction of mine today. It is *so* hot in this room.

I subconsciously twirl my pen around between my fingers and then tap it loudly on my desk. I look down at my dog-eared paper and whisper to myself, "Concentrate. Think."

With my ink pen, I scribble down my tenth goal for the summer.

"Completed and ready for summer to officially begin," I continue to whisper to myself as I look over my annual list of summer goals one last time.

*Goals for summer vacation -*
*June 15, 1978*
*By Ruby Tuesday Vander*

*1) Learn how to swim.*
I'm not sure if I've avoided learning or have just never had the opportunity, but in that neglect, I'm almost 16 years old and still don't know how to swim. Every year it becomes tougher for me to go to the beach or someone's backyard pool party and make up reasons to stay out of the water. I can't continuously use the lame excuse, "I'm on my period," it just doesn't work for three months straight. But really what is worse than any excuse is if I don't learn to swim, someday I might not be able to save someone I love from drowning. Like maybe my own child. So my first goal of the

6

summer will be to sign up for swim lessons at the community center. This goal will help me learn to be more responsible for myself and to the people I love.

## 2) Earn my black belt in Karate.

When I was younger, my mom would enroll my brother Ian and me, in karate class every fall. We both had just received our brown belts when I got sick with a hellacious stomach flu. That flu led to a double ear infection, double pneumonia, and then pleurisy which all landed me in the hospital. Ian finished the class and earned his black belt, but I couldn't because I was too weak for so long after that I just couldn't finish. Learning self-defense is important to me, and really for every girl to know, because it makes us both physically and mentally strong, which are two important factors that we need every day in our lives.

## 3) Learn how to darn my socks.

I seem to always have holes in my clothes lately, but none irritate me more than the ones in my socks. When my heel, or especially my toes, gets caught in a hole in my sock, I feel instantly annoyed. I twist and pull my sock, turn it, and even gather and tuck it between my toes, but it never feels quite the same as a good darn repair. I have to lean on my Grandma Dotti for anything in my life that relates to sewing. She's always sewing something for someone, and she's the only person I know that knows how to darn. This goal might sound silly, but it will help me re-create something new from something old or lost. To reclaim simple things in life that we take for granted is important to our character, and to re-create the greatest things in life (socks, of course, being one) is essential, and we should all try and do it as often as we can.

4) *Write at least ten songs.*

As long as I can remember I have a solid and deep love for music and my Grandma Dotti. My very first memories of my life were of my grandma beside me as music played in the background. Both music and my grandma have made me feel peace in my heart when I'm sad, given me strength when I've felt weak, made me laugh, made me cry, and made me see life and love in a lot of different ways. And because of that, I've let them both guide me, and they both have become two of my biggest inspirations. So, with that love of music and the love and encouragement from my grandma, I've decided that I want to be a songwriter. Maybe I'll even become the next Bernie Taupin. Becoming a songwriter is a lofty goal, I know, but my grandma has always told me, "If you stay true to your heart and listen to what it is telling you, it will lead you to your destiny with all life's happiness attached." So every day I listen hard to what my heart is saying, and every day I am reminded of how important music and my grandma are to me.

5) *Read volume Q, R, and S of the encyclopedia.*

Philosophy could be my middle name. It's not, it's Tuesday, but because I have such a deep love of reading and learning, one of my goals is to read the entire encyclopedia in full. I have read volume A through P in previous summers, and by doing that, one of the most important things I've learned is, the more you read, the better you do in school and everywhere else in your life. I'm hoping this goal will someday help me become the well-rounded polymath I hope to be.

## 6) Hitchhike to Elisa Howell Park.

I know it sounds like a completely idiotic idea. And it is. But it was last January when my best friend, Bonnie Lenzer, and I decided that we needed to be a little more adventurous with our lives. We were snuggled up on her couch watching the snow fall during the biggest snowstorm to hit Detroit. As we watched all the kids in our neighborhood shag cars that cautiously went down her snow covered street, we realized that we've both become a little too overly cautious about life which made us think we might be missing out on some fun. We both admit that we seem to play everything safe so we won't upset our parents and disrespect the life they've made for us. Bonnie's brother, Clyde, says he falls asleep just looking at the two of us, but Bonnie and I take pride in being more sensible than most other kids we know. Especially Clyde. But we decided that snowy January afternoon that we should do something dangerous this summer to help us both become a little more daring and a little less afraid of life. We thought if we hitchhiked to Eliza Howell Park, which is just a couple of miles down the road that could, possibly, force out some bravery. Putting ourselves in a scary situation, one that is dangerous and could potentially harm us does not sound at all smart, but Bonnie and I think it will give us some needed courage. So we think. The sensible part of our possibly hazardous adventure is that we both plan on taking a weapon with us. However, it's still undetermined what the weapon will be. We have thought of everything from a nail file, to a butter knife, to a can of Mace hidden in our knee socks.

*7) Sign up to be a Reading Buddy at the library.*

Mrs. Mulroney, the head librarian, asks me every summer to join the Reading Buddy program. I love to volunteer and help the people in my neighborhood with their reading abilities, but because I learned Braille a couple of years ago, Mrs. Mulroney asked me if this summer I would teach a blind child in our neighborhood how to read. As emotional as that sounds for me, I know that sometimes you have to set your emotions aside and do things that you never thought you could do to help someone who is struggling. I believe there is a time to cry, in private, but I also think compassion is important in this world of ours, and if you're able, you should always be willing to extend yourself to someone who needs you. A loving and empathic heart is one of the most important things in life.

*8) Paint my bedroom ~YIKES!*

My pink and yellow bedroom screams "little girl," whereas a black and purple bedroom that is heavily draped in shag or velvet hollers "refined teenager." But painting anything has never been my strong point, and years of dreadful art projects at school have proven that. I don't know why, and I won't question her, but my mom just gave me the okay to paint my room this summer.  Over the winter Grandma Dotti and I made plans to make a purple bedspread with black pillows and hook a purple shag rug. And even though I'm a *horrible* painter, painting my room will help me practice patience. Finding patience has sometimes been hard for me, especially with things that I'm not good at, but if I'm determined to do a good job, patience somehow has a way of surfacing.

*9) Sew teddy bears for the pediatric ward at the hospital.*

My friend, Leanne Jones, whose mom works at Newsted Hospital, told me the hospital is always looking for volunteers to sew teddy bears for the children who have extended stays. Now that Grandma Dotti has taught me how to sew, I think this would be a nice thing to do for the kids who are sick and away from their families. And even though I find sewing extremely frustrating, (it sometimes makes me say the worst kind of swear words), I'll try it again, because dedicating yourself to something that makes someone else happy is worth all the temporary frustration.

*10) Get in shape to join the high school track team.*

If I train over the summer and make the tenth-grade track team at school in September, it will be a huge challenge for me. It would involve facing my biggest fear, which is standing in front of a crowd and competing. Life is very comfortable for me, and it's easy to quit something once you feel a second of uneasiness. I'm like everyone else in this world; if your life feels perfect to you, why change it? But finding the strength to face your fears matures you, and helps you grow into a person who's good for this world. Sometimes we're forced to face challenges in life, whether we like it or not, and I have to be brave enough to do that.

A secret goal I have every summer is to make sure I overindulge in lime slushes, which are one of my favorite things in the world. Bonnie's parents own a restaurant around the corner from my house, Chicken-N-Joy, where they sell five flavors of slushes. Her mom, Lauren, and stepfather, Charlie, never mind that I stop in to get one. They are two of the sweetest people I know, and even though I never mention this annual secret goal to anyone - it's always my favorite one of the summer.

I draw my last doodle heart on my paper and read over my list one more time, and hope these summer goals will help me grow more into the person I want to become. Responsible, physically and mentally stronger, creative, true to my heart, smarter, courageous, compassionate, patient, dedicated, and one step closer to fearless.

My summers are usually consumed by just two things: my dedication to my goals and my nightly sleepovers at Bonnie's house. And now that I am graduating from ninth-grade, and moving on to high school, I want to challenge myself to a strong list and have the best summer vacation ever.

I look up at the clock and smile.

**RRRIIINNNGGG!!!!!**

There it is. The dismissal bell has finally rung.

It's now official. No more Harding Middle School for me. I'm sure that I will miss this great school that has attached itself firmly to my heart, given me an incredible education, and facilitated my growth, but I purposely erase the thought and the emotions attached, and gather up my English book and folder.

As I head towards the door, the sound of books slamming shut and chairs rearranging continues to fill the room. Everyone pushes passed me and out the door, eager for the instant sensation of summer freedom.

"Goodbye, Mr. Tichik," I say as I place my English book onto his desk.

"Ruby, I'm going to miss you," he sings to me as he abruptly stops quoting Shakespeare, "but I'll see you later tonight at graduation, kiddo!"

I smile at my great teacher, who has just reminded me that I need to hurry home, iron my favorite dress, and find my favorite black patent leather sandals that are hidden somewhere deep inside my bedroom closet.

I meet up with Bonnie in the hallway, and we exit the first double doors we see.

As Bonnie and I start our walk home, she immediately pulls out a Newport cigarette from the back pocket of her jeans, ignoring Principal McCarthy's rules about smoking on school grounds. She gathers up her long black hair and pushes it to one side. The freckles on her nose seem to glow in the sun, something I know that bothers her, because she constantly complains about them, but I sometimes wish I had a row or two. She pulls out a pack of matches from her tee shirt pocket, slowly lights her cigarette, and then tosses the match into the street.

A lot of people around me smoke. My friends at

school, Bonnie, Mom, Grandma Dotti, my favorite uncle, and because I love them so much, I really wish they wouldn't.  Cigarettes are filled with chemicals, they deplete all the essential vitamins in your body, and they can do extensive damage to your heart, lungs and arteries. You are inhaling nothing positive when you smoke, and I worry about the outcome later in their life. But, I am far from perfect myself. My addiction to black licorice may throw me into a diabetic coma one of these days.

Smoke and swear (ass, being her favorite word) are the two things that most people think define Bonnie Lenzer. And when her tough exterior gets her in trouble sometimes, I notice a lot of people judge her too harshly for that. But I know Bonnie better than most anyone, and I know she has a very beautiful heart.

It was a snowy January day, over six years ago, that I waved to Bonnie and her family as I watched them move into the house directly behind ours. We became friends immediately, and now we are inseparable. Every morning before school we meet at the same spot, on the corner of Outer Drive and Kentfield, and start our three-quarter mile walk to Harding.  After school we meet in the Science hallway. Occasionally we will see Ian and Clyde, on their way home from Redford High School, at Checker drugstore while Bonnie and I shop for snacks. But today we decide to postpone Checkers buy-one-get-one-free Banana Flip sale and hurry home instead. We make our split at my corner-where she goes one way, and I go the other. We are both anxious to get ready for graduation tonight.

We need to shower, shave our legs, double up on deodorant, updo the hair, and get back to the school gym by 6:00.

I share my house on Kentfield with my Grandma Dotti, my mom Lilah (Delilah Daniela McAuley - given name at birth), and Ian. My Grandpa Kip bought our house when my mom was born and lived here until he died in January of 1966. My parents' marriage had just broken up at that time too, and with my mom struggling on her own, Grandma Dotti asked us to move in. Though sadness and heartbreak, it turns out that being together has been perfect for all of our hearts.

Since I've lived here, I have made many an observation. Everyone in our neighborhood works hard and plays hard: true salt of the earth type people. All the houses in our community, for the most part, look the same. They are small three bedroom bungalows with asbestos siding painted yellow, beige or blue. They all have aluminum awnings and a small concrete porch, and if you're lucky, you have a garage. But my house is different. Not because it's the only four bedroom, aluminum sided, black and white house on the block; it's just *extra* beautiful in every way.

I suppose it is because I've emotionally attached myself to everything about my house: the smell of a freshly baked homemade pastry lingering over the kitchen or the shrilling sound of our weather-beaten windows as they open and close when we let the smell of summer fill the house. The vibration of our archaic refrigerator or the soothing hum of our old antique fan on a hot day makes my heart feel incomparable warmth. The tranquil night sounds of an ageing house "settling" and the celebrated sound of the furnace "kicking on" for the first time on a chilly fall morning always fills me with unrivaled comfort.

Every spring Grandma Dotti and I plant zinnia, cosmos and daisy seedlings around the entire exterior of the house. Our flower beds also sporadically line the chain-link fences that separate our house from our neighbors, the Hardy's and the Morgan's. We nurse the peony, lilac and rose bushes in our yard until they are hearty and in full bloom. We plant a small vegetable garden and watch our strawberry, blackberry, elderberry and blueberry bushes flourish deep into the fall. Everything about my house, I love.

I run across my lawn and wave to Grandma Dotti as she fights with the overgrown lilac bush on the side of the house. She is holding a bouquet of fresh cut daisies, but she manages to give me a wave back as she delicately dabs her nose with a tissue. The smell of what could be a possible cheeseburger filters outside onto the front porch and immediately pulls me into the house.

I dump about half of my school folder into the kitchen garbage can and sit down at the table across from Ian, whose mouth is full of a ketchup-saturated cheeseburger. He has considerately set a place for me, which includes a
tall glass of chocolate milk.

My mouth waters as I load up my cheeseburger with every condiment allowed.  I take only a couple of bites, because each one seems to slowly be forming a knot in my stomach. I had the same problem with my meatloaf

16

at lunch, so I know I couldn't possibly be full. After my poor attempt of an early dinner, I jump in the shower to cool off.

The tepid water feels good on my face, and as I try to wash my graduation jitters down the drain, I shake my head free from thoughts of the nervousness and tension and transfer them to the back of my brain.

I'm quick in the shower, always have been, so I shave my legs and underarms, wash and rinse my entire body in record time-just under six minutes. Just as I start to dry off in our wall-to-wall pink bathroom, I hear the sound of my mom's voice coming from the kitchen. I sigh into the oversized roseate towel that gently covers my face. My heart always fills with relief when I know my mom has made it home safely from her job as a bank teller in downtown Detroit.

With my towel wrapped tightly around me, I sprint down the hallway and get a quick glimpse of my mom as I hurry into my bedroom. "Hi, Mom, traffic good today?" I shout.

"Not too bad. Got out of downtown in record time, Ruby, just for you," she shouts back.

She is smothered in orange today. Her tangerine-colored dress falls perfectly to her knees, which compliments her perfectly matched shoes. Her hair is wrapped tightly in an orange plaid headband and her orange earrings complete her always sparkling brown eyes and flawless face. She always looks great and has great style. I know that I get my love of fashion from her, but when I wonder what it is I get from my absent father, everyone always tells me the same thing: "his gorgeous green eyes and gorgeous face."

In my room, hanging from the knob on my closet door, are two of my favorite dresses. I am grateful to Grandma Dotti who neatly pressed both of them for me. I always have trouble deciding on which one to wear, but I decide on the white spaghetti-strap sundress with the big black belt that has a giant black flower attached.

I wiggle my legs into a brand new pair of nylons, sprinkle a little baby powder on my feet, and then slip them into my black patent leather sandals. As I towel dry my hair, one of my favorite songs comes on the radio that sits on the nightstand by my bed. I start to sing along with Sly and the Family Stone as they sing *Hot Fun in the Summertime* and say to myself, "There's *nothing* sweeter than summertime!"

I start to brush out my medium-brown hair and let my natural side part align in place. My bangs slightly cover my eyes, and my lighter streaks of hair fall evenly around my face and down the middle of my back. I'll continue my search for the perfect hairdo as Grandma Dotti and I look through all of our favorite magazines this summer because, as every girl knows, good hair changes everything!

Until then, the heat from this prematurely hot summer forces me to once again wear a ponytail high and tight on the top of my head. My attempt to perfect' a high and tight updo from a picture of Faye Dunaway that I found in my latest issue of *Rona Barrett's Hollywood* magazine falls short, as a few strands of hair fall down on my face.

I pull out a few fresh daisies from the overflowing vase that Grandma Dotti put in my room this afternoon. I pinch the stem and then strategically place them into my slightly messy updo. I'm ready to go, but before I do, I pin my completed list of summer goals on to the corkboard that hangs by my bed. I place it directly on top of the last five years of completed goals. I'm anxious to start on my list, but first, Mom, Grandma Dotti and Ian are waiting for me. Ninth-grade graduation is just an hour away!

# PAINT IT BLACK
♥♥♥♥♥♥♥♥♥♥♥♥♥♥♥♥♥♥♥♥♥♥♥♥♥♥♥♥♥♥♥♥♥♥♥♥♥♥

When we arrive at the school gym, I look for Principal McCarthy right away. When I find him, he is rearranging the rows of black metal folding chairs that the Student Council organized perfectly earlier today. My initial thought was to help him, but as he feverishly adjusts them, and knocks into them at the same time, I wonder if I would just make matters worse.

His crisp ebony suit and signature checkerboard bow tie, make him look his usual handsome and distinguished self - even with his hair a hoary, thick, sweaty mess. When he sees me, he gives me a firm salute.

"Ruby! Does everyone know where to sit?" he asks me.

"We sure do, Principal McCarthy," I reassuringly say back to him, even though the entire class did their fair share of goofing off during rehearsals this week.

He quickly abandons his reorganizing attempt and starts to greet the new crowd of people who are slowly filing into the gym. As I walk with Mom, Grandma Dotti and Ian to their chosen seats at the very top row of the bleachers, I notice Bonnie coming in with her family.

Jodi, Clyde, Bonnie, Rollie, Rosella, Hawley, Toby and Ellery, along with Bonnie's mom and stepdad, make up the Lenzer-Smith clan. One of the many reasons that I love Bonnie and her family so much is that you would never know there are step and half siblings living together. Most families I know who are

20

labeled "broken," refer to each other as half and step which sounds divided and never fully coming together as a family. But in all the years Bonnie has been my friend, I've watched her family blend themselves perfectly together, acting genetically connected with equal amounts of love and respect for each other. Like *all* families should be.

I don't see Bonnie dress up too much, but her multi-colored floral dress and hot pink pumps perfectly match her hot pink lipstick. Her hair is coiled high on top of her head with a little bit of curl around her face: a hairstyle we have practiced *numerous* times on each other and the very patient Rosella, Hawley, and Ellery. We try to exchange a quick wave, but are interrupted by Principal McCarthy's deep voice over the speakers. "All ninth-grade students need to find their designated seats," he anxiously says.

On my way to my seat, I stop to steal some cool air in front of the only industrial-size fan that Harding owns. Today it is sitting in front of the first row of chairs and is oscillating heat evenly to just the first five rows. The blast of heat that hits my face makes a few more strains of hair fall in my face. I pull them back and tuck them around a daisy or two. I'm glad I decided on an updo, but I'm wondering if the daisies have stayed as fresh as when I put them in earlier. I artfully wave my hands to get Bonnie's attention as she takes her seat in the section of "L's." I point to my hair and she gives me a nod and a thumbs up, giving me the validation I need.

I slowly make my way through my crowd of friends and look for Warren Umbaugh, whom I've sat alphabetically behind in every class, my entire time at Harding. When I find him, I give him a quick wave and my biggest smile of the day.

"Hi Ruby, you really look pretty," he says shyly.

I want to hug him goodbye, because I'm a hugger, but I'm not sure if that will make him uncomfortable or not, so I just tell him, "thank you." Warren's normal bushy raven hair is slicked back and tucked behind his ears. His pinstriped charcoal suit fits him snugly as he towers over me by at least 10 inches.

"You look handsome yourself. I love your snazzy suit and tie," I tell him.

"Thanks, Ruby, and thanks for always helping me in class. You're the sweetest person I know. I'm going to miss you next year. I don't know what I'm going to do without you guiding me through World History."

"Oh, I know you'll do great." I say dolefully at Warren's reminder that he is going to a different high school next year. The split between Redford and Cody High Schools will force me to say goodbye to a lot of good friends today, and that was something I was trying not to think about too much. Warren has always been a good buddy to me, and as I try to stop any tears from forming, I listen closely as he starts to whisper a summary of our ten years together.

Some stories made me laugh, some made me cringe, like when Hunter Eaton was chewing on a pen in class and it busted open in his mouth. Black ink shot everywhere, and when he accidentally swallowed some, Sandy Pierson threw up the liverwurst sandwich she had for lunch. Or when John Lyndon jumped from the second floor library window and our entire class was pretty certain that he died from the fall. He didn't; he was just suspended for a week. Or the time Loretta Acacia's drug overdose on the playground got Harding on the local news. It was exciting to everyone I knew, except Loretta Acacia's family of course; they were embarrassed out of the neighborhood.

As Principal McCarthy finishes up his speech on "Building up your Dreams in High School," Warren and I continue to giggle with stories about the school's Salisbury steak, the "glue" that holds it together, and the very questionable gravy. He reminds me too about all the dangerous and illegal things everyone would do to Harding's fire escape, and the time Ben Kendall got caught smoking marijuana backstage in the auditorium. I never believed the rumor that his father murdered him that night (I saw him a few days later at Joe's Department Store), but I do believe that he got kicked out of Harding forever.

Warren and I subtly try to hold back our laughter as he reminds me of the time the two of us were dissecting a pig in science class. As I delicately tried to remove the liver, and keep my breakfast down at the same time, it slipped from my hands and slid at least seven feet across the floor. He also mentions the grand slam I hit in gym class last year, which at the time, I really wasn't aware I had even hit. I saw the ball go into the street, but I just ran the bases and hoped for the best.

And when he reminds me that Ryan Burt, who was legally able to drive to school in eighth-grade, proudly parked his car next to Principal McCarthy every morning, it takes everything I have inside of me not to laugh out loud.

I fan myself with my hands and try to kick off my shoes that are stuck with sweat to the bottom of my feet. It may be today's heat, or maybe it's all the thoughts of my impending high school years that are making me sweat from head to toe.

I've never felt nervous about school. I always look forward to it, but when Ian gave me a tour of Redford over spring break, I had to tell myself not to think of all the changes it will bring with its enormity and unfamiliarity. Right now I have to remind myself to stay determined to have a great summer.

Warren G. Harding Middle School is made up of great teachers, with great students, and situated in a perfect part of Detroit. It's a tough neighbor and a tough school, but because of that I feel proud that it's been such a big part of my life. I've made forever friends, and these last ten years of great education has helped me grow in so many ways. My heart may feel melancholy right now, but it also makes me feel like the luckiest girl alive.

I slide my shoes back on to my feet and think of all the changes directly ahead of me. I remember what Grandma Dotti once told me, "Life is not meant to stay the same and change is expected. Embrace the good changes, and look to your inner strength for the not-so-good changes. Both however, will make you grow."

But I admit to myself as I sit here that I'm a little nervous of change. It can make your life completely incredible or it can make it utterly frightening. And one thing that I have always known about myself is that when life suddenly alters itself, it becomes incredibly hard for me to let go or say goodbye. It's something I'm just not good at.

Most of this graduating class of 87 students has been together since our first day of kindergarten, so as we all begin to line up to receive our graduation certificates, I clap along and say a silent goodbye in my head to each one. Some though, have left a mark on my heart, so as they take their turn, I smile and think to myself...

Christopher Chavez. *Even though I have a distorted view on marriage, I really thought our "wedding" in third grade was nice. You've been a great "husband," no complaints, but I've already decided that you'll be the only one I'll ever have.*

Aaron Franklin. *I hope you realize that your incessant stealing, even if it's just someone's belongings (my lunch, for example), might end you up in jail someday. Oh, I'm sorry about all the times Bonnie called you an ass. She didn't think you needed my lunch more than I did, but I thought otherwise. That's why I let you keep it.*

Marvin Gardner. *Thanks for the ringworm in fourth grade. I appreciated the time off from school.*

Sylvester Johnson. *I'm pretty sure that I'm gonna miss you the most. When you told me that you were moving to Atlanta this summer, it felt like a punch in the stomach. You are the one person who has made me laugh the most in my life. Every day since kindergarten you would tell me the funniest stories and say the silliest things to me that would make me laugh and give me the giggles all day. Even if it got you in trouble with the teachers, you happily made that sacrifice, and I love that about you. I'll forever picture you in my mind wearing my lavender button-up sweater and my pink barrettes in your giant afro. That will always make me smile. We are complete opposites in every way possible, but proudly, that never stopped us from being great friends. We're proof that prejudices are taught in life, and I'm happy to say, not by either of our families. I will always be proud to call you my friend. You're someone I'll never forget and I'm sure that I'm going to need you down the road in life to make me laugh, as life is sure to get tougher.*

I clap a little bit harder and a little bit louder for my wonderful friend Sylvester, and I quickly wipe away a tear that I didn't realize was on my cheek.

Franco King. *My first kiss, and the only ninth grader here shorter than me. I don't believe I ever thanked you for that wonderful kiss. It was so good that I still think about it years later. It was so amazing, that it's making my eyes twitch just thinking about it. I remember it was the beginning of fifth grade and you had made it clear to everyone that you were going to do whatever it took to kiss me. However, your constant stories about the funeral home your parents own made me uncomfortable. Formaldehyde, embalming, rigor mortis, draining of blood, are all things that NEVER pull a girl in. But I somehow pushed them aside (a little) during the kiss. Your soft grab of my waist, your tight hold into your chest, and your long hard kiss. Incredible. After that day you nicknamed me, "Fiancée," which always made me blush. Whatever we had together, I thought it was sweet.*

I let out a heavy sigh.

Bonnie Lenzer. *As we grow up, and our friendships mature, you begin to realize who your true friends really are. They're the ones who remain by your side unconditionally and genuinely care about you: no jealousy with each other, no disharmony, only respect and support. Sincere friendship is rare, I know that already, but I also know that Bonnie and I have that. I am honored that she calls me her very best friend. Truly honored.*

I clap hard and try to whistle for my forever friend, but really, the whistle falls short to a muffled screech and a moderate spray of spit.

Eve Mahoney. *I know that you are not here at graduation today, but this would be your turn in line. You haven't been at Harding for years now, but thanks for being the first best friend I ever had. I remember we became best friends on the very first day of Kindergarten. Then one day near the end of second grade, without any warning, you were gone. Rumors circulated that your dad had killed your mom, but I will never believe that anything bad happen to you. I felt my heart break for the very first time because I missed you instantly. I've thought about you a lot through the years, and I hope that you are happy and are having the best life. Wherever you may be.*

I twist and bite my bottom lip, which is something I've always done when I've felt the urge to cry.

Alecia Payton. *I respect your decision to keep your baby. I would never judge you, nor should anyone. It must have been an emotional, yet critical decision for a fourteen-year-old girl to have to make. I hope you have lots of people who love you, because no one knows when the toughest part of life is going to hit them. When it does, you need a ton of love and support standing behind you, and I hope you have it.*

Roxie Sheppard. *You are a mean and evil bully. I realize that you are the way you are because there is someone being mean, evil, and bullying you in your life. But you should now know how terrible it feels and stop the hate cycle. You will become happier and find your deserved love. This world needs fewer mean people and more nice. Oh, and all your threats to me- they never bothered me. I was never afraid of you.*

Cole Thompson. *Damn you're cute. Your beautiful wavy brown hair and big brown eyes have caused quite a wonderful distraction for all us girls at Harding. I'm pretty sure I can speak for all the girls here today when I say that we all have had a crush on you at one point or another. I know that you haven't a clue as to who I am, but thanks for the one and only valentine you gave me at our first-grade Valentine's Day party. I realized quickly that your mom wrote it out, but that's not what I used to see when I would stare at it when it was stuck to my bedroom mirror for years. It somehow has disappeared in the last year, and I guess that says it all.*

*And to the person who stuck the little valentine pillow in my locker in seventh grade. I never had a chance to thank you because I don't know who you are, but I do love you back!*

I stand close behind Warren as we wait our turn in line. When he walks up to receive his certificate of graduation, he shakes Principal McCarthy's hand, waves to his family, and then exits the stage. My stomach churns with nerves, and my legs start to shake as I, somehow, walk over to our much loved Principal.

"Ruby Tuesday Vander," he calls out.

I extend my hand to him, and he holds it tight. "This one will take awhile," I think he says, as he starts to read off some academic awards that I have won during the school year. The fact that my brain is floating somewhere else besides in my head where it should be, has muffled my hearing.

He winks and affectionately tells me, "You made Harding proud, Ruby. Good luck to you."

"Thank You, Principal McCarthy," I say quietly but appreciatively.

He hands me my certificates, and I quickly leave the stage and take my seat next to Warren. I, again, kick off my sandals as I try to calm the shuddering of my entire body.

I sit up straight in my chair and look around the gym. My heart feels overwhelmed and as I push my sentimental sadness aside, I let the enormous amount of love and pride that I'm feeling fill up inside of me.

I hope I'll be able to hold on to this part of my life forever.

"Eleanor Roosevelt once said, 'You must do the thing you think you cannot do.' I say... go do them. Congratulations class of 1978," Principal McCarthy says as the gym simultaneously erupts with screams and applause.

I think about making my way to the bleachers to look for Mom, Grandma Dotti and Ian, but my legs are still shaking, and I want my tears to dry up, so I stay seated and count up all my awards that I have cradled in my lap. Twelve this year. That might be a record for me.

When I see Bonnie, I start to inch my way over to her, but because my entire class is all leaving in the same direction, all at once, I get stuck in place a few times. From behind I heard someone start to sing - very loudly.

*"Goodbye, Ruby Tuesday!"*

I turn to see my friend, Julius Hampton, trying to do his best Mick Jagger impersonation, but because that's the only part of the song Julius knows, it's not quite capturing the iconic Mick's distinctive excellence. But I love the song and the effort.

Once anyone learns my name, they always try and sing *Ruby Tuesday* to me, but no one ever seems to know *any* other line but that one. *Ever.* I smile at Julius and say, "Goodbye, Mick."

Ruby Tuesday Vander is my name now, but not the name I was given at birth. The story of my name goes like this...

I was born Ruby Rachael Vander on December 18th, 1962 but my mom changed my name when I was four years old. Apparently, my dad had a girlfriend around the time I was born whose name was Rachael. Years later, when my mom found out, she was so angry that she became driven to remove Rachael from name. When The Rolling Stones released their song "Ruby Tuesday," the first time my mom heard it, she instantly fell in love with it. The added bonus that I was born on a Tuesday, and on Keith Richards' birthday, all compiled into my newly legally-changed name. A *very cool* Mom consideration, I think. Some might say it's a scandalous story I suppose, but I just tell everyone that

30

Mick Jagger wrote the song for me.

I know - I wish!

I twist my way through the crowd and finally reach Bonnie, "What an ass! He sounds like an ass trying to sing that song to you," she complains while rolling her eyes back and forth.

"Oh, I think it's kind of sweet. You know, I should marry the first guy that can sing *any other* part of that song to me. It might just change my view on... " I say as we are interrupted by some commotion in the back of the gym. We both turn to see what it is, but because I have always been one of the shortest people in my class, even on my tiptoes, I can't see a thing. Bonnie shrugs her shoulders at the sudden noise; however, slowing moving through the crowd, I get a funny feeling in my stomach. Kind of like the one I had when I was trying to eat my cheeseburger earlier.

I feel a soft pull to my left shoulder from my friend Lucy Sage, "Ruby, I think your grandma just fell down the bleachers." She hesitates. "I think she really hurt herself."

I must have panicked, because I really don't remember if I acknowledged her or not. With Bonnie behind me, we indelicately shove our way through the chaotic crowd.

I climb the bleacher stairs, taking two at a time, and rudely push myself through the small crowd of people gathered around Grandma Dotti.

"Grandma, are you okay?" I ask her as my mom interrupts.

"Mom, did you pass out? I think you did. I'm not sure what you hit your head on. It's left a mark." she says.

"I'm not sure, Lilah. Maybe...," Grandma Dotti says as she turns to me and grabs for my hand. "I'm sorry, Ruby. I surely don't want to ruin your day."

"You could never ruin my...your nose. Your nose is bleeding. "

I don't remember ever seeing my grandma this way. Her skin is marshmallow white, and her already dark brown eyes look darker and ghostly deep-set. But she nods her head and says, "I'm so proud of you, Ruby girl. Really proud. How many awards did you get this year? I lost track at seven."

"Ah... I... don't...remember," I say, as I sit down next to her, placing my certificates on the other side of me.

My awards and graduation, both so imperative to me all year, just don't seem very important to me at all right now as I watch a thin stream of blood trickle from Grandma Dotti's nose. Someone behind me hands me a tissue, and I gently start to dab the blood from her face.

As I sit with her, I notice her hands are shaking as she tries to hold a cup of water. I help guide her hand as I hold the bottom of the cup. I look around at what's left of the dwindling crowd.

"We need to get you home." I tell her, "So you can lie down. You need to lie down."

"Let's get you some fresh air, Mom," my mom says looking distracted.

"Hold on to me, Grandma. I'll help you down the stairs." Ian says, placing his hands on the small of her back.

I gently take hold of her arm. Once she is off the

stairs, we sneak Grandma Dotti out the back door of the gym as discreetly as we can.

My legs instantly stick to the vinyl seat in the back of my mom's black Ford LTD when I try to slide in. I carefully pull them off, adjust my dress, and then lazily slouch down in my seat. Ian and I sit completely still, never saying a word, as Mom starts the two-minute drive home.

I watch Grandma Dotti wipe her nose with a bloody tissue and then stare out the passenger's window.

"It must have been the heat, Lilah," she says quietly to my mom. "I can't take the heat."

And as we all listen to my mom's prediction of, "If it's this hot in June - August will be atrocious!" I daydream out the window.

My mom turns the radio down to just about a dead silence, but I can faintly hear that one of my favorite songs is on. I don't feel like singing out loud, like I usually do, so I softly hum along with the great Temptations as they sing *You're My Everything.* It's interesting to me that certain songs fill your head, or come on the radio at certain times in your life, because coincidentally, my grandma is exactly what The Temptations are singing about - she is my everything.

I've stood proudly beside my grandma all of my life and watched her treat every person she meets with equal amounts of respect, but she also shows great self-respect with those who have been tough on her. Her nonjudgmental and humble heart has taught me a crucial lesson in life. The sweetness, the loyalty, and the generosity of her heart are inserted into everything she does, which makes her love apparent every day in each of our lives. She has a genuine and loving heart which has made her a perfect role model.

I look up at the fading afternoon sun that sits slightly above the trees, and my eyes instantly squint. I have always thought that life has colors to it. Some days are sunny yellow; some days are dark and black. Today I would say that my day started off painted in multi shades of yellow. The anticipation of graduation and summer vacation made it that happy shade. But seeing my grandma in pain has now changed the color of my day. The day now seems dark, like someone decided to instantly paint it black and remove all the happy yellow from it. The colors of your life change when someone you love is hurt.

When we get home, my stomach starts to growl uncontrollably the minute I step in the house. I walk directly into the kitchen, swing open the refrigerator door and see a homemade lemon meringue pie sitting on the shelf next to Mom's paper bag lunch. Grandma Dotti always bakes a pie on a special occasion, but I talk myself out of a snack. I really don't feel like celebrating anything tonight, so I decide to just go to bed hungry. It's been a long day, and a long school year, so I really think I should just try and get a good night's sleep.

Just as I crawl into bed, my mom opens my door and peeks her head in.

"Ruby, I'm going to take Grandma to the doctor's in the morning. Just for a checkup."

"Oh...sure, okay," I say wondering if Mom has a greater concern that she's not sharing.

Her voice seemed uneasy and insecure, so as I lie there on top of my bed a hundred thoughts go through my head. *Why would Mom think Grandma needs a doctor from just a fall? Or maybe it wasn't a simple fall? Did she lose her balance? Did someone push her? Am I overreacting? She was probably overwhelmed from the heat. Or is it something more serious? I'm very protective of her. Why was her nose bleeding? I remember now that she had a nosebleed last week that she ignored. And was her nose bleeding earlier when I came home from school and saw her in the backyard dabbing her nose with a tissue? Now I think it was. Maybe not. Is she bleeding internally? She did hit her head after all. Does she have a concussion? I remember Ian had a concussion once, and we had to keep waking him up throughout the night. What if she passes out in bed, and we don't know? I'd better check on her through the night.*

I toss and turn on top of my cotton drenched bed as I force myself to erase all the negative thoughts from my head. I take a deep breath, close my eyes and talk myself out of anything bad that could possibly happen to her. *No one would trip her. Nothing serious caused her to pass out. The humid air just overpowered her. She's always been fairly healthy, so she couldn't be suddenly ill. Tomorrow I'm sure Dr. Cantrell, will give her a complete physical and assure us that she is in the best health.*

The good thing about this dark evening is it is almost over, and tomorrow when I wake up it will be a new day that I can paint any color I choose.

# I JUST WANT TO SEE HIS FACE
♥♥♥♥♥♥♥♥♥♥♥♥♥♥♥♥♥♥♥♥♥♥♥♥♥♥♥♥♥♥♥♥♥♥♥♥♥♥♥♥♥

There is a perfect spot for me under the sycamore tree in our backyard. The surface roots have formed a perfect circle that my butt fits into perfectly. The crooked branch that unintentionally grows low to the ground makes it the ideal spot to hang my radio. The giant leaves and their clustered blossoms shade the nice soft grass below and adds peace for me as I read, write or listen to music.

The massive trunk on the aged sycamore makes it hard to see me; so on days when I want to hide from the world, that's where I go. Today is one of those days, so I decide this is where I want to spend my first day of summer vacation.

As I sit peacefully concentrating on the sounds of the neighborhood, I hear the rattle of our cyclone fence interjecting into my thoughts. I peek my head around to see Bonnie acrobatically climbing over. It's always been the quickest way to each other's house, even though the blueberry bush sometimes gets in the way. I know she can't see me, so I get up to meet her.

"How's your grandma?" she immediately asks.

"Okay, I think. She felt good this morning. She's at the doctor's with my mom right now; they should be back pretty soon."

"Let me know what the doctor says."

"Thanks, I will."

"You coming over tonight?" she asks me as she blows a couple of smoke rings from her cigarette into the already humid air.

36

"Yeah, later. After dinner."

"K. We're leaving pretty soon to go get my cousin, Wesley. His mom doesn't want him this summer, so he's coming to live with us."

I shoot Bonnie a look of confusion. *What?* I think to myself. *Who doesn't want their kid?*

"Oh well, I guess we're stuck with him... for a little while anyway," she says laughing, and I hope teasing, while making the same acrobatic move back over the fence.

Bonnie usually makes me laugh, but not today. I stand there a little stunned, thinking about how sad that sounded, and also, *how in the world can they fit any more people in her house?*

I quickly take my spot back under the tree and start to think about the anticipation of summer. We wait months for it to arrive as we let fall, winter, and spring graciously pass us by, so we can wallow in it. "Summer vacation" are two beautiful words that bring any school-aged kid instant happiness. There's such freedom in knowing that you have no ties to school for 80 straight days, and you can do whatever you want, whenever you want, because you're not obligated to anything. Your allegiance to school instantly vanishes from your mind and is happily replaced with tranquil mornings, blistering hot days, and sweltering hot nights that you never want to end. Summer. Glorious summer.

My summer days are usually spent with Grandma Dotti and working on my summer goals' list. Mom works full time at the bank, and Ian spends most of his summer with his girlfriend, Patty, working at the bowling alley, or with his friends playing baseball at Stoepel Park.

Grandma Dotti and I have somewhat of a regimented schedule every day. We start each morning by cooking a big breakfast together, then water and weed our never-ending flower beds and pick fresh bouquets for every room in the house. We make weekly runs up to Checker drugstore and always come back with a Hollywood movie magazine that we sit on our front porch swing and discuss in great length. We watch our favorite TV show *The Gong Show,* together, and on rainy days, we watch old black and white movies that sometimes make us laugh, or sometimes make us cry.

We go for a lot of walks together and always hold hands along the way. I'll never feel like I'm too old to hold my grandma's hand. We talk about everything, but mostly about school, books we're reading, baking, The Marx Brothers, Montgomery Clift (and how truly gorgeous he was) and the trip we're saving our money for, to Ireland.

We listen to my radio together too, and even though I'm certain Grandma Dotti likes softer music, she listens intently as I keep her informed on all my favorite bands. Sometimes she surprises me and later quotes me on a particular one. There have been times a certain song will come on the radio, and we sing and dance together while laughing hysterically at ourselves. My favorite thing she does is when she messes up the lyrics, which she swears is not on purpose.

On Saturday mornings we do chores together while

Mom goes grocery shopping and runs errands. For some reason Ian always gets out of helping us, but that's okay because Grandma Dotti and I put on an old Glenn Miller album of Grandpa Kips and dance like flapper girls to *Hallelujah, I Love Her So,* while vacuuming, dusting and polishing the house. It's kind of "our" song.

"Look at me go, Ruby!" She always says to make me laugh.

We cook together every night and wait for Mom and Ian to come home so we can all have a nice dinner together, which is important to Grandma Dotti. I admit - I'm her constant shadow.

After I help with the dishes, I grab my packed-to-the-max tie-dye sling bag, give Grandma Dotti a kiss goodnight, and hop the back fence into Bonnie's yard.

There is usually one house in the neighborhood that is distinctive, and in my neighborhood - it's Bonnie's. With Mom and Grandma Dotti's approval, I spend almost every night in the summer at that distinctive home of hers. It's probably the oldest house in the neighborhood, and it is in constant need of attention. Whether it's a sheet of shingles that has seceded itself from the roof, a scattered glass window in need of replacement, or the endless painting of the flaked weathered exterior, Clyde is relentlessly trying to fix it.

The front screen door is constantly swinging open and shut which echoes through the already noisy house. With Rollie and Hawley playful running and laugh-screaming their way throughout the house, and Rosella and Toby's continuous game of "who can climb the highest, scream the loudest or run the fastest," makes it a house of no rules.

I have never really mentioned to my mom or Grandma Dotti that there are no rules in the house, and riskily, no adult supervision around. Clyde and Bonnie are pretty much in charge most of the time; as Mr. and Mrs. Smith are preoccupied with Chicken-N-Joy. I guess I've never mentioned the lack of supervision because I've never been in any trouble in my life, and I know Mom and Grandma Dotti trust me. They know I will always do the right thing, and I don't want to do anything that would break that line of trust.

My summer nights there are spent sitting on the flat part of the roof outside Bonnie's bedroom window. We talk deep into the night as we listen to music, the crickets in her yard, the frog's croaking in Mr. Morgan's backyard pond, and the sound of her neighbor Mr. Norcross', pulsating sprinkler that seems to be on constantly. Like Grandma Dotti, we're best friends who talk about everything. Music, boys, sex, cliques, pollution, serial killers, famous authors, the President of the United States, *Saturday Night Live, Saturday Night Fever,* what color we would paint the White House if it were up to us (Bonnie-fuchsia, me-lavender), her dislike of fish and mine of wax beans. We talk about the growth of our feet and bras (as far as size, she wins in both areas), moms, dads, Clyde, Ian, and how mean dodgeball is.

We give ourselves homemade facials, paint our toenails, and borrow each other's clothes. We pull all-nighters while eating popcorn, chicken legs and sometimes chocolate cake into the early morning hours. We watch movies, invent recipes, laugh hard, cuss hard, tell clean and dirty jokes, and sometimes cry together all night long.

I lay back into my comforting sycamore tree, close my eyes, and breathe in the silence of the morning. The fluttering of a butterfly around my toes tickles me and then reminds me that whenever a butterfly does that, something good soon happens to me.

Once a butterfly landed on my shoulder and, that night, as I walked up to Checkers, I found a twenty dollar bill on the sidewalk. It brought me relief because then I could spend a little more on Mom's birthday present, and get her something she really wanted.

In early summer of 1973, I was sunbathing in my backyard. I fell asleep, and when a butterfly flew into the mess of hair that was piled on top of my head, it woke me up to discover that I had a severe sunburn. Later that day while I was reading *The Detroit Free Press,* I discovered I had won a drawing contest that I had entered. My "first place" drawing, which won me a $25 worth of free Kool-Aid, was of President Nixon sitting on the roof of The White House (Lavender House, actually) as Pat, Tricia and Julie Nixon barbequed on the thick chartreuse Presidential Mansion lawn.

Last spring a butterfly followed me to school, and later that day my gym teacher, Mr. Jameson, continued his ongoing quest to find Harding's fastest runner. I had been nursing a muscle pull in my left calf for weeks, but it was down to two people: Fran Nelson and me. I turned on everything I had inside of me and beat her by just four feet. I was then declared the fastest

41

runner at Harding Middle School. I humbly accepted my award and then thought of that recurring butterfly and its meaning.

A butterfly was present the morning I hit the grand slam and again the morning I won Student of the Month. I'm not sure if crediting the touch of a butterfly is the cause for my sudden fortunate situations. Maybe it's just a coincidence, but it would be great to start my first day of summer vacation with a touch of fortuity.

The morning is still, which I've always found is the perfect time to write. Mom and Grandma Dotti are at the doctor this morning, and Ian doesn't have to leave for work until noon, so I know he's sleeping in. As I sit there and tap my pen on my blank piece of paper, I'm a little stumped on what to write about so, I turn on my radio and search for a good song. Sometimes I just need one word to get me started, but absolutely nothing is making its way into my brain today.

I'm still under the tree, staring down at a blank piece of paper, when I hear Mom's car pull up in the driveway. I decide to abandon my writing attempt and make a nice healthy lunch for everyone. Tomatoes are a good source of beta-carotene, so a batch of fresh tomato sandwiches should get Grandma Dotti on her way to feeling better.

Bread toasted, mayonnaise thick, tomatoes even thicker, and a sprig of spinach sticks out of all five sandwiches that I pile high on our biggest dinner plate. Tomato sandwiches are everyone's favorite, so it was an easy choice for lunch.

As I try to manipulate my fat tomato sandwich, I notice a small bandage on the inside of Grandma Dotti's left forearm that slightly covers a fresh purple bruise. I know it's just procedure for Dr. Cantrell to take blood from his patients that come into his office as your blood tells a lot about your health, but I do wonder what he's looking for.

Grandma Dotti dressed nice for Dr Cantrell today wearing her favorite pink polyester short set with her bright yellow sneakers that she just recently bought at Thrifty Hardware. Last night's rest has brought the pinkish hue back to her cheeks and also the beautiful smile that she always shares with everyone.

Today's 92 degree temperature doesn't feel as stifling as yesterday, so after lunch Grandma Dotti and I sit on our front porch swing so she can rest and get her strength back. We snuggle up close together and I hold her tender arm in my lap, only leaving her once to make her some fresh squeezed lemonade and a bowl of fresh fruit mixed with yogurt.

As we sit and wait for the ice cream truck to come down our street, Grandma Dotti lights her first cigarette of the day. I watch her mouth pucker and see her wrinkles form around it. Her thick and wavy chocolate brown hair that is slightly peppered with gray has fallen around her face from the humidity. She tucks it into her matching pink headband and then taps her finger on her cigarette. I watch the ashes slowly roll off the porch and then hold her thin hand in my lap again.

I'm not good at guessing people's weight, but I'd guess Grandma Dotti is not much over 100 pounds.

Her petite frame of five-foot-two inches, a gene that I'm certain I get from her, makes her just two inches taller than me. But it's also a delicate gene that, unfortunately, makes us have to fight harder when we're sick.

Although I'm still feeling the shot to the gut from yesterday, after dinner I grab my radio, a couple of magazines, my loaded sling bag, kiss Grandma Dotti goodbye, and I hop over the back fence into Bonnie's yard.

I'm almost at Bonnie's backdoor when I see Toby hopscotch his way up the driveway and then directly over to me. He wraps his arms around my waist, and his thick brown hair tickles my arm as my fingers get caught in his knotted-up hair. I can always count on cute little Toby for a sincere dose of affection. He may only be six, but he's a great hugger.

Bonnie and I are always anxious to official kick off summer, so when she sees me wrapped up with Toby she waves me into the house. She gives up her attempt to help Ellery finish her demolished chicken pot pie and gets up from the table, drops her plate in the sink, grabs hold of my arm, and starts to pull me through the kitchen.

Her forcefulness, in that microsecond of time, forces me to only get a quick glimpse of Ellery's big smile, the heavily-engrossed-in-his-food-Clyde, and... someone else at the table. My peripheral vision notices a boy, who looks around my age, sitting at the end of their long oak table. He must have been hungry, because he never looked up from his dinner plate. But in just that short amount of time, for some reason, I noticed a lot about him.

He had a dark green knitted stocking hat was pulled down tight around his face. Surely, he is uncomfortable with it on in today's heat. The sleeves of his green plaid flannel shirt were rolled up to just above his elbow which exposed some cuts on his arms. His fingers were long as he barbarously held his chicken drenched fork.

"Wesley? Is that your cousin...? Wesley?" I whisper to Bonnie halfway up the stairs.

"Oh, yeah, that's Wes. Hey, I heard Doyle Avery wants to ask you out. Would you go? It would be a nice summer romance for you. He's cute, and he has his own car."

"He is cute, but Eugenia O'Connor dated him last summer, and she said he used to hit her. She even showed me the bruises."

"Really? What an ass."

Bonnie and I continue to slowly maneuver our way up the muddled steps to her bedroom and then out her bedroom window to our normal spot on the roof. I hand Bonnie my latest issue of *Creem* magazine and then immediately turn the chunky dials on my radio to find a good song. I sing along to *My Angel Baby*, my favorite song of the summer, and it instantly relaxes me. Bonnie is used to my singing so she puts up with it nicely.

"How did your grandma's doctor's appointment go?" Bonnie interrupts me, her eyes heavily fixated in the magazine.

"Okay... for a doctor's appointment. They're always bad. Needles, syringes, loss of blood, you know." That's

45

all I say. I don't feel like talking about it too much, so I just daydream into their backyard through two more songs.

My dreary thoughts instantly vanish, when I hear Clyde climb out the window behind me and onto the roof. He adoringly taps me on the head and says, "What's up Ruby?" I'm so distracted by Wesley cautiously following him that I couldn't form an answer.

"Wes, this is Ruby," Clyde says as his thick dish water blonde hair falls in his face covering his dark eyes. "She lives behind us, over there," he says pointing to the sycamore tree in our backyard.

I watch Wesley sit down next to Bonnie, and when he glances up from under his hat, I think I saw a shy crooked smile. I want to get a better look at him, but he continues to keep his head down and didn't say a word.

He's got a cute hat anyway.

"Wes doesn't have to go to summer school this year, so his mom let him come live with us," Bonnie announce to everyone. "Lucky us. First time no summer school?" she laughs.

"No," he says at a whisper.

And that would be the only word he spoke all night.

I don't laugh along with Clyde and Bonnie and their relentless teasing of him, and even though he keeps his head down, I smile at him anyway.

I know it's rude to stare, but I couldn't force myself to look away from him. I couldn't help it. I was drawn to him. I just want to see his face. My heart kept repeating the same thing. *I want to see your face. Look up at me.*

I watched Wesley play with his broken shoe and then readjust his hat by sliding it lower on his face. He pulled his knees to his chest and rested his elbows on top of his dirty ripped jeans and then stared out into Clyde and Bonnie's grassless, bicycle sprawled back yard in complete bewilderment.

He reaches his slender arms over to Bonnie's pack of cigarettes and then slaps two out into the palm of his hand. He tucks them in the front pocket of his flannel shirt and then fixed his crooked collar on his shirt. I watch him continuously pulled on a loose piece of shingle and then readjusted his hat again, which this time, helped reveal some of his face.

I close my magazine in my lap. I couldn't look away from him.

I'm not sure if it was the weight of my stare, but after a couple of minutes he finally looked over and smiled at me.

His pale green eyes are soft and sleepy, and even though they are the most beautiful eyes I've ever seen, they look filled with sadness and worry. The horizontal scar that is hidden in his left eyebrow is long and thin. The vertical scar below his right eye, that is short but wide, makes him look tough but alluring at the same time. His concaved dimples make me want to fall right into them and the dissimilar structure of his nose tells me that it might have been broken at one time - yet it's still perfect. The smoothness and fullness of his lips are exactly what defines kissable lips and the light stubble around those kissable lips tells me that he may have just started to shave.

My recurring stomach fullness is back, and this time, it's accompanied by labored breathing.

He's gorgeous.

The clock on Bonnie's tall oak dresser glows 2:20 in red digital numbers when we all crawl back into the house from the roof, but Bonnie and I still decide on pickles and celery for our very late night snack.

As we start to make our way downstairs to the kitchen, I glance into Bonnie's oldest sister Jodi's bedroom. I don't know why I did; Jodi had moved out three months ago to go live with her boyfriend, so I know she wasn't in there. But I know that's where Wesley went twenty-two minutes ago. I slightly tilt my head to look for him, but the room is too dark.

With just one look at his face I already feel that my heart is snagged. Cute but tough looking boys always get a girl's heart in trouble - oldest news in the world. And as I skip down the stairs and into Bonnie's kitchen, I hum and sing quietly to myself, The Ronettes' *Be my Baby*.

What made me think of *that* song?

I rub my temples and remove the song from my head and remember the butterfly that visited me earlier today. Another coincidence? Or has the touch of that butterfly brought me something to smile about again?

"Ruby, you okay? You're quiet tonight." Bonnie says, instantly opening the panty door as we enter the kitchen.

"Yeah, I'm okay," I tell her as I grab a brand new jar of hamburger dills from the second shelf of the refrigerator.

Bonnie grabs a bag of celery and a sleeve of saltine crackers and rips open the crimped end to test their freshness. "Your grandmas' gonna be alright," she says muffled with a mouthful of crackers.

"Yeah, she will. But I think I'm gonna stay home with her the next couple of nights."

"Yeah, sure. I understand... Wow, fresh crackers. That's rare in *this* house. Good find tonight though."

*Rest my heart. Situate my brain - is really what I need to do*, I tell myself.

On our way back upstairs I want to get one more look at Wesley - maybe offer him a pickle or some celery, but I quickly changed my mind when, through the darkness, I see a dark green hat resting on a stack of pillows. I wonder why he sleeps with his hat on? It just makes him all the more mysterious to me.

# HAPPY
♥♥♥♥♥♥♥♥♥♥♥♥♥♥♥♥♥♥♥♥♥♥♥♥♥♥♥♥♥♥♥♥♥♥♥♥♥♥♥♥

I dream funny sometimes; multi-colored snowflakes falling from the sky; Clint Eastwood as our mailman; bowling with Lynyrd Skynyrd; taking a bath in a tub full of chocolate jimmies; all the toes on my feet the same size as my big toe; and my very favorite dream – I'm an Indy Racecar Driver - Winner! But last night I dreamed of the immune system, and it reminded me that Grandma Dotti might just have a vitamin deficiency. If I boost her immune system by adding the right foods to her diet, she might get on the road to feeling better.

This morning Grandma Dotti sits at the kitchen table in her faded pink nightgown watching me as I slice a grapefruit in half for the two of us to share. She cautiously sips her morning coffee as her face grimaces from the warmth that tickles her face. I delicately chop up a red pepper that I picked early this morning from the garden, and then pour a half dozen vigorously beaten eggs into a sizzling fry pan. I sprinkle the peppers on top and then watch them disappear into a giant, flat, pale egg. I fold it over to form the perfect red speckled omelet.

All week I dedicate myself to cooking the healthiest foods in the food chain. With Grandma Dotti always by my side, I make a big batch of mashed sweet potatoes for an important dose of vitamin A; oatmeal mixed with bananas for vitamin B, stuffed green peppers and strawberry bread for a heavy amount of C, salmon for the healthy D, blueberry and blackberry salad for necessary E, and mashed cauliflower for the forgotten K.

I challenge myself to multiple variations of the tomato sandwich and make broccoli, cabbage, bean, and barley soup for various quantities of multivitamins. I even add "multivitamins with iron" to the grocery list.

So after Monday night's dinner of baked garlic chicken, mashed rutabaga, and a spinach salad, I'm tired. Bonnie called me earlier and asked me if I wanted to go to the show with her tonight, and I told her I would because I think I need the mental break. Also, it would be a good time to jump back into our summer sleepovers.

My brain feels resituated, but my heart? We'll see.

"Spending the night at Bonnie's tonight, Mom," I tell her as I align the last dinner plate neatly in the cupboard. She sits down at the kitchen table with her glasses, a pen and a handful of bills.

"Grandma has a doctor's appointment tomorrow. Her results are in from all her blood work. You wanna come along for the ride?"

"Sure, I'll be home early."

"Ooo...k," she says squinting at the water bill.

I grab my sling bag, kiss Grandma Dotti goodbye, and I'm off to Bonnie's.

When I hop the fence into Bonnie's yard, I stop after only two steps. My feet hesitate to go any further when I see Wesley with Clyde and Bonnie waiting for me in their driveway. Bonnie never mentioned Wesley coming with us, and it's fine that he does, but I feel the urge to want to run back home and change my clothes... or fix my hair... or change *something* about myself. I forgot to pay attention to myself today, and as I quickly readjust my bangs and barrette, I realize that my hair is messy and dirty. I've been so busy around the house the last couple of days that I completely forgot about taking care of myself.

I swing my flip flops around in my fingers, quietly hum *Gimme Shelter* to myself,
nonchalantly walk over to the three of them, and we immediately start our walk to the show.

The line outside of the Brightmoor Theater bends and twists down Fenkell Avenue. As we take our place at the end of the line, the evening sun hits my shoulders and sends warm tingles down my spine. Or maybe it's Wesley who is standing approximately seven feet and four inches behind me.

When we start to inch our way inside, I inhale the intoxicating scent of freshly buttered popcorn. There's almost nothing better in life. And even though my stomach is doing some unrecognizable things right now, I'm planning on ordering the biggest bucket my money can get me.

I stare at the movie poster for *The Buddy Holly Story* that hangs in the lobby. I've been anxious for its release since Grandma Dotti and I read about it last summer. I squint my eyes - the standard look of reading hard - and check the movie times on the wall around the poster. Because my stomach feels very nervous, I'm purposely trying to look anywhere but where Wesley is. Which is now approximately five feet eight inches behind me. I know Bonnie loved the movie *Jaws* so much that I know she's anxious to see the sequel, so I've already decided to see *The Buddy Holly Story* later with Grandma Dotti.

"*Jaws 2*, okay, Ru?" Bonnie says excitedly and already knowing my answer.

"Sure. Perfect."

The scent of popcorn leaves my nose for a quick second and is temporarily replaced by a fresh, woodsy-piney-type scent. I recognize it from the few times that Ian has worn cologne. It *could* be Clyde that smells that good, but I think it's Wesley, because he is now standing roughly three feet ten inches behind me.

Bonnie's smile instantly disappears and her face freezes. "Oh, shit!..." She stops suddenly.

"What?"

"Margo Turner. Walking this way."

Margo Turner is a girl Bonnie and I know from school. Every school has a girl like Margo Turner, and Harding's certainly not exempt. She's a confident girl. Extremely confident. Okay, *overconfident.*

But from what I've seen, in the years I've known her, her confidence seems to only escalate around guys. As her posture suddenly gets better, her enormous boobs come into play. She plays with the charm on her necklace more, she wears the wrong size shirt, and of course, the occasional bending over to pull up her perfectly aligned knee socks. She always tops the conversation off by throwing her head back with fake laughter over things that are not really funny. She touchy too.  Always putting her hands somewhere on a guy.

The reality of Margo Turner has nothing to do with the insecurity of us girls because that part-time

53

confidence is nothing but lack of respect or consideration for other girls' feelings. We can all like whomever we want, but they're always going to end up with her because she sets out to become their "First." And she gets them. Every. Single. Time.

Ian - two summers ago. Clyde – three summers ago.

Last year when she individually dated a family of brothers - twins Jose and Manuel, and then their older brother, Javier, who all had girlfriends, the genuineness of her relationships with males was questioned. Bonnie jokes and says that Margo is waiting for their younger brother, Roberto, to get of legal age so she can snag him and make a clean sweep. She gets every guy she's ever wanted, but hurts a lot of girls along the way.

I suppose she's looking for love like everyone else - after all - love tends to make you happy, but I don't think she realizes that she's going about it the wrong way.

Bonnie has taken her games a lot harder. She doesn't always call her the nicest names, and that started when Bonnie had a crush this year - a HUGE crush - on a guy named Nick Hartley. He sat next to Bonnie in art class, and Bonnie was sure things were going her way. She said he flirted with her a couple times, brought her art supplies to the table for her, and even made her a cassette of Bonnie's favorite band, the Faces. Then, out of the blue, we (we - meaning the entire school) heard that Nick and Margo were "going out." Bonnie was devastated. I had never seen her cry so hard. I helped her through it best I could, and then I noticed my feelings about Margo had become the same as all the other girls at Harding. And that was something I wanted to avoid.

Now, here she is....

"Hi, ladies," she says, as I try and pull out some finesse from deep inside of me.

"Hi Margo," I say quietly. Bonnie says nothing.

"What movie you ladies here to see?"

"Ja..." I try to say as she turns directly to Clyde, ignoring my answer.

"Hi, Clyde. Who's your friend?" Margo says.

Wow. She just used me to get to... Oh no! Wesley! Wesley's next!

"This is my cousin, Wesley. Wes, this is Margo." Clyde says smugly.

Clyde *had* to introduce her to him. Anything other than that is bad manners. But as I watch her take two giant steps towards Wesley, landing close to his feet, I can't help but notice that
Wesley takes three giant steps back. I counted.

Hmmm. Maybe he's not interested in her. Or maybe he has a girlfriend to whom he is faithful. That's nice. But I sure don't want to continue to fall for someone who has a girlfriend. That's double the pain.

I feel my dinner completely roll over in my stomach. I've never felt jealous over anyone in my life, but I think right now I may be living the definition of the word.

I'm suddenly sick in my stomach, a mental uneasiness, a nervous feeling running through my entire body and a serious twinge to my heart that makes me want to projectile vomit on the back of Margo's head. That all has to be jealousy. I don't swear too much, but this was definitely a "Holy Shit" moment! This. Feels. Horrible!

Margo continues to talk to both of them, but is clearly directing her questions to Wesley, as Clyde tries to answer all her silly questions.

"Oh, I'm seeing *Jaws 2*, too," Margo laughs at herself. "But it looks scary; maybe I can come sit with you? I won't be able to eat all of this popcorn. You wanna share with me? Oops, I forgot to get a pop. Who wants to stand in line with me? Maybe we can stay after and try to sneak into that Buddy Holly movie?"

"Gasp!" I'm not sure if anyone hears me because I am too concerned with the lack of oxygen flowing through my lungs. *Keep breathing, Ruby; because I'm sure she did not just say what I thought she said.*

"You okay?" Bonnie says to me from a few feet away.

I don't answer her, because my voice box wasn't working either, so I just mouth, "Yup."

*Why do I care that Clyde introduced them? Why do I care that she's all over him?*

*Why do I care if she and Wesley sneak into the movie that I've been waiting to go see?*

So, the answer to my question this morning is no. My heart has not rested.

Bonnie and I always lean on each other for support in these situations, but because I haven't mentioned my growing interest in her cousin, I wipe my face with my hands thinking, that's somehow going to change how my face must look.

"I don't think she's with Nick anymore," I quietly say, looking at the popcorn line like I'm looking for someone or something in particular.

"They can both kiss my ass," she snaps back.

I need to get back to my original distance of approximately seven feet four inches from Wesley because I'm not going to stand here and watch Margo hypnotize him, or whatever she does. "Let's get our popcorn," I say, as I grab hold of Bonnie's hand.

Every time I go to the show with Clyde he wants to sit in the same seat. It's the seat where he had his first make-out session. It's important to him, I guess. He claims it took him as far as third base, so sitting there brings back good memories. So as the four of us make our way up the dark stairs (I notice immediately that we somehow lost Margo), to the very last row - five seats off the aisle on the right-hand side of the theater - I purposely saunter behind and nibble on my popcorn.

I sit the opposite end from Wesley, with Clyde and Bonnie between us. I force myself not to look his way, but I find myself peeking at him through my bangs. He sits low in his seat and has pulled his green stocking hat down so low that it almost covered his eyes. He stares expressionless at the movie, but smiles at all the scary parts. His legs bounce uncontrollably and never once stayed still. When he whispers a couple things to Clyde throughout the movie, our eyes meet which makes *me* instantly stare expressionless at the movie.

I stare down at my half full popcorn bucket, as the movie credits roll. I don't want the rest of it, but there are still a lot of glorious hunks of butter-saturated popcorn too beautiful to waste. Wesley didn't get any popcorn or pop, so this might be a perfect opportunity

57

to share with him. It would be a nice way to talk to him (for the first time) and have him talk to me (for the first time), but girls like me don't like to make the first move. Or really, the second or third. So when we start to exit the theater, and with Wesley directly behind me, I look around for a garbage can.

I don't know why I changed my mind, but I do.

"Would you like the rest of my popcorn...before I throw it away, or..." I nervously ask him.

"Ah... sure. Thank you," he says with the sweetest smile. A gorgeous smile. Dimples are cute on anyone, but on his face - beautiful. So beautiful that I feel myself stop breathing.

It would be the first time of many that summer that he would take my breath away.

"Let's stop at Checkers," Clyde says scuffling his feet along the sidewalk as we start our walk home. "I need some Fritos, beef jerky and maybe a Yoo-hoo."

I'm not hungry at all, but I think I might get some black licorice for my midnight snack tonight. My nervous stomach has intensified in these last few hours and black licorice always seems to cure whatever ails me. From a broken ankle to menstrual cramps - it always works.

"Hey, Ruby Tuesday!" I hear someone shout from across Checker's parking lot.

I turn to look and see my friend, relay partner from gym class, and Harding's biggest flirt, Jimmy Drew, waving me over to him.

"Hey, Ruby baby, how's your summer going so far?"

58

he says leaning against a car that I know isn't his.

"Pretty good. How 'bout yours?" I say walking over to him, and at the same time, watching Clyde, Wesley and Bonnie disappear through the double glass doors of Checkers.

"Hey, I wanted to ask you something. I'm having a Fourth-of-July party. My parents are going up north that whole week. Why don't you come by? We'll be there all night partying. Come by anytime. You can bring Bonnie, I guess."

"Yeah, sure, we'll come," I say trying not to be rude, although I'm distracted.

He was talking about roasting some corn on a barbeque, some "amazing weed," his sister's new baby (never caught the gender), and his breakup with his "dumbass girlfriend," but all I really was concerned with was Wesley.

"So you gonna join the track team at Redford?" he asks me.

"Ah... Yeah. I think. Gotta get in shape first though."

"It doesn't look like you need to get in shape. You look perfect to me."

"I haven't run in awhile...ahhhh...since...March? Thanks though," I stutter while turning around to see Bonnie violently swing open the double glass door of Checkers holding a small paper bag. Clyde and Wesley are immediately behind her.

"You look good, girl." Jimmy says ignoring Bonnie's glacial stare, strictly intending for him.

"Well, I gotta go," I say nervously. "I'll see you at your party... and at track practice... and I'll... uh, see you later."

Walking with my head down, knowing that I was just extremely rude, I catch up to Bonnie. I've never acted this way before in my life. What's wrong with me?

"What did that ass want?" Bonnie asks, pulling a package of peanut M&M's from her bag.

"He invited us to his Fourth-of-July party."

"You gonna go?"

"Yeah, I told him we would. It'll be fun."

The sun has gone down, but I still feel sticky from the afternoon heat. Suddenly I realize that I put very little makeup on today. I can't remember if I combed my dirty hair at all today, but I do remember that the barrette in my hair is the one I've had since Kindergarten. My favorite jean shorts have a ripped back pocket from one of my failed strategic leaps over the back fence, and the plain, old, white T-shirt that I wiggled into this morning has an old mustard stain on it. Today's lackadaisical attitude is all based on Bonnie and I being best friends. We don't care about that kind of stuff with each other - It's part of our unconditional loyal friendship.

But when it comes to a guy that makes your heart quiver - it's everything. So considering today's haphazard attempt, I casually stroll behind Wesley to hide from him.

But I can barely take my eyes off of him. I watch everything he does.

He pulls hard on miscellaneous tree branches that hang over the sidewalk. He rattles every fence that he passes and kicks everything in his way out into the street. He walks along the edge of the curb, and as I watch him gracefully balance himself, I smile at his unwavering concentration. But when he went into his shirt pocket and pulled out a package of black licorice twists and turned to me, I immediately look down and felt my whole body freeze with fear.

"I bought you something," I think he said.

He was talking at normal volume, but I could barely hear him. It was like someone hit me in the side of my head or my double ear infection was back. I think I thanked him, not sure, and if I did, I'm certain I stumbled through it.

I'm pretty sure that June night, sitting on Bonnie's roof, was the night I fell in love with Wesley. Love is something everyone anticipates in life. Some people even plan their life around it, but really, you never know when it's going to hit you. You just hope you're ready when it does.

This summer, it caught me by complete surprise.

It's never one thing that makes you fall. It's a hundred little things.

His soft, but deep voice, his laugh and his smile. The way his shoes and pants don't fit him properly, but look so cute on him. His very kissable lips and his habit of lightly rubbing the stubble around his mouth. His quiet and shy demeanor and the confidence in his walk. His broad shoulders, his chiseled face, his perfectly toned skin and all the little cuts on his hands that tell me he works hard at something. His striking green eyes, his long eyelashes, his nose, his height, his weight. The fact that he constantly readjusts his hat, the way he slowly licked the salt off the corner of his salted popcorn lips and the way he gnawed on the black licorice twists we shared. The way he looks up, the way he looks down. The way he listens, the way he talks. The fact that he sits next to just me and smiles at just me. I love all that about him.

In my head I start to sing one of my favorite songs, *Baby, I Love Your Way*. Peter Frampton sings it better than me, and I wouldn't dare sing it out loud, but I want to tell Wesley all the things that Pete is singing about. But, because I have spoken very few words to him, and I don't believe any were a complete sentence, I remove the song from my head.

Tonight Wesley seems happier. He nonchalantly laughs off Clyde's constant teasing with a cute shrug and continuously takes Bonnie's pack of cigarettes from her. His long fingers pull two cigarettes from the pack; one he dangles from those kissable lips of his, and the other he tucks into his shirt pocket.

"Hey, Wes, how does Holden like the Army?" Bonnie asks him, sliding her cigarette pack back onto her lap.

"Not sure. I haven't heard from him in awhile," he says slowly lighting a cigarette. "Holden's my brother," he says turning to me.

*Brother. He has a brother. He has a brother who's at least 18 because he's joined the Army. What else?*

"Has Grandma Alice heard from him?" Bonnie continues.

"Don't think so," he says, looking around for a safe place to throw his match.

*I know that Bonnie's maternal grandma's name is Alice, so that would mean his mom and Bonnie's mom are sisters. What else?*

62

"How's Aunt Kristine?" she nonchalantly asks.

"My mom," he directs to me again. "I don't know."

*His mom's name is Kristine. What else?*

"So, you ever gonna take that stupid hat off?" Bonnie asks snickering.

"Probably not," he says, inhaling his cigarette hard and exhaling slowly.

All those comments directed to me and I had nothing to say back. I just sat next to him, watching him talk, and realizing that I've fallen hard for him.

"Hey, did you pass anything in school this year?" Clyde says with a smirk.

"Ah. Not... positive," he reluctantly says. "Algebra kicked my ass, I do know that. I don't get it, don't like it, and I'll never need it." His voice grows quieter.

"You should ask Ruby to help you with it. She's good at all that stuff," Bonnie says as my head shoots up. "She's in some kind of tutoring club at school... Problem solvers club.... I don't know what it is. What is it, Ru? She can probably help you read a little better too. You read like shit, Wes."

Wesley glares at her, but doesn't say anything.

I'd *love* to help him, but she just caught me by surprise and I'm not really positive he would want me to. Some people just don't want help from other people, and I get the feeling that he might be one of them.

"Ah, it's...I'm in the," I say, stumbling to remember the club I've been in for five years. "Quandary Club. We try to help other kids with any problems they may have or solve some school issues. And, well, sometimes, when you struggle at something, it might

63

depend on the teacher. A good one or bad one can make all the difference," I say to him as I stare directly into a loose shingle. "I will help you. If you ever wanted... help. I...," I stop suddenly. What am I saying!? I know better than to make myself available to a gorgeous guy like him. It would be setting myself up for heartbreak.

I would help anyone I know, especially my best friend's cousin, but what if it looks different to him? What if he has a girlfriend and it looks like I'm trying to step in between them? I would *never* do that, but he doesn't know that about me. But what if he doesn't have a girlfriend? It would be a nice way to get to know him a little. Helping him doesn't mean he'll necessarily fall like I'm hoping he will.

All this commotion that's going on in my head sounds nothing like the commotion that usually swirls around in there.

But when Wesley turned and smiled at me - and my palpitating heart - and said, "Yeah, sure. Thanks. That's really sweet of you," the commotion instantly subsided and I felt completely different inside.

"Let's go find a snack, Ru," Bonnie interrupts, as she simultaneously stands up and flips her cigarette off the roof, "Whatcha feel like tonight?"

I didn't answer her. My entire body felt suddenly anxious and suddenly amazing at the same time. I wanted to stay out on the roof all night with Wesley, but that would have made my feelings for him obvious I'm sure, so I follow Bonnie back through the window, down the stairs, and into the kitchen.

"Hey, you're right about Doyle Avery. I heard the

same thing about him hitting Eugenia O'Connor," she says leering into the kitchen pantry. "But you know who would be a better summer romance?"

"No, who?" My eyes focus on a basket of glowing orange cheese in the refrigerator.

"Wes."

"What?" I say, inadvertently slamming the refrigerator door shut.

"Wesley. He likes you, Ru."

"What?"

"Well, his exact words were, 'I really like her. She's beautiful, and she is so sweet.'"

"What?"

"Ruby, who in their right mind would agree to do *anything* related to school over summer vacation? Especially fuckin' algebra? And do you realize that you just said the word 'what' three times in a row, Mrs. Charles Dickens Hemingway Poe?"

We both laugh at my bad grammar, but my laugh is a different laugh then I normally have. It is the happiest laugh and the happiest smile I've ever felt.

Bonnie and I shared a bag of Cinnamon Red Hots, some glowing orange cheese, and some maybe not-so-fresh eggnog. I remember, when I fell asleep I had a *great* dream. A dream that made me feel so - Happy!

# HAND OF FATE

When I arrived home the next morning, I jumped right into the shower. I danced my way through it, and I sang the entire time. I cut my legs shaving. Twice at the ankle and once at the knee. But that didn't matter. I felt so happy inside. I know only a few things about love, but enough to know that I've fallen head first into it!

Grandma Dotti's doctor's appointment is at 12:30. As we wait for Mom to come home from her shortened day at the bank, I make blackberry muffins, papaya milkshakes, and tuna fish sandwiches for lunch for an overload of nutrients. I set a plate out for Mom so she can eat before we leave. I arrange it nicely with a cloth napkin, a Hershey kiss and a fresh cut daisy to the left of her plate.

But when Mom comes home, she seems anxious to leave. She walks directly over to me as I pour and equally divide the papaya milkshakes into four tall glasses. She drops her purse onto the kitchen table and ignores it as her keys fall out and hit the floor.

"I want you and Ian to stay home this time while I take Grandma to the doctor's." she says somberly.

"Why?

My mom doesn't answer me and ignores her decorative lunch plate. Both make me a little concerned.

She turns to Grandma Dotti and abruptly asks, "Ready, Mom?"

As they quickly leave, and Ian disappears into his

bedroom, I stand alone in the kitchen staring down at my disregarded lunch.

I eat by myself and then wash and dry the dishes. I rearrange all the glasses in the cupboard by size and shape into perfect rows, then refill the napkin holder with alternating blue and yellow napkins. I wipe down all the fingerprints left on the refrigerator door, cupboard door and oven door.

I look back and forth at the kitchen clock and watched the time go by as I play four games of Clock Solitaire. I lost all four, so I gathered up all the throw rugs in the house and hung them on the clothesline. I beat them clean with a black Louisville Slugger and then put them all back in their exact spots. I threw a load of whites in the wash, vacuumed the house - upstairs and down, hung the whites out to dry, and then sat on the front porch swing by myself and looked out at the marbled gray sky while hoping for rain.

I sit in the driveway and watched the ants eat the nectar from the Peony buds and then trim all of our five unruly Evergreens with hedge clippers.

Nervous energy, I guess.

I think a lot about dinner and then had an instant craving for spaghetti. Grandma Dotti and I canned a lot of tomatoes last fall, so the canning room is filled with jars of our homegrown preserved tomatoes. I decide to make a big batch of spaghetti sauce along with some sautéed green beans. I'll add extra garlic to our homemade sauce to fight any germs and continue to build her immune system.

I check the kitchen inventory and notice that my mom forgot a couple of things at the grocery store on her last trip. No spaghetti noodles (only elbow), not one can of green beans (only corn), and no Parmesan cheese (only cheddar). I know Mom has a new guy in her life, so I think she might be a little preoccupied these days. I haven't met him yet - he's that new - so all I know about him is that his name is Reed Something-that-is-long-and-hard-to-pronounce.

I grab a few five dollar bills from the emergency money jar that's hidden behind the cookie jar and shout up to Ian to come with me.

We're not long at Shrubland Market. I go directly to the canned goods and grab two cans of green beans, one box of spaghetti noodles and the smallest jar of Parmesan cheese I could find. Ian follows behind me and fills his arms with things we don't need. Doritos, Bosco, Chow Mein noodles, Fruit Float, cocoa butter tanning lotion, and Pop Rocks.

"What?' is all he says to me as I stare into his arms and try to calculate his frivolous spending in my head.

We hurry and check out and start our two block walk home. I look up to the summer sky and watch the platinum gray clouds swell and move in directly above us. Ian and I start to hurry to get home, almost running with our bags. Grandma Dotti is always right when predicting that the rain will cool things down. It always does, and we are in desperate need of a cool down. And even though I love a good summer rain and a booming thunderstorm, I hate when my paper grocery bags get wet.

My mom's car is back in the driveway, so Ian and I run up the porch, and as a few raindrops hit our shoulders and sprinkle our bags, we let the screen door slam behind us.

My mom has always been strong. She's got great confidence and there's nothing shy about her, but right at this exact moment she seems different. I don't know that I've ever seen her like this before. Her forehead is creased with worry. Her pretty brown eyes look tense and tired and when she starts to speak, it's at a vibrated whisper, "We got some pretty tough news today. Why don't you two dry off and come sit down."

Ian and I do neither. "What's wrong?" Ian says.

I look at Grandma Dotti who is sitting at the kitchen table. Her head is down and her hands are folded tight in her lap as she stares down at her bright yellow sneakers. Her normal smile that greets me every day, no matter where I've been, has not surfaced. Something's wrong.

My mom is distracting as she fumbles around in the kitchen cupboards like she's looking for something important. It actually looks like she's trying to hide her face. My heart is racing and my stomach instantly twists and forms into a heavy knot. I place my hand on my heart and slightly rub it as Ian and I continue to stand there nervously waiting for what she seems hesitant to tell us.

"Mom, you're starting to scare me," Ian says.

A sick and uneasy feeling instantly filled my stomach. I feel lightheaded so I take a deep breath, but really, nothing could prepare me for what I was about to hear.

"Grandma has... Leukemia. Acute Leukemia," Mom says finally shutting the cupboard door as her trembling voice goes flat.

Ian and I just stand there. Shocked. Frozen.

I don't remember what I did with the bag I was holding, but I remember the front door slammed shut from the wind, and the rain instantly changed direction and started to spit on the front windowsill. My mom hurried over to shut the window as Ian and I stood motionless. Everything suddenly seemed distant to me at that moment.

I know that Leukemia is cancer of the blood, and even though it might sound horrible to all of us at this exact moment, people do survive it. Grandma Dotti will, because I could never imagine anything else. Cancer medicines are powerful and are sure to be tough on her, and that will break my heart to see, but she'll be okay because I know that I'll do whatever it takes to get her better.

I grab the multi-colored green crocheted blanket that drapes over the chair in the living room, and wrap it around Grandma Dotti shoulders. I kneel down next to her and kiss her flushed cheek. Her hands shake as she tucks a tissue into the sleeve of her sweater. I hold her hands, squeeze them tight, and then give her the biggest hug of my life.

"Everything's gonna be okay," I tell her as I swallow back tears. "Whatever it takes Grandma, we'll get you better. I'll make sure of it. The doctors will help you. They'll give you some medicine. Chemotherapy, I'm sure, and I know you'll be fine. I've read a lot about cancer and they have a lot of success with it."

I stare at her sad brown eyes and watch them fill with tears. Mom's, Ian's and Grandma Dotti's tears always, under every circumstance, instantly make me cry. It's like our Lacrimal glands are somehow all wired together.

I bit my lip to hold back the flood of tears that have instantly formed in my eyes. I feel at this exact moment that I should be strong for her, but really how can I? How do you try to hide devastation that hits deep down into your soul?

"Love my Ruby girl," she says, as she puts her hand to my face and softly rubs her finger on my cheek.

"I remember what you said to me once," I say, as my voice begins to shake. "You said, 'When life gets tough, Ruby... you get tougher.' Well, prepare to see me at my toughest, Grandma."

I hug her tight and she hugs me back tighter. We love each other the most in the world. That's what makes this so incredibly hard.

It was a quiet night at the dinner table. No one spoke except for the occasional, "Could you please pass the whatever." I made the spaghetti and green bean dinner along with a spinach salad for a healthy dose of vitamin K, but I played with most of mine. I kept twisting my spaghetti with my fork and then watched it unfold back off. I lined up my green beans to form my initials, and over-tossed my salad once I realized I put too much dressing on it. Nothing tasted good. Maybe it's because I completely lost my appetite somewhere around four o'clock this afternoon.

After dinner I sat alone at the kitchen table as the stove light fiercely glowed behind me. I memorize all three prescription bottles that the doctor gave Grandma Dotti. I double checked their dosage and then read every inch of the pamphlets that Mom had stuck underneath them.

"Living with Cancer," one pamphlet shouted. "Beating Cancer," hollered another. "Cancer and the One You Love," rang loud in my head.

So did the word- acute.

I turned the pamphlets over and placed them neatly under the flour canister on the kitchen counter. I didn't want to look at that iniquitous word cancer.

To see it written in print, lying in my very own house, pertaining to someone I love, made my heart sink. I refuse to believe that she has been given an inauspicious hand of fate with just one blood test, or an expiration on her life.

I line the gold plastic prescription bottles in a row on the kitchen counter and then make a promise to myself that I will follow every one of the doctor's orders.

It rained heavily that night. I lay in my bed and listened to the rolling thunder softly shake my house. I watched from my window, the cold, hard rain beat down on the sidewalk and then roll into the street instantly flooding it. I counted the splashes of rain left on my windowsill from that cold, hard rain, and still refused to close the window when it hit a hundred. I looked up into the night sky as its ugly shade of black hovered over my house disinclined to move east. I felt like I was stuck in a scene from an old black and white movie that Grandma Dotti and I watch together. A scene filled with desolation and gloom, where perfect love goes disastrously wrong. One that makes you cry heavy.

I'm thinking about precious time wasting away. Why didn't the doctors send Grandma Dotti directly to the hospital to start an immediately blood transfusion? We need to strictly focus on getting her blood healthy again by eliminating her cancerous blood cells, but at the same time getting her healthy ones to multiply. And what about her bone marrow? We need to concentrate on that first and foremost. We can't wait - she might get sicker. All they gave her were a few prescriptions and an appointment for next week. That's doing next to nothing.

Lying there, staring into the pitch dark night, I make an important, but not difficult decision. My summer of 1978 will not be devoted to a list of goals or my nightly sleepovers at Bonnie's. My summer will be devoted to getting my grandma better. Bonnie will understand. She knows I can't be anywhere else except beside my grandma.

As I listen to the thunder drown out my radio, I rearrange my pillows and snuggle my head deep inside them. I close my eyes and try to fall asleep, but my eyes fill with tears. I rub them, and then squeeze them tight. The tears roll past my ear and tickle my neck as I wipe them with my palm. Tears that don't go away for me usually tell me that I'm scared of something. And I am. I'm scared that someone I love is sick and might get sicker.

I flip through the dials to search for a good song, but find there is nothing but commercials. It's a gloomy night all the way around. My heart beats loudly as my tears now run uncontrollably.

And to think I woke up so happy.

I wake up early the next four days and immediately throw myself into the strict routine that I've set for myself. I start my mornings off by making everyone blueberry pancakes, scrambled eggs, and fresh squeezed orange juice. I always remember to have Mom and Ian's homemade granola bars wrapped up and waiting for them on the kitchen counter when they leave for work.

I let Grandma Dotti rest as much as possible, but I've noticed that when it's quiet in the house, I find myself starting to cry. I sometimes have to go outside with my radio and sing to myself.

On Thursday I edged the sidewalk, mowed the front and back grass, raked up all the clippings, then swept the sidewalk and porch. Grandma Dotti helped me water and weeded the flowerbeds and then we picked fresh bouquets for every room in the house.

I picked fresh vegetables from the garden for lunch and Grandma Dotti and I snacked on all the berries from the fruit bushes all day. I made our mailman, Mr. Russell, fresh blackberry muffins when he promptly delivered our mail at 1:10, and then I stripped everyone's bed sheets and hung them on the clothesline to dry like Grandma Dotti does from March to October.  I promise myself to never slow down - Because that's when it starts to hurt.

I made Grandma Dotti laugh when I wheeled the heavy galvanized garbage cans out to the curb early Friday morning and vigorously hosed them down when I mistakenly took a small Daisy pedal for a maggot.

74

"You're such a corker," she says, laughing. Grandma Dotti uses that word when someone does something funny or unique.

I also gave the garbage can lids a fresh coat of neon orange paint. I hem a couple of Ian's pants, sew all new buttons on one of Mom's sweaters and then iron five of her favorite dresses so they would be ready for her when she goes to work on Monday.

But most importantly, all week I've made sure that Grandma Dotti is taking her medicines, staying hydrated with Strawberry Lemonade, and watching *The Gong Show* and *The Four O'clock Movie* with me.

After our beef roast dinner, Mom pulls me aside.

"Ruby, you've been great with Grandma this week and with helping around the house. Thank you." she says appreciatively, "But it's important that you spend time with your friends too. You worked hard at school this year, and it's your summer vacation. You haven't been to Bonnie's in awhile, and I think you need a break. Why don't you spend some time with her tomorrow? You always have fun together and she makes you laugh, and that's important right now. Ian has the day off tomorrow so he'll be here all day with Grandma."

"Being with my friends is not my priority, Mom. It's getting Grandma better."

"I know that, but I want you to try and squeeze in a little fun this summer. You need a distraction, Ruby."

"I... guess..." I reluctantly say, as I think about Wesley who has been constantly on my mind. I would love to see him again. I found him floating around in my heart this afternoon while I was changing the light bulb in the laundry room. I think seeing him might make me smile a little, which is something I noticed today that I haven't done in awhile. Plus, I did tell him that I would tutor him in algebra, and I've never reneged on my promise to anyone and I certainly wouldn't start with him.

I stand in front of the mirror attached to my dresser in my bedroom and comb out my tangled hair. My eyes are slightly bloodshot from my shower cry as I pull my favorite summer pajamas over my head, and let it slowly glide down me. The soft worn cotton feels good as it lands at the middle of my thigh.

I stand on my tiptoes and pull down my old algebra book from the top shelf of my closet and stretch my feet until my toes ache. My algebra book falls down, along with a couple of sweaters which seem to soften the blow, as they all land on my head. I place the book on the floor by my bedroom door and then belly flop onto my bed.

Every night of my life I've slept with my radio on. I had a radio in my crib, and I now have one along the side of my bed. Sometime
s while the music plays in the background of my sleep, I dream that I'm on stage in front of a half-million people at Woodstock singing and playing guitar. Or sometimes my dream takes turns imitating Ann and Nancy Wilson of Heart, because I'm still not sure which one I admire more. I turn my big chunky radio dials to find a good song and then place it back on my nightstand.

I remember as I fell asleep, I was singing along to

The Stylistics, *You Make Me Feel Brand New.* That's a song that always makes me think of Grandma Dotti and all that she has done for us. It makes me think of the sacrifice, and the love, and the truly wonderful life she has given Mom, Ian and me from my earliest memories.

But somewhere in my dream, Wesley appeared. My tired brain wonders if we could ever have something that defines love. No one ever knows how love will grow, but I will say, I am so incredibly lucky and grateful for all the love I do have in my life. So grateful.

# TORN AND FRAYED
♥♥♥♥♥♥♥♥♥♥♥♥♥♥♥♥♥♥♥♥♥♥♥♥♥♥♥♥♥♥♥♥♥♥♥

I wake up to the soft hum of Mr. Hardy's lawnmower and glance over to my alarm clock which foggily looks to read 10:31. I never sleep this late unless I'm sick.

I hear the faint whispers of Ian and Grandma Dotti watering the flowers outside my bedroom window as I inhale the smell of fresh cut grass passing through my room. I roll to the edge of my bed, turn off my radio, and nonchalantly stroll to the bathroom.

I spend forty-two minutes in the shower and I am so sleepy that I wash my hair with Ian's dandruff shampoo by mistake. I exfoliate my entire body to where it is beat red and shave my legs twice and, surprisingly, didn't cut myself.

I nonchalantly stroll back to my bedroom.

The heat in the house seems suffocating already today, as I sit on the edge of my bed with a fuzzy pink bath towel wrapped tightly around me and my wet hair dripping on my back and shoulders. I stare into my closet, not able to decide what to wear. I guess I should just go casual with Wesley; I don't want to look like I'm trying too hard with him – which - of course I am.

Whenever I have a hard time deciding what to wear, for some reason I start at my feet and go up.

Because I go barefoot 99% of the time in the summer, I usually don't give my feet much thought, but this time I give them a quick coat of soft pink nail polish. I lotion up my nicked-free legs, slide on my undies and button up my new white shorts. I slip into a white silk bra, and shake out a black and white polka dot T-shirt from the bottom drawer in my dresser and glide it over my head. I think I need to give my hair a lot of attention to recover from the last time Wesley saw me, so I blow-dry it for extra volume, gather it all up into a high ponytail, and curl it.

I dab a tiny bit of Chantilly Lace on four of my pulse points - my neck, my wrist, behind my knees and the tops of my feet. I don't want to overdo it; I just want to get rid of the dandruff shampoo scent that's stuck in my hair.

Ian and Grandma Dotti come in from outside just as I saunter into the kitchen from my bedroom. Ian starts to look in the breadbox, and Grandma Dotti sits down directly in front of the fan, pulls her dark bangs away from her face and starts to situate the fan to the ideal height.

I know the heat sometimes bothers her, but she looks sad to me today. Her eyes are lost into the spinning blades and her smile is short and tight. I always have a hard time leaving her, but today feels worse.

I know Ian will do a good job while I'm gone - he's plenty capable - but my heart feels heavy and lost. I can't let a cute boy, like Wesley, get in the way of what's important in my life even if I've fallen hard for him. So I remind myself of that, and then hope Ian will ask me to stay and help him.

"Ian, make sure you put some strawberries in Grandma's lemonade today. I'll go get some from the garden," I tell him as I take a kitchen knife and start to whittle a point into my yellow Ticonderoga pencil.

"I'll get 'em," Ian says, staring captivatingly into the refrigerator.

"Oh, and it's Paul Newman week on the *Four O'clock Movie*," I say as I watch my pencil shavings fall into the garbage.

"Got it."

"Don't forget Grandma's medicine schedule. It's on the counter, and I left notes," I say, as my fingers fumble through the kitchen junk drawer looking for one of my many purple pens.

"Yup, saw it."

"Oh, and I washed all the vegetables from the garden with soap and water, but make sure you wash them again because Mr. Morgan sprays chemicals on his garden and he sometimes, accidently I hope, sprays our garden. Anyway, they'll need a second rinse. I guess I can stay and do that."

"Ruby, I got it," he says, exasperated.

"And...," I pause. "Of course you do. I'm sorry."

"Go. Just go. You and Bonnie go get in trouble for once," Ian frustratingly says.

"If you need me, I'm just...,"

"Goooo!"

I find a purple pen and then stick five sheets of lined paper into the pages of my algebra book. I kiss Grandma Dotti goodbye and then take baby steps out the back door.

Halfway through the back yard I stop. I look down into the grass, turn and look back at my house, and then down at the grass again. I should go back.

But then I look up and see Wesley at our back fence. I smile and just about race walk over to him.

"Hi, Ruby," he says so quietly that I barely heard him. "How are you?"

"Pardon? Oh, hi, I'm fine." I say,

"Bonnie told me about your grandma. And I'm sorry. I haven't seen you in a while and... I was just coming by to see if you're okay. I hope you don't mind that I was coming over?"

"Oh, no, of course not. I was actually on my way to see you. I thought it might be a good day for an algebra lesson. Thanks for asking about me."

With just those few words from him, the exact spot in my chest where my heart sits felt warmer than the rest of me. The genuine concern I felt from him hit me in that tender spot in my heart. "I have a lot of work to do to get her better," I shyly tell him. "But I'm gonna do it. I'm determined."

He smiled the most beautiful smile at me and even though I'm feeling sad today, his smile made me want to reach over the fence and hug him. I didn't, instead I decided to change the subject. "So, do you think you're ready for an algebra lesson?" I say, suddenly shaking from nerves.

"Sure," he says hopping over the fence with one leap.

He follows me to my favorite spot under my sycamore tree, and we sit down on the fresh cut grass. He sits his usual position; knees pulled up, elbows resting on top. And I sit my usual position; legs crossed Indian style.

He distracts me for a minute because he smells really good. I take a deep breath and then readjust my ponytail. I hand him a pencil and a piece of paper, and then open my algebra book.

"The letters you see in algebra, usually an X or a Y, are called variables. They are a placeholder of an unknown number."

When I glance over to him, his eyes are slightly squinted and his very kissable lips are completely still. I wonder, as a lot of girls he knows must wonder, actually how soft are those very kissable lips? I need to stop wondering and concentrate on algebra.

"You start here and cancel this number out." I point. "What you do to one side of the equal sign, you have to do to the other side - like this.' I scribble. "If not, the equation will be wrong."

He drums his pencil on his knee and when he wrote something I stopped talking and watched the arc of his left hand slowly glide along the paper. It's never mattered much to me that I'm right-handed until this very minute. My newly discovered benefit of being right-handed is that it forces me to snuggle up close to him.

"You add or subtract your way through it," I slowly show him, as my sudden brain fog takes over my entire head.

I inhale a quivering breath.

After a couple of hours, we take a break. I run into the house to get us both some strawberry lemonade, check on Grandma Dotti, and run back out. I did it in record time - just under three minutes.

I hand him his tall glass, wiggle back into my spot next to him, readjust my ponytail again, and watch him take a long, soothing gulp from his glass.

Strawberries softly touching his lips. Ice cubes sliding behind. His Adam's apple slowly pulsating up and down.

I must look ridiculous.

"Thanks. Strawberries in the lemonade. I've never had that. Your own recipe?" He asks, arching his eyebrows while waiting for my answer.

"Um... don't remember where I got... the idea from." But I can't remember what my middle name is at the moment either. God, his eyes are beautiful. "Ah... how about a little bit of homework?" my intoxicated brain says, thinking that giving him homework would force him to see me again.

"Homework already? On my first day?" He smiles.

"It won't be too bad. Nothing scary. Remember, just add or subtract your way through them."

He's so distracting that I have to force myself to heavily concentrate as I write five algebra problems on a piece of paper. "Make sure you put your name in the top right-hand corner or I'll automatically have to flunk you," I tease.

*And anything else you might want to add - last name, middle name, birthday, hearts with Wesley and Ruby floating around in it, you know - anything like that.*

"Yes, Miss Vander."

I look back at my house and have a sudden urge to be with my grandma. I honestly don't want to leave Wesley, but I feel I need to get back to her. I get up and dust off my now dirty shorts.

"I have to go now; I have to help make dinner," I say.

"Sure. Oh... Um... Ruby?" He says slowly getting up. "I was wondering if I could take you someplace... later. To thank you... for helping me," he stammers, looking at, I think, my kneecaps.

"Oh, yeah, okay. That's really nice of you, but you don't have to," I say now looking at his kneecaps.

"I'd like to. Can we meet back here at around seven? Is that alright?"

"Sure, I'll be here at seven."

Our eyes meet, and we share five second of silence.

"Thanks," he says softly then quickly turns and disappears over my back fence as I run back into my house.

*Wait. How does he know my last name?*

I butter four pieces of bread and arrange then, butter side down into a greased fry pan. I open up eight slices of American cheese and four slices of Swiss and distribute then evenly across the bread. I butter four more pieces of bread and place them butter side up on the slightly melted cheese. Ian places a saucepan down on the burner next to mine and spoons out the contents of a can of tomato soup. As he stirs in some milk to his bubbling pot, I flip over my grilled cheese sandwiches with a spatula and watch them sizzle.

I eat most of my sandwich and watch Mom and Ian eat all of theirs. Ian has even made himself a second sandwich, but Grandma Dotti eats very little. She smiles at me all through dinner, but seems preoccupied, and as I watch her stir her soup, I actually felt my heart ache.

I pick at the rest of my sandwich. I silently blame my heart ache on my diminished taste buds so I throw the rest of my sandwich into the garbage can.

It's uncomfortably hot in my room as I sit on the floor by my closet with a small assortment of clothes surrounding me. I fan myself with my favorite issue of *Rona Barrett's Gossip* magazine.

"One, two, three, four, five, six," I count out to myself. "I just changed six times." I pick the blue jean skirt up off the floor and pull a light pink T-shirt from my drawer. I'm thinking we'll probably go somewhere I'll need shoes, so slide into my pink sandals with the big daisy on top. They will match the five little daisies that I have stuck in my newly combed updo.

It's almost 7:00, so I give Grandma Dotti a hug and a soft kiss goodbye, and I head out the back door.

I run so fast through the back yard that I hear the screen door slam behind me just as I reached the sycamore tree. When I see that Wesley is already there, leaning against the tree, I can't help but instantly smile at him. His brown, button-up shirt looks freshly pressed, and the short sleeves fall just above his elbow, slightly gripping what looks to be very toned muscles. His clean blue jeans and broken shoes continue to go perfectly with his green knitted hat.

As we start our walk towards Fenkell Avenue I have no idea on how to start a conversation with him. Weather? Sports? Movies? It all seems silly. The only thing bouncing around in my head is the reoccurring Ronettes' singing *Be my Baby*.

It wasn't until four blocks into our walk when we finally spoke.

"Thanks for helping me today," he says shyly. "You're so patient. I need that. Thank you."

"Sure, anytime you need help, just ask," my voice is deliberately casual.

"You look nice."

"Thanks, I think you look really nice too." And he really did, I didn't say that because he said it, even though I'm sure that's what it sounds like.

He pulls on the front of his shirt and says, "Clyde's shirt."

Funny, I don't remember Clyde ever wearing that shirt. I've known him for six years, and I've never seen that shirt before. "It's nice. You look nice in it." I'm repeating myself; I'm saying the same words over. What is happening to me?

"I like the flowers in your hair. Are those from your yard?" he asks, looking down at his shoes.

"Yeah, they are. Thank you," I tell him softly. All of the sudden I find myself being exceptionally shy with him. Whenever I wear flowers in my hair, someone always seems to have something negative to say about them. It's my first time someone has complimented my hippieness.

"You look very pretty," he says, looking up at me.

I smile back at him and secretly take pride in my nonconforming ways. He just said I looked pretty. Wow. Your heart feels at its very best when the guy who owns it compliments you. There's not much in life that feels better than that.

Continued nervous stomach, increased shyness, heart palpitations, shortness of breath, paying entirely too much attention to what I wear - this is absolutely love that I'm feeling and I would love it if he were to

86

fall in love with me.

Going to the movies in the summer is one of my favorite things to do with Grandma Dotti so as I breathe in the smell of fresh summer air and fresh buttered popcorn at the same time, my mind immediately thinks of her.

She should be here with me.

Wesley turns to me, pulls out his wallet and says, "I wanted to show you how much I appreciate your help today, so I wanted to take you to the movie you wanted to see the other night." He points to the Buddy Holly movie poster that's hangs in the theater showcase.

My eyes slightly squint and my mouth dropped open slightly - which is never a smart look.

Can I throw my arms around him, hug him tight, and kiss him right here in front of all these people? Of course I can't.

"Yeah... I... would love to see it," I say. Sweet of him, but I feel bad about taking any of his money. "But, you don't have to pay for my ticket."

"Oh, I want to," he says, turning to the ticket window.

As I stand next to him, I try to sneak a nonchalant glance at the two pictures in his wallet. I don't get a good look, but one is of a lady that looks a little like Bonnie's mom. Must be his mom, Kristine. The other picture is of an older lady and someone who looks like an older version of him. Must be his Grandma Alice and his brother, Holden.

If he carries a picture of his mom, his grandma, and his brother in his wallet, I swear I'll start making out with him in the middle of this theater.

So I better not ask.

"Thank you. Can I buy you some popcorn or a snack or something?" I ask him instead.

"No, I'll get that. Can we share? I like extra butter on mine too."

I didn't answer him, because it occurred to me right then, that the night the four of us went to the show; he was paying attention to me, not Margo Turner.

Girls love that. Girls love when a guy pays attention to them and all the things that are important to us. I did want to see *The Buddy Holly Story,* and I do love extra butter on my popcorn. I have to say, I'm a little surprised that he would choose me over Margo, but maybe he knows, like all smart people know, that girls like Margo are trouble and have some very disrespectful traits.

Bonnie said he liked me, but how much?

In the theater, as we watch the movie, we sit next to each other, but we both lean the opposite way in our chair. I nonchalantly stick my hand in the popcorn bucket, purposely, after each time he takes his enormous handful.

As I sit nervously in my seat, I think to myself - It's hard for me to understand how my heart can feel all the elation of falling in love, and at the exact same time, it also can feel the anguish of the deepest pain in life. It doesn't seem like your heart could survive such heart confusion.

So, maybe, there are two sides to your heart. One side recognizes love in every form and all of life's beautiful things grow there. And the other side, a magnet to all the darkness and ugliness in life. The only way your heart can survive that confusion is to spin around and try to make love the dominant side. My heart must be continually spinning, because the last couple of weeks it's been hurting so badly.

I also wonder if Wesley thinks of this as a date. I've never really been on a date before, but I suspect he has. It's not that I never wanted to go on a date or never wanted a boyfriend, I have, but it's just not happened for me. I've had a few situations in my life where they seemed like dates, but they really weren't. I don't think so anyways.

The first one that comes to mind was Ian's friend Dexter Robinson. He was friends with Ian and one day he called me and asked me to meet him up at the bowling alley with Ian, and a bunch of their friends. I really like to bowl, and Ian has some nice friends, so I thought it would be fun. It wasn't.

Dexter ignored me the entire night and flirted with someone else's girlfriend and then the waitress who brought us some pop. He told me I was a "shitty" bowler, which confused me, because in the end I had a higher score than him. Ian said he got really mad when he told him to never call me, which confused me even more. I thought about it for awhile, and I came to the conclusion - not a date.

I came close with Harold Murrell. We had been good friends for years when he asked me to the seventh-grade Halloween dance. He told me he was going as Elton John, because he knows how much I love him. I thought that was incredibly sweet, so I thought it would be perfect for me to go as Kiki Dee.

But a couple days before the dance, I got sick with Shingles. I was in so much pain that I couldn't go to school for three weeks. I couldn't go to the dance with Harold or see Clyde and Bonnie go to the dance as Bonnie and Clyde. Bonnie said Harold danced with Margaret Jackson all night, and seeing that they're still going strong after almost three years together, everything worked out perfectly.

Then last summer my friend, Daisy Flanagan, wanted to fix me up with her brother's best friend, Paul, which immediately made me uncomfortably. He had tickets to see a local rock band play at a nearby college campus and had no one to go with. I was a little uneasy about being "fixed up," but I really wanted to see the band I keep reading about in the paper. Daisy made Paul sound fun, so I agreed to meet him there. When I did finally meet him, he barely spoke to me. I gave him money for my ticket (which he gladly took) and then he didn't even walk with me to our seats on the lawn. He didn't stand anywhere near me, and he barely spoke to me. However, I do remember the first thing he said to me.

"I really wanted to see this band, but I had no one to go with, so I guess you'll do."

The next day Daisy called me and went on and on about how much Paul was in love with me.

"Really?" I told her, "I didn't get that feeling."

She said he was going to call me later that day for a second "date," which he did, but my Grandma Dotti answered his call for the next four days and simply said that I was not around. So really, no first or second date ever happened.

Van Williams was number four that almost happened. It was the first day of school, and he was in my social studies class. I did think he was cute, but one of the first things he told me was that he couldn't decide between me or Jennifer Swenson for a girlfriend. I did secretly want it to be me, but when he took weeks to decide and made his decision with Jennifer, I felt a little hurt. But everyday as we sat in class he would tell me in a really sincere voice how much he was in love with me and not Jennifer. I never told him, but his words never made me feel flattered. They exhausted me. I never expected him to break up with Jennifer for me - he made his decision - but his weeks of "contemplating" between me and Jennifer made me feel like I was not quite good enough. *Close,* but not quite.

Also, all his pointless affections for me told me what kind of boyfriend he was. Horrible. He's with one girl while he's expressing his feelings to another. He's wasting his time, and Jennifer's time, because his heart is not entirely with her. It's a big disrespect all the way around. Jennifer did eventually breakup with him, and when he asked me out a day later, I said no. It hurt to tell him that, but it hurts worse when you're made to believe for months that you're someone's second choice. Not a great feeling. You can ask *anyone* that. So - no date.

Number five came just last January. Harding had a winter dance called the Winter Snowfest where the ninth-grade class elected a court with a King and Queen. I won Snow Queen, but later that night, I developed a fever and felt sick to my stomach. I really wasn't comfortable being crowned "Queen" of anything, so my diagnosis of whooping cough was my not-so delicate way out of the dance. I was happy to excuse myself and give the crown to the runner-up, Cheryl Warddell. The whole "Snow Queen" thing would have been too hard for me anyway. It would mean that I'd have to go to the dance and well, pretty much, stand alone in a corner and feel Roxie Sheppard's constant glare weigh me down. And then sometime in the evening, stand on stage and get a picture taken for the yearbook, and I think the local newspaper. The spelling bees' hard enough on me every year - I just couldn't do it.

However, I didn't realize that Cole Thompson won King (everyone I know voted for him, so I shouldn't have been all that surprised), and according to the rules of the dance, we would have been forced to couple up that night. I would have had to get my picture taken with him, eat dinner with him (and the principal), and best of all - slow dance with him. At the time I would have desperately called it a date, but of course it never was.

And Clyde - what's his deal? I would never date him because he's like a brother to me. A few times I thought he was going to ask me out, but it turns out he was just trying to look down my shirt.

After the show Wesley and I start to walk home. I would love to hold his hand, and certify this as an official date, but he keeps them in his pockets the whole night. I suppose that's fine; my palms are sticky and sweaty, and I have a funny feeling in my stomach that's getting more intense.

"You wanna come over, or did you wanna go home?" he quietly asks me.

"Ah, yeah, I'll come by for a little bit. Check in with Bonnie." I want to get home to my grandma, and I swear, if it was anyone else I was standing here with I would tell them that, but I wanted to squeeze in just a little more time with him.

All these excuses that I find to be with him, I find unusual about myself, but not shameful. Which is even more unusual.

Wesley opens the front door to Bonnie's house for me, and I immediately notice the tranquility of the house, which tells me that no one's home. The TV is off, and no one is running up to me or away from me. First time for both.

I fan my face from the stuffiness of the house, even though the windows are open, and as I step over Hawley's Barbie Doll camper into the kitchen, Wesley offers me a drink.

"Coke or 7-Up?" he asks, closing the refrigerator door tight. "Sorry, that's all they have."

"Coke, please," I say as I sit down at the kitchen table and watch him take a bottle opener, secure it tightly around the bottle cap, pull it upward, and then hand it to me. "Thank you," I say mesmerized.

He pulls out a chair and to my surprise, sits down next to me. When Bonnie's cat, Roderick, jumps on the table, Wesley picks it up, puts it in his lap, and pets the top of its head.

"You know Roderick is a girl?" I tell him, taking a sip from my pop.

"Roderick? He is?"

"Yeah, Bonnie wanted a boy cat, thought that's what she got, named him Roderick, and then one day it was laying on her bed, and well... we discovered it was a girl."

Wesley's eyebrows draw together, "Discovered... it was a girl?"

"Bonnie was... well, it was.... we just figured it out. Bonnie explained her love of Rod Stewart to Roderick and told her that she just has to accept the name." I tell him, barely able to control my laughter.

*Bonnie's gender-confused cat? That's the best conversation I can come up with?*

As Wesley starts to talk, I think about his dog - or maybe his cat - I rest my elbows on the table, cup my chin with my hands, and for the next twelve minutes I stare at his face, which is both cute *and* handsome. He looks like he has a really nice build under his shirt, so the mental picture that is developing in my head of him holding me in his arms is in *no way* leaving my brain like it should - no matter how hard I try to transfer it to another part of my brain - it just won't move.

I'm not concentrating on what he's saying, I just watch his ruby lips move and wonder what it would be like to kiss them. Bonnie and I have talked about guys a lot, and we both have always wondered what a great feeling it must be when someone likes you so much that he wants to kiss you, and only you, for long periods of time.

We have also wondered what it would be like to make-out with a guy. To have him hold you in his arms and move his hands around you as he touches all your trigger spots. Have him whisper in your ear things that make you blush. Bonnie and I have always wondered what it feels like to get the love you deserve.

Seeing that the world is overpopulated, I bet it's the absolute best feeling when you're loved that much.

Falling, falling, falling.

My pensive thoughts are interrupted when both the front and back doors swing open and the Lenzer-Smith's instantly fill the house. Rollie and Rosella viciously chase each other through the house as Clyde walks frantically to the bathroom with Ellery in his hands. Toby runs directly to me for my much anticipated hug, and Bonnie fights to get something out of Hawley's hair as Hawley tries to run away from her. Mrs. Smith's arms are so full with packages of assorted breads, that I can barely see her face.

"Need any help, Aunt Lauren?" Wesley asks standing up.

"No thanks, Honey. It's your day off, continue to enjoy it. Hi Ruby," she says, smiling at the both of us.

Mr. Smith has both arms full of boxes of chicken and exhaustingly drops them on the kitchen counter. "Busy day today, Wes," he says to him. "Lucky for you it was your day off. Toby, get in the tub, Buddy. Hawley, let Bonnie help you, Honey. Rollie, Rosella there's some leftover coleslaw if you kids want it."

Wesley turns to me and says, "You wanna go upstairs? Someplace quiet?"

"What? Sure."

Oh, no. My bad grammar is back.

As I slowly follow him up the stairs, I can only hope, in this clouded head of mine, that it would be his bedroom I'm following him to. We could sit on his bed, hold hands, possibly share a kiss or two, and hug each other so tight that we can feel our hearts beat. But as we both zigzag our way up the cluttered stairs and down the hall, I follow him into Bonnie's room, and we crawl out her window and on to our spot on the roof. And this time, it's just me and Wesley listening to the crickets in the yard, Mr. Morgan's frogs croaking and the sound of Mr. Norcross' pulsating sprinkler.

"So, do you like working at Chicken-N-Joy?" I shyly ask.

"Yeah, I'm saving my money for a Camaro... and because we had to move I really don't have a place to live right now, so I'm kind of saving for that, too. The next time I see my mom, hopefully I'll have enough money to get us a place. Not anywhere near Toledo. That's where I'm from. What kind of music do you like?" He says as he takes a cigarette from his shirt pocket, dangles it from his mouth and then tilts his head at me.

"Well, I fell in love with The Rolling Stones when I was just a baby. I love Otis Redding and The Temptations. I love all Motown. It's my heart. What's wrong with Toledo?"

He pats the pocket of his shirt, pulls out some matches, and then lights his cigarette. "Bad memories," he says. "I hate it there and won't go back. You're too sweet to hate anything. I bet there's not one thing you hate."

"Wax beans. I can't figure them out. But that may be due to a bad wax bean experience I had once. I mistakenly ate a fuzzy one years ago. It changes everything once you throw them up out of your nose. But I feel the complete opposite with Fettuccini Alfredo. Genuine love. What is it that you love?"

"Boxing. Basketball. Peanut butter, Toasted ravioli, Waffles, and watching cartoons. Not in any order though, because I love them all equally. Led Zeppelin, my mom, Holden, Grandma Alice. Oh, and I feel the complete opposite about peas. I hate 'em, and I have never thrown them up out of my nose. And school. I hate school. Bonnie says you're the school genius."

I retained everything he said, especially the list of people he loves. No girlfriend or ex girlfriend was mentioned - got that - and even though I feel a little more comfortable with him, I still select every word carefully.

"School, like anything, is what you make it."

"That's a genius answer right there."

"I've tried to make it a great time in my life, because I know it's only temporary, and I think I have so far. I like your hat, but aren't you a little toasty with it on?"

"I guess I fa...messed up too much. Fifth-grade. That's when it happened. My dad, died and I flunked because my mom never sent me back to school. She stopped..." he paused for a minute. "I hate my new haircut. So I'm hiding behind this hat until my hair grows out."

"You should never hide behind anything."

"Genius answer again. But I do. I can't help it. I hide behind a lot ever since...."

"Since your dad died?"

"Bonnie says you know every Marvel character ever

97

created."

"Did she tell you about a specific R-rated Spider-Man dream I had?"

"No, but if I take my hat off will you tell me?"

"I might."

He puts his cigarette under his right shoe and then pressed on it with his foot. And when he took his right hand and slowly slid his hat off, it certified all the feeling that I've been having for him.

He's so gorgeous.

I stare at him and his really short, blonde hair as he rubbed all the little cowlick hurricanes that are growing ever so cutely the wrong way. His hair, which has now become the cutest hair I've ever seen on anyone, is a nice scissor cut, not a bad razor cut like Grandma Dotti's brother, Uncle Levi. His is always a little too "porcupine."

"My grandma Alice," he says, trying to rub his fingers through it. "She somehow managed to take my already bad hair and give it the worst haircut of my life. I swear my head was bleeding by the time she was done."

"I love a cowlick head." I say with a soft giggle. "Your grandma didn't do a bad job at all. It's...really cute." I could barely say it, because I fell completely out of breath.

I can see the scars on his face a little clearer now, and I try not to stare. They are just as adorable as his hair, and I've grown instantly curious how he got them.

He gives me a cute smirk, propels his hat off the roof, and we watch it land in Bonnie's   backyard.

"Okay, what happened with you and Spider-Man?"

"Well," I try and begin, "it's actually a little X-rated. I was at his high-rise apartment in New York. He had rescued me earlier that day from Tar Water Lake. I was kidnapped by Bullseye and dumped there. It was a very romantic night at his place. We were eating White Castle hamburgers and drinking Pabst Blue Ribbon Beer. We started to make out and, well, then he took off more than his mask. If I knew you a little bit better, I'd tell you more."

"Incentive," he tells me as his dimples light up his face. He really cannot get any cuter at this moment.

Wow. I sound like such an idiot telling that story.

I don't know what time it was, but it was dark when he walked me home. We took the long way around the block and walked slow, taking baby steps at times, and we even stopped a few times to comment on the sensational speckled moon. But I wonder, as I watch him with his head down, hands in his pockets, kicking small piece of gravel into Fenkell, how healthy he will be for my heart? Love can make your heart feel perfect, but it can also completely shut it down.

Will he fall in love with me and help sooth my conflicted heart? Or will he just help tear it completely in half? Will he stay here in Detroit and be my high school sweetheart? Or will he go back to Toledo to the life he left behind? And to all the girlfriends I'm positive he's left behind.

Wesley's guaranteed a girlfriend on his first day at Redford, and I'd love to be it, but maybe I should just limit my heart to friendship with him. I have lots of friends - who are boys - and even though he feels completely different to me, great looking guys like him are known to hurt ordinary girls like me. My heart certainly doesn't need to unravel any more than it has so far this summer.

"Always listen to the core of your heart, Ruby" is what Grandma Dotti repeatedly tells me. And right now the core of my heart is telling me that he has a tight grip on it, and I've fallen in love with him. But maybe, for the first time in my life, I should forget my grandma's words for the sake of my very fragile heart. My heart feels torn and frayed, but in love too. What do I do? How should I feel?

I step on to my front porch as Wesley pulls out a piece of paper from his back pocket.

"I got my homework done on time," he says, handing it to me.

I instantly smile and say, "Wow. I'll check for you. Goodnight, Wesley. Thank you for everything."

As I close the screen door behind me, I turn to watch him leave. I give him a quick wave as the street light glows above him. When he waves back, it wasn't my stomach that fluttered this time - it was my heart.

I *think* I brushed my teeth. I *think* I washed my face. And I *think* I brushed my hair. But I really don't remember doing any of it. As I slip my red cotton nightgown over my head, I smile as the gold rick-rack at the bottom tickles my thigh. I climb into bed with Wesley's homework still clutched tightly in my hand.

I flip through the channels on my radio to find a good song. I find the perfect one to sum up the night. I listen to The Three Degrees sing, *When Will I See You Again?*

When will I? Wes, are you lying in bed wondering the same thing right now? Are you falling in love with me or am I just your new friend? Is this the beginning of "us," or is this the end of "us?"

I unfold his homework paper and look for his name in the right-hand corner.

### WES EVERETT

Everett. Wesley Everett. Wes Everett. I keep repeating his name in my head. I stare at his signature for awhile, even rubbing it gently with my thumb.

I hold the paper tightly in my hand as I run my pencil down, correcting his work in my head. I smile at his one wrong answer, which gives me the excuse to see him tomorrow. The thought of running through my house, through our backyards and into Bonnie's house to tell him how proud I am of him, quickly vanish when I realized how desperate that sounds. So instead, I mark it with a B ☺

Then I erased the B ☺ and write "Great Job!"

As I lie on top of my bed I feel the humid air float over me making it a no-covers night. I lie on my left side and then switch to my right. I get up and then lie back down diagonally across my bed, first on my back then on my stomach. I'm distracted, but not by the heat this time. I can only think of one thing.

Wesley.

I'm so worried about my grandma, but I can't seem to shake him from my mind.

I feel stuck between the two of them. I certainly don't have to choose between them, and the love I feel for each of them are two different kinds of love, but wanting to be with Wesley makes me feel almost disrespectful to my grandma. She needs me more right now, and there's no way I'll waver on my dedication to getting her better. It's still the most important thing in my world. But it's hard to not want to be with Wesley. I just can't seem to push that aside right now because, honestly, I really want him in my life.

Each day with Grandma Dotti I feel the saddest I've ever felt. Her being sick is the epitome of heartbreak. But when spending time with Wesley I feel the complete opposite; I feel the force of love trying to break through.

But there is something for sure that I know about love. Love isn't always convenient, and it's sometimes hard to find. So when we feel love, we should all take a chance with it.

It's the timing of this love that really worries me. It certainly doesn't feel like the right time to fall in love.

Or, is it the perfect time to fall in love?

# THAT'S HOW STRONG MY LOVE IS
♥♥♥♥♥♥♥♥♥♥♥♥♥♥♥♥♥♥♥♥♥♥♥♥♥♥♥♥♥♥♥♥♥♥♥♥♥♥♥♥♥♥

My heart feels funny when I wake up the next morning. It feels like it has been stretched and pulled in every direction. I put my right hand over it and give it a little squeeze. The collision going on in my heart, between love for Wesley and fear for Grandma Dotti, hits directly in the middle. It feels injured, but at the same time, content. I think at any second I will implode inside, but yet my heart feels stronger and secure, perhaps even bigger.

I think it's a tangled mess.

I know I've fallen hard for Wesley, I really think we're perfect for each other, but there's always a chance he doesn't feel the same. Love is funny. It sometimes grows unevenly. Sometimes one person loves more than the other, which is eventually what breaks you up, and then, your heart in half.

Even though I know we all play the fool in love sometimes in life, this is *not* a good time for me to experience rejection. I should push my feelings for him aside and stay strong and levelheaded and - most importantly - devoted to my grandma.

So with this confusion swirling around my heart, I decide to stay close to Grandma Dotti for the next few days. I'll never leave her side and give myself a Wesley break. I'll clear my heart and brain of him, and I make a new promise to myself of an even stronger commitment to getting Grandma Dotti better.

When I hear the distinctive sounds of the fruit and

vegetable man's truck trumpeting through the neighborhood announcing his fresh daily produce from two streets over, I grab a handful of singles from the kitchen counter, run out the front door, and wait patiently at the end of the driveway for him to turn down our street.

Grandma Dotti sits on the front porch, fanning herself with a magazine, as I wave the fruit and vegetable man's truck down, I ask for a half a dozen snow apples, a spinach bunch, a pound of bananas, and a giant watermelon that was *way* too big for me to carry back up the driveway.

I strategically position them in my arms and stumble into the house.  I had to rearrange everything in the refrigerator after I found a spot for the enormous watermelon. I wipe down all the shelves, both drawers, and defrost the freezer. It takes me two hours to do and I don't think of Wesley once, so I decided to keep myself busy around Grandma Dotti all day and not give my brain a second of Wesley time.

I untangle the garden hose and then pulled it around to the front of the house to wash all the windows. I drag the ladder from the garage, lean it against the house and fix the clog in the gutters with a butter knife.

Grandma Dotti watches me as I pick all the weeds from the cracks of the sidewalk and then I touch up the address that Grandpa Kip painted on our curb 23 years ago. I use yellow neon paint, because that's the only paint I could find.

I keep Grandma Dotti hydrated with unlimited strawberry lemonade, and we snack on yogurt, carrots, oranges and red grapes. I constantly check our bright yellow kitchen clock so I never forget to give her her medicines on time. Mom even remembered to pick up a bottle of multivitamins with iron, which Grandma Dotti graciously takes.

"Feeling good today, Grandma?" I ask, sitting down next to her on the front porch swing.

"Okay today, Ruby. Just my bones aching a little," she tells me as she takes my hand. "And I'm worn out. But I'm sure it's all those darn pills I have to take. They're just making me so tired."

"It sounds like they may be working, so it's important, more than ever, that you rest up."

"It must be my nurse. She's taking good care of me."

"Always," I say as I hand her, the 2:00 pill.

It's been amazing to me that she hasn't once complained about the leukemia. Not once.

While I watch her take her medicine, I think about how drugs affect the body. I'm hoping that her body is fixing itself just like it does when you have a cold or flu. You take your medicine and sleep the day away while the medicine goes to work, running through your bloodstream and destroying the virus. These last few days that I've been with her have been a little overwhelming for me. It's hard to look at her and not break down and cry, knowing that she has a horrible sickness running head-to-toe through her body. But I have to remain strong for her, so I bite my lip to hold back tears.

I remember all the times she has taken care of Ian and me when we've been sick, had stitches or a broken bone. I wish that was all she had to battle. I look up to

105

the sky and make a wish to the sun that her pain is minimal.

"Grandma, you have a doctor's appointment tomorrow, remember?"

"I start chemotherapy, don't I?

"Yeah," I say as my voice fades quickly. Her doctor thinks she needs it, and even though I think her body is too small for such a strong drug, Dr. Cantrell insists that it's going to help her. "We'll see how it goes. I bet you won't have to take it long."

One of my favorite songs comes on the radio. Grandma Dotti taps her foot and I sing along to *Sweet Love* by The Commodores. It's a song so fitting at this moment, as I hold her hand and think about how "sweet" love really is.

When true love touches you it gives you a heart connection. The sweeter the love, the deeper the connection. And when that love grows wide, high and deep, there is never a detachment. My heart is so connected to my grandma that as I watch her fight her cancer I feel my entire body ache as well.

That's how strong my love is for her.


Later in the day, when Ian gets home from work, I start to think about dinner. I peek in the freezer and find a package of pork chops wrapped tight in freezer paper, so I lay them in the sink to thaw. The kitchen cupboards are filled with paper products and nothing that would go along with a pork chop dinner, so I grab my purse and head out the door to Shrubland.

Shrubland Market is made up of only three short rows of food, two walls of coolers and fruits and vegetables down the middle, so I'm never in there long. But today as I casually stroll through the aisles looking for something healthy to make with dinner, everything I pick up seems to be loaded with preservatives, or artificial, or imitation *something*.

I inspect every label from each item I pick up.

I leave with a gallon of whole milk, a loaf of whole wheat bread; a giant box of cereal that is filled with granola and a bag of red beans. I've read that they're really good for you, and I think they will go well with the pork chop dinner.

I have underestimated the weight of my grocery bags as I leave Shrubland. I wiggle, cradle and rearrange them in my arms three times before leaving the store.  I look up at the sweltering sun and smile as its warmth covers me. Today is exactly what summer should feel like, and it's a typical summer day in Detroit. It's hot, humid, and exactly perfect.

So perfect that I decide to take my time walking home, admire my amiable neighbors and my charming neighborhood with all its beautification.

I wave to my friend, Mr. Pete, who is busy pumping gas at the Standard Gas Station.

"Hey, Ruby!" he shouts, moving quickly between two cars. Mom gets her gas there, and Mr. Pete is forever fixing her "ongoing windshield wiper problem," so he knows me well.

I smile at the only lady waiting at the bus stop. She has on a beautiful lime green hat and a lime green coat dress to match.

"Beautiful hat and dress," I tell her

"Thank you," she smiles, as the gap in her teeth

makes her look even more beautiful.

I wave to my neighbor, Helen, who lives on the corner of my block. She is walking spryly through her yard. Her sweaty, dark hair covers her face as she inserts yet another lawn decoration into her flowerbeds. She must have over a hundred by now, which is a lot for the size of her lawn, but I *love* all the creativity. It's art at its finest.

I cross the street and see an ex-friend of Ian's named David skateboarding in the church parking lot. He glares at me, his eyes as stinging as the sun, which made me uncomfortable, so I look up to the sky, smile it off, and start walking a little bit faster.

"Hey, Ruby," I hear Rollie say as he vehemently rides by on his bike, swerving to miss me.

"Sorry, Rollie. I didn't see you. Careful! Don't hurt yourself," I yell at him, even though he drives by me so quickly that I know he doesn't hear me.

I readjust my bags again and then inhale the wonderful smell of roasted chicken. I must be hungry, because it grabs a hold of me a little firmer today. As my feet and heart pick up speed, I follow its scent down Fenkell Avenue.

As I find myself standing directly in front of Chicken-N-Joy, I realize that I completely missed my street. How did I get here? How did I miss my street?

Wesley.

That's how strong my love is for him.

I know he's working today, and even though he might be a healthy diversion from my grandma right now, I have tried all day to push him away from my mind. But the fact is he's never left it since the very first day I met him.

When I defrosted the refrigerator this morning, I wondered what he likes with his pork chops and what his favorite ice cream might be. When I washed the windows this afternoon *I thought* I saw his reflection in the glass. After I fixed my bangs, I turned around to look for him, even though I knew he wasn't there. And when I was fixing the gutter earlier I thought about climbing up on to my own roof just to see if he was sitting outside on his.

Earlier when I was picking weeds from the cracks in the sidewalk, I wondered how he viewed dandelions. Does he think of them as an annihilating weed or a medicinal flower like I do? When I was painting the curb, I almost painted a heart with our initials in it next to our address. I really thought about him every second of the day.

It doesn't seem like I'm able to push my feelings for him aside. I feel drawn to him wherever he may be. Like there's some type of magnetic pull.

As I stand there staring at Chicken-N-Joy, I try to talk myself out of going inside and buying my first lime slush of the summer.

*I won't go in. But really, the slush would go great with my pork chop dinner. I don't want to bug him, but I haven't had a lime slush yet this summer. I'll just peek inside. Just a quick peek- that's all.*

I shield my face from the sun, but I'm not able to see much from the glare on the window. My paper bags start to slip, and as I fumble to get a grip of them, the door opens in my face.

"Do you need some help?" I hear.

"Oh... Hi, Wes," I called him Wes. I'm not sure he would want me to call him that, that's what his family calls him, but it just fell out of my mouth that way. "No, I'm good. I got 'em, thanks."

"How's your grandma? Is she feeling better?"

Ouch. That just hit me directly in the tender spot of my heart, and I think I might break down and cry if I talk about her. I don't want him to see that side of me, so I go with the vague and ordinary answer, "She's okay. Thanks for asking." I'm sure he saw the tear that suddenly appeared, so he sweetly changed the subject as I rest my grocery bags on the ground.

"Are you on your way home? I can help you carry your bags home," he says, as he squints his eyes from the sun.

Boy, he sure looks adorable squinting his eyes from the sun.

"Yeah, no... I'm on my way home...but I don't need help... thank you, anyway."

"How bad did I do on my homework? I was thinking about it and...I think I really messed up."

"No, you did great. Only one wrong, but I see your mistake, so we'll just need to go over a few things before we move on in the book. If that's alright?"

"Sure. Oh, I have something for you. Can you wait a second?"

I nod yes as I watch him go back inside.

Can I wait a second? Are you kidding? I would wait all night and day out here for you.

The sun is warm and clammy on my back. I delicately move my hair that is stuck to my shoulders and then slowly try to wipe the prickle of sweat that is forming on my forehead. When I wipe my hands on the back of my sundress, the door swings back open.

"Thought you might like this... 'cause it's so hot." His arms extend and he slowly hands me a lime slush. "It's really hot today."

I stop breathing for a second, or maybe two. He seems to have that effect on me. It's like he shoves a spear into my heart, and I instantly become breathless. "Yeah, it is. Actually, I was just coming to get one."

He knows I like lime slushes. That means he's asking about me. Girls like when guys do that too. That means they want to find a way into your heart.

I smile at him and my lime slush and forget all my manners. "It's my favorite.... I gotta go," I say, quickly gathering my bags. A wave of emotion fills me, reminding me that I have been away from my grandma too long. I need to get back home. And even though lime slushes always make me happy, I feel a sudden urge to cry. I, once again, rearrange the bags in my arms, so I'm able to sip on my lime slush, and then turn to walk away.

"Oh, Ruby? There's this place that I wanted to go tonight. I thought maybe you could come with me... maybe later... if you can. I understand if you can't."

I stop quickly, using my toes as brakes. I want to scream out the loudest "yes" that my 90-pound body can produce, but I just slowly turned around and said, "Sure, I'll come with you. Sure. Do you want me to come over at a certain time?"

"No, I'll come pick you up at six. Is that okay?

"Sure, six is good. See you then. Thanks," I say as I unsuccessfully try to give him a wave goodbye with my

111

hands full.

I force myself not to turn around, as I take a sip from my lime slush. I put the straw to my mouth, and even though I've had hundreds of lime slushes in my life, this one tastes different. It tastes sweeter. Maybe because his DNA is all over it, is why it tastes like the best one I've ever had.

With a smile stuck to my face, I inhale a long sip on the straw.

It's funny how love can instantly make you smile when you're just about to cry. It's so powerful.

I squint at my bedroom clock. It's a few minutes before six. I'm ready. I think. Because of the slight drop in temperature and the fact that Wesley didn't say where we would be going, I decide to wear my black cotton bellbottom pants that Grandmas Dotti and I tie-dyed the year we learned to tie-dye. Everything in the house got it that year, even Ian's underwear. I throw on a white button-up blouse and tie it in a knot at my waist. I put on some big silver hoop earrings and muddle up my ponytail.

I'm ready to go, but my body starts to shake from nerves. As I leave my bedroom I sigh heavily and tell myself, *"Wesley's just a new friend. I have a lot of them at school - boys who are my friends. It's always been pretty simple for me to have a platonic relationship with them, so this shouldn't be that hard."*

"Mom, I'm going out for a little bit. I'm sure I won't be too late," I tell her, talking over TV.

"Okay. Yeah, if you're not going to spend the night at Bonnies, don't be out too late, "she says, listening more to Jimmy Carter's speech on toxic landfills. "You're coming to Grandma's appointment with us tomorrow, aren't you?"

"Of course."

"Tell Bonnie Hi."

"I will."

I haven't mentioned Wesley to my mom, so I let her assume that I'm off to Bonnie's. *Close.* I don't offer any more information, and she doesn't ask.

I kiss Grandma Dotti goodbye and head out the front door

As the screen door slams behind me, I see Wesley walking up our sidewalk. He tilts his head and smile. I smile back trying not to stare at his clean sneakers, perfectly-fitted jeans and his navy blue short-sleeved shirt which has one button unbuttoned at the top. His casual and relaxed attire make him the most handsome guy I've ever been with.

Wesley's hat looks officially gone, and as he puts his head down and tucks both hands deep into the pockets of his jeans, we start our walk toward Fenkell Ave.

When we get to the bus stop, it immediately arrives. He pulls out his wallet, pays for two tickets, and we sit down on the worn vinyl bench seat directly behind the bus driver.

"How was your lime slush?" he asks me.

"It was great, thank you, but they're always great." *But today's was somehow even better than great.*

"Chicken-N-Joy busy today?"

"Not really. What did you make for dinner?"

"I went with pork chops."

113

"How do you cook your pork chops?"

"I fry them in an electric skillet. How many loads of dishes did you do today?"

"I don't know. Maybe... nine"

"What does Clyde do all day at Chicken-N-Joy?"

"He doesn't do anything but eat. Do those earrings hurt your ears?"

"No they're not too heavy. Do you think I could ever own my very own slush machine?"

"Sure, I don't see why not."

"I'm gonna have to talk to your Uncle Charlie about that."

As I sit next to Wesley, I watch the bus driver take us deeper into the city. This reminds me of all the times Grandma Dotti, Ian and I would take the bus downtown. We would go to Hudson's Department Store when Grandma Dotti had to buy a dress for a special occasion. Along with a new dress, she would get an oversized hat and low heel pumps that all matched perfectly. At the end of our shopping day, she would take us to Sanders Ice Cream Parlor for some ice cream. I remember we ordered the same thing every time. Ian gets a hot fudge cream puff with vanilla ice cream; Grandma Dotti has a hot fudge sundae with butter pecan, and I get two scoops of chocolate almond ice cream that I always ask for in a sugar cone. Grandma Dotti would always grab a chocolate bumpy cake and a jar of hot fudge sauce before we headed back home on the bus.

When Wesley and I hurry to change buses, and quickly board the one that glows "Warren Ave," above the windshield, I think about how Mom and Grandma

Dotti stress to Ian and me to "Never go into the city alone or without an adult." It's a command that, surprisingly, Ian has obeyed, but as I sit there, the sun slowly descending and the impaired city moving behind me, I feel excitement running through my veins. I feel safe with Wesley and most importantly - I trust him.

I can't stop thinking about my grandma tonight, though. It seems whenever I'm with Wesley, she's heavy on my mind. But when I'm with my grandma, he's the one heavy on my mind. Love just doesn't leave you alone; it seems like it just constantly has to sit alongside you. And even though I feel this is a date for Wesley and me, I wish my grandma was here with me.

The bus stops and Wesley gives me a slight nod and says, "This is us."

I follow him and as I gingerly make my way down the three steep steps, Wesley grabs my left hand to help me down.

But then he never let go.

His nice soft hands held on to mine as we slowly walked down Warren Road and then around the corner to Cadieux Avenue. When we arrive at a place that looks like a cute corner bar, it's dark inside, so I squint my eyes to adjust to the immediate darkness and let Wesley lead the way. He stops to talk to a man cleaning some highball glasses behind the immaculately arranged bar, then he takes my hand and we step around the corner.

We enter a room that's long and narrow and consists of just two slightly concaved dirt alleys. A row of bright fluorescent lights above the slab of cement divides the concaved alleys. Wooden wheels - about eight inches in diameter - lay sporadically on the ground. As I watch Wesley bend down to get one, he asks me, "Have you ever been Feather Bowling before?"

"No, I've never heard of it."

"I came here once with my dad, Holden and Jodi. It was a long time ago. My Grandma Janet used to live around here actually. See those feathers down at the end?" he points.

I nod yes as I look down the elongated alley to see a lone feather sticking out from the dirt. This room is really just a two-lane bowling alley with dirt floors instead of the wooden alleys and a lone feather instead of pins.

"Feather Bowling is just like regular bowling, but you roll a wooden wheel instead of a bowling ball and try to get it as close to the feather as possible. You go first," he says handing me the, surprisingly, light wheel.

I wish Grandma Dotti was here. She and I would have so much fun at this, and next to Wesley, this is the cutest thing I've ever seen.

After our four games of Feather Bowling, which I lost every one, we sat at a table by the bar to have some pop before we had to catch the bus back home.

Sitting next to him, our arms consciously align together, drinking the Vernors he bought for us, and laughing about the last episode of *All in the Family*, we share stories of our life-so-far. All of our fears, triumphs, accomplishments, failures and dreams. And as I sit and listen to Wesley Everett's heart unfold, I found my own heart filling up with something that surprised me. Courage. A lot of times in life you need courage, and falling in love is one of them.

All night he's been giving me such a sweet feeling inside, and I love how I feel with him. I want this with him. I want to be the one he shares his heart with. He makes me feel good about myself and really, really happy, which is hard for me to understand with my grandma being so sick.

Tonight my newfound fortitude that's growing inside of me tells me that I can get close to him, and stay close to my grandma, and love them both at the same time. Right now my grandma is safe at home and ready to start her cancer treatments - that I'm confident will help her - so I feel that I can be more than just friends with Wesley.

I fall more and more in love with him each time I see him, and I'm unable to push my feelings aside. They're just too strong. I can only hope that he would want the same with me. Wish and hope. Exactly what life is all about.

Wesley and I hold hands, tighter this time, as we walk back to the bus stop. His grip feels just like my grandma's. A firm, warm, perspiring clutch that sometimes hurts your knuckles. Signs of a serious hand holder, I think. Grandma Dotti always told me that she held on to my hand so tightly because she never wanted to lose me.

I could only dream that Wesley shares that same sentiment.

We wait twenty-two minutes for the bus to arrive, and when it did, we let everyone else board before us. Still holding hands, I follow him to the last row on the bus and sit down next to him. He never let go of my hand, even when he notices his shoe is untied.

With the lights from the city flickering over us, we sit in the dark sharing shy glances and amorous smiles with each other. It feels like the perfect opportunity for a kiss, I thought, but I would never go first.

I was never aware of the time, or how long it took us to get back home, or how mad Mom might be when I walk in the house too late. But I do know that I don't want this night, or the feeling I have inside, to ever end.

"Thanks, Wesley, for a great night," I tell him standing on the bottom step of my porch. "I had such a nice time. Thank you," I say.

He looks into my eyes and I waited for his response. He says nothing.

His eyes transfix with mine. He cups his hands on my face and leans into me. I feel the strength in my knees slightly weaken. We tilt our heads in the opposite direction - at the same time - and I doubt it happen in slow motion, but it felt like it did- we kiss the greatest kiss ever. It is soft and tender, warm and sweet.

I don't remember exactly how long it lasted, and even though I wasn't prepared for it, I did my best to give him a great kiss back. There really is nothing you can say after a much anticipated kiss like that, so I just watch him walk away.

It's official. I'm in love. Yup, I'm in love, and it doesn't matter what my brain is telling me to do about him, because my heart can't seem to stay away from him.

118

# PAIN IN MY HEART
♥♥♥♥♥♥♥♥♥♥♥♥♥♥♥♥♥♥♥♥♥♥♥♥♥♥♥♥♥♥♥♥♥♥♥♥♥♥♥♥♥♥

I always check the weather for Grandma Dotti the first thing in the morning.

Grandma Dotti follows the weather religiously, like a diehard sports fan would follow their favorite team. I think she missed her calling in life; she should have been a meteorologist.

I turn the TV on and listen from the kitchen as Grandma Dotti's favorite TV weatherman predicts a hot week. "Temperatures in the ninety's and getting hotter next week," he foresees.

Ian has the day off and Mom takes another half day from work, so we all leave at noon for Grandma Dotti's first chemotherapy appointment.

A blast of stale air hits me in the face and I instantly feel "car sick" as I climb into the back seat of my mom's car. Before my mom starts the engine, she lights the cigarette that she had been clutching in her hand for twenty minutes, and then fumbles around for a pack of gum in her purse for two-and-a-half minutes.

She rolls down her window, only turning the handle once around, which allowed very little fresh air to come in. Her cigarette filled the car with poisonous gases and unhealthy tar that circulated around the car looking for a healthy lung to land on. I loosely cupped my hand over my mouth and nose and fought to breathe. I sat patiently the entire ride to the hospital and waited for my mom to turn on the radio.

She never did.

I love hot summers, mainly because Michigan

winters are so long, but today I'm annoyed with the heat. On a scale of 1 to 10, my level of annoyance is a solid 15, and it's only 12:05 in the afternoon.

Newsted Hospital is cold. In more ways than one.

A nurse with pale blue scrubs, and curly blonde hair so long that it covered her name tag, sends us down a maze of hallways on the third floor. She never spoke or smiled, just her shoes squeaked in rhythm. We end up in the very last room in the north wing.

The ice that's  instantly forming in my veins made me check the rooms wall thermometer the second I entered. It reads 52 degrees. Anything under 70 degrees is *freezing* in my world, so I wrap my arms around me and hug myself tight.

The walls in this lonely room are a dirty beige and are bare except for some medical equipment that haphazardly circles them. There are no windows, so the only light is from a large fluorescent lamp that hangs directly above the lone bed. It seems extra bright and extra irritating to me today, which gives me an instant headache.

It's loud in this part of the hospital too. Infusion pump alarms are going off, squeaky wheels on metal carts are moving at high speed through the hallway, and everywhere I walk I smell either urine or bleach, which now pushes my annoyance level to a solid 20.

Grandma Dotti sits on the edge of the bed that is tainted with unidentifiable stains as the nurse tightens a blood pressure cuff to her arm. The layer of dust under the bed makes me sneeze twice and everywhere I step I seem to be in someone's way, which is irritating

120

me more than them. You can almost see and taste the thickness of germs floating in the air which makes me wonder how anyone could come here to get better.

Grandma Dotti smiles at everyone who greets her and even those who don't. Mom, Ian and I stand at the edge of her bed and watch the nurse stretch a tourniquet around Grandma Dotti's bicep and tie it tight. She places a thermometer in my grandma's mouth, takes another vile of blood from her already visibly worn arm, and then injects a needle into her protruding vein to start her treatments.

They are in 30 minute sessions, so we wait patiently with her as I steal glances at the watch on Ian's left arm. I always try to look for something positive in a negative place, but this one is hard.

I'm ready to go home.

I'm so uncomfortable. I'm restless and agitated by everyone and everything today. I know because of all the hurt that I'm feeling inside, I'm seeing the world in such a negative way. I guess when your heart hurts, so does everything else in your life. My head hurts, my stomach, my knees, my feet - everything. The little patience I do have has completely vanished, and I'm finding that my mood swings are now out of control. I'm in a full blown pisser.

Ian and I nervously pace in and out of Grandma Dotti's room, as Mom rapidly skims through a magazine that clearly doesn't interest her. I give Grandma Dotti's toes a little squeeze and she smiles her way through her wretched treatments.

Ian leans into my ear and says, "I'm going for a walk. You wanna come?"

"Sure," I droningly say. Walks usually clear my head, and I'm in desperate need for that right now.

We walk to the elevator, and Ian presses the "1" button as the elevator doors close on us. "Remember when we were here, maybe seven or eight years ago..." he asks, looking up at the row of descending numbers above the elevator door.

"When you put the eraser up your nose?" I interrupt.

"Yeah... what would make me stick an eraser up my nose?"

"I don't know," I laugh, "but I know I couldn't get it out, even with the vacuum cleaner hose."

"Yeah, you've always tried to save me. Thanks," he says, as the elevator doors open, and we're hit by the aroma of fried food.

"Remember the time I dragged your ass home from Stoepel Park when you, for some reason, jumped off the swings, while you were in the air, and landed directly on a broken glass bottle hidden in the grass?" Ian asks, almost in disgust.

"The disadvantage of my commitment to be barefoot for life," I say, inhaling the smell of steamed macaroni and cheese. "I remember the glass got wedged so deep in my foot that I couldn't walk, so you threw me over your shoulder and carried me all the way back home."

"Yeah, you barely weighed anything, but three blocks of you on my shoulder was killing me. I was just about to pass out when I dropped you in the middle of our front lawn. You have to admit, though, that the trail of blood that you left for those three blocks was pretty cool."

"Yeah, so was the story that we told Grandma when

she saw all of the blood all over my foot."

"Yeah," Ian interrupts, "We told her that some crazed lady was trying to murder us. We even made up a name for her - Diana Smuckinghole. Grandma never bought the story, not for a second. She looked at your face, which was porcelain white, and just about shoved me aside." He laughs.

"I remember she cleaned my foot, bandaged it, gave me a Fudgsicle and sat with me on the front porch until Mom rushed home from work to take me to get stitches."

"Favorite," Ian says, with his smirky smile. "And all those bee stings to your head! That had to hurt."

"It did hurt. I think it made me delirious, because I was certain that Al Pacino was my doctor. I'll never go outside and trim the hedges after shampooing with my homemade honey shampoo in my head again. Lesson learned," I accentuate.

"How are you doing through all of this, Ruby? You doing okay?

I don't answer for a minute. "Of all those times here that you just mentioned, Ian...today's visit hurts the most."

Ian Kipton Vander was born just 11 months before me. My young and eager parents had him in January of 1962, and then me, I'm sure accidently, that following December. I'm sure we were a great tax write-off for them that year. Everyone says that Ian and I look alike, but I don't see it too much. Ian is slender like me, but a lot taller. We do have the same hair color and the same long eyelashes, but Ian has dark brown eyes like Mom and not green like our dad and me.

Ian drops some change into the vending machine, looks over the first row and then pulls the level for a Nestle Crunch bar. It slides out, and he tosses it to me. His hands dig deeper in his blue jean pocket as he pulls out more change and makes another selection of a Reese's Peanut Butter Cup for himself.

While I munch on my glorious, but inglorious lunch, I think about Wesley. Wesley feels different to me than other boys I've talked about to Ian, and he will pick up on that right away. If I tell Ian, I have to tell Mom. I've thought about telling her, but I know she has a lot on her mind these days. Her daughter falling in love with the cute neighbor boy could possibly stress her out even more.

Plus, for all parents in the world, teenage love scares them to death. They are afraid all the morals that they have instilled in us immediately disappear upon eye contact, that the trust that's been built between you completely vanishes, and, sex or no sex, it's something they're worried about more than you. I guess they know that love sometimes equals pain, and they're afraid for our heart.

Instead of sharing anything with Ian, I hum a song, The Spinners, *Could It Be I'm Falling In Love*.

I don't have to wonder if I'm falling - I know I'm there.

When you never have to question your love for someone, and the word "doubt" never enters your mind - you're in love. When you think about destiny and your future together, no matter what age you are - you're in love. I feel lucky that Wesley has come into my life because I love the feeling of loving him.

I want to tell Ian about our date, but decide not to. It doesn't seem important and appropriate today. I think I normally would want to tell everyone I know how perfect it was. A trip into the city on a beautiful summer night with the perfect gentleman. Feather bowling and sharing a bag of chips and some pop while talking about music and holding hands. Perfect. Perfect because it gave me a happy and peaceful feeling, and every time I've thought about him today, I find myself smiling inside. Human nature I suppose, to have your body instantly smile inside when you think of the person you're in love with.

But then a sudden feeling of discontent sets in and I feel the puncture that my grandma's illness has left on my heart. Pain and heartbreak all take over.

Ian and I make our way back to Grandma Dotti's room using the same elevator. I lean against the hard paneled elevator walls as the metal bar presses uncomfortably into my back. I hug myself and think about Wesley once again.

What will he do to my heart? It's already so tender over my grandma's cancer, and I hate how that feels. I can't have more pain enter from somewhere else in my life; it would be the ultimate heart disease. I know he gave me a sensational kiss good night, but was it just a courtesy kiss?

The elevator doors open and a big blast of frigid air-conditioning sends a shiver down my spine. A big blast of heartache is really what it is.

Later that afternoon when we're at home, Mom starts to make dinner. Grandma Dotti and I sit on the porch, holding hands and watching the rest of the day

125

pass as the perfect summer sky hovers over us.

"I sure hope this will all pass soon, Ruby," she says to me. "I don't think I can take too much of that chemotherapy. I'm already looking forward to the day I won't need it anymore," she says softly as I rub her battered arm.

"Me too," I say even softer.

"But I'm going to fight this. You always have to hold on to hope, Ruby."

I look directly into her eyes that are filled with worry. My eyes start to water, so she smiles a bright and beautiful smile at me which always controls my tears. I think of all the times that I've had the urge to cry, but her smile made my tears instantly stop and gave me the strength I needed.

Like my first day of kindergarten when I knew she was about to turn around and leave me in a room filled with little strangers. Or when I got my ears pierced. Or my awkward and inflated braces that seemed welded into my mouth. When I started my period for the first time, or the time I went on my very first sleepover at my friend Gloria Tyler's house that was only six houses away, but felt like six states over.

The time I had to give a speech to the entire school on ecology, and when I was forced to play the "broken doll" in my third-grade Christmas play, I nervously stared out into the audience for her support.

Every year at the school spelling bee when I'm down to just one word - which happens to be the world's *hardest* word - I always looked for her and it was always through her incredible smile that my tears would vanish.

Cancer is a horrible disease, and everyone knows that. People have to fight it with everything they've got. Sometimes you win that fight, and sometimes you lose. It hurts and destroys people and changes their lives forever. It grabs hold of your soul and never lets go. It changes your life forever.

I know how chemotherapy works. It's supposed to stop her cancer cells from reproducing and help repair her damaged bone marrow. But chemotherapy hurts all her blood cells - good and bad - and it can stop her immune system from working properly. It is already fragile, and I'm worried it will make her sicker.

I don't share any of what I'm thinking with her - I would never want to worry her - so I just give her a kiss on the cheek.

The pain in my heart feels different tonight. It's deep to the core. My heart feels bruised and deflated. It's never felt like this before. It hurts so bad.

I've learned a lot about the human heart in my life. It's a muscle that is not only red, but also yellow and white. Your heart sits in the middle of your chest slightly tilted to the left side, and given enough oxygen, it can continue to beat outside of your body. The only sound you hear from it is the four values that are opening and closing as it beats approximately 100,000 times a day. A newborn baby has a faster heartbeat than the average adult heart. Your aorta is as large as a garden house, and sex actually does help it stay healthy, which explains all of Uncle Levi's jokes after his heart attack a few years ago. A man's heart is slightly bigger than a woman's, and because it sits protected by your rib cage, you wouldn't think it would get damaged as easily as a lot of hearts do.

One more thing I know about the heart - any damage can sometimes be irreparable.

I woke up suddenly the next morning to the sounds of Grandma Dotti throwing up in the bathroom. I hurried down the hall, tripping on Ian's baseball spikes along the way, which stubbed my toe horribly. I hazily continued into the bathroom where Grandma Dotti is sitting on the edge of the bathtub, wiping her mouth with a piece of toilet paper.

"Grandma, are you okay?" I ask, not thinking too much of my stupid question, but too much about my throbbing toe.

"I need to lie down, Ruby... not feeling too good."

"Sure... okay..." I say, as I gently help her up, hold her tight, and walk her back to her bedroom.

I tuck her in bed with just a light cotton sheet to cover her. I open both her window as wide as they go, and then place a plastic wastebasket next to her bed. I close her door behind me and then listened for her to call my name.

I stand by her door for an hour.

I tiptoe down the hall and sit alone at the kitchen table with my hands folded tight in my lap. Mom and Ian are both at work, so I sit in silence and don't move once. I didn't speak. I look at nothing and listen to nothing. The only thing my body could produce was a straight stream of tears that roll down my face and onto my lap.

I let her sleep most of the day, and when I hear her get up to go to the bathroom; it was the first time I moved in hours. I kneel down next to her on the bathroom floor and as the pink floor tiles dug into my knee caps, I hold her, rub her back, and watch her dry heave for a half hour.

I tuck her back into bed, give her two tablespoons of coke syrup and help her eat a sleeve of soda crackers. It was all I could think of to help her.

When Mom came home I asked her to call Dr. Cantrell. She did, but he repeated over and over that she is having a normal reaction to the chemotherapy.

But it doesn't pacify me. My thoughts about chemotherapy are hitting me deep and harder than ever. Medicine should never make you sicker. And if it does, then isn't it obvious we should try something else?


After two days of nothing to eat, Grandma Dotti finally nibbles on a small piece of apple cake I had made. I felt very little contentment because her already petite frame looks diminutive, and her skin has changed colors - from pearl to eggshell -to beige- in just a few days. It's been almost two weeks since we found out about her leukemia, and I don't feel we are on the right track to getting her better. My entire body hurt so badly today that I doubled over in pain. A few times today I felt nauseous and fought to breathe.

As hard as it is for me to leave, I gather up my algebra book, grab my radio and hop over the back fence into Bonnie's backyard.

# LOVING CUP
♥♥♥♥♥♥♥♥♥♥♥♥♥♥♥♥♥♥♥♥♥♥♥♥♥♥♥♥♥♥♥♥♥♥♥♥♥♥♥

Everyone I know loves summer. And summer nights are one of the very best things in life. The day's hot sun has gone down and the temperature sits perfect. The night sky glows in the deepest onyx, the sparkle of the stars are extra vibrant, and the glow from the sagebrush-covered moon - incredible.

The mixture of sounds from the city are distant, but clear. Ernie Harwell's distinctive voice announcing Tiger baseball games on the radio soothes even the non baseball lover. The faint sounds of TV laugh tracks and laughing neighbors in their homes quietly fill the neighborhood while the scent from the night's barbeque still lingers in the air.

There are so many things tied to summer nights that make then great, but when it's shared with someone you love - it becomes one of your greatest memories of life.

Wesley and I sit on the roof outside of Bonnie's window, share a lime slush, and eat cookies that I made for him before it got too hot in the house. I baked a couple dozen peanut butter cookies hoping it would make him smile - which would make me smile.

I glance over and watch Wesley work on his algebra and stare out into the tranquil night sky.

We talk about random things like- his neighbor's 40 pound cat; Toby's crush on me and all of the wonderful things that he does for me; Mr. Morgan's congested frog pond, and my first grade teacher who died in class after having a massive heart attack.

We talked about his album collection, my album collection. His favorite birthday, my favorite birthday. The story of his name, the story of my name. His favorite President, my favorite president. His favorite jelly bean flavor, my favorite jelly bean flavor. His brother, my brother.

But when I talked about my mom and dad. He said nothing back.

"I could really go for a pickle loaf sandwich right about now," he says with a smile that shows off just one dimple. "You want one with me?" .

Heavy sigh. The romance of it all. Sharing a pickle loaf sandwich with Wesley Everett under the heavily inflated moonlight. Almost nothing better.

"I *love* pickle loaf sandwiches. But I have to go."

"You do?" he asks sadly.

I nod my head because his sad face takes my breath away. "Yeah, I'm not spending the night tonight. I want to get home to my grandma and make sure she has a good night sleep. The last couple of days have been rough for her, and I want to make her a nice healthy breakfast in the morning. Get her back to feeling better."

"Sure, I understand. I just thought if you were spending the night, maybe you could be my cartoon-watching buddy in the morning."

I twist my lips and take a deep breath. Cartoon-watching buddy? That would be one of the greatest things that ever happened to me. The two of us snuggling up on the couch together. Me, feeding him breakfast with our pajamas on, kissing between sips of orange juice, and nibbling on the same piece of toast

131

while I watch him watch cartoons.

"I better go," I say, so quietly that I'm sure he didn't hear me. I pack my algebra book into my sling bag and tuck Wesley's papers deep into the middle.

My life has never moved in slow motion - if anything - it's going too fast, but when Wesley leans over and cautiously slides his arms around my waist, my world suddenly stopped.

I look down at his already tanned arms that fit so perfectly around my waist. His arms are warm and soft and, as I feel his fingers squeeze the side of my shirt, I look up at his beautiful green eyes. My brain was thinking *so* much, but I'm glad it knows not to say a thing.

I slowly put my hands around his neck, and as our foreheads slide together, so do our lips. In the kisses of my past - I usually count the length - not this time. I concentrate. I concentrate on the softness, the slow movement and the spectacular taste.

That's what love does. It makes you lost.

I hear no music, no crickets, no frogs, and no all-night sprinkler. Nothing.

I rank our kiss as not only one of my greatest moments in life, but the hug was equally as great. His arms feel amazing and so comforting to me that I lean in closer to him. His hug takes away all my horrible thoughts of the hospital and Grandma Dotti's cancer for just half a minute. I feel all the ugliness of her sickness lift up and float away from me. His kisses seem to push it far away from me.

I would love to be his girlfriend.

When we walk to the back fence, he waits for me to

get into my house. I don't turn around this time. I feel such a strong urge to run back over to him, have him kiss me just a little bit longer, a little bit harder, and much deeper. It would push my grandma's cancer even further away from me if he did.

I run up the steps of my back porch, swing open the screen door open, and let it quickly slam behind me.

I love - love.

The next morning I let everyone sleep in. Mom had filled the coffeemaker the night before so I tiptoe into the kitchen, press the start button, and listen to it instantly start to percolate. I pull four bowls from the cupboard and four spoons from the utensil drawer and arrange them neatly around the kitchen table. I tuck the box of Granola cereal under my arm, grab a bowl of fresh fruit and a gallon of milk from the refrigerator, and set them in the middle of the table. I run the bowl of fruit under warm water for double germfree reassurance and then sprinkle them with ice cold water. I take four pieces of whole wheat bread from the breadbox and dropped them into the four toaster slots of our stainless steel toaster. Grandma Dotti and Ian like their toast burnt, so I adjust one dial to eight and leave the other on four as I press down both levers at the same time.

I sit at the kitchen table inhaling the combination of warm toast and coffee and the stillness of my house. I pull out Wesley's algebra paper from my sling bag that I casually dropped on the kitchen table last night.

As I start to look over his algebra paper, I slowly glide my index finger down the page and calculate, in my head, all his answers. I turn the paper over and see this...

You + Me = ♥

I feel my heart stop for a second, and when it started back up it felt completely different. It has a different temperature than the rest of my body. Maybe 10 degrees warmer. It feels lighter, but heavily coated in something I can't describe. Perhaps it's what love must feel like in liquid form. It's beating differently, like when you hear your very favorite song. It feels absolutely incredible!

I place the paper over my heart and then kiss it and wonder - could he love me as much as I love him?

For dinner that night I bake some whitefish that I sprinkle with dill. Fish has good oils in it and dill will help soothe Grandma Dotti's stomach. As the fish bakes in the oven, I mash my boiled garlic sweet potatoes next to a pot of steamed beets. Garlic is good for your blood, and beets are high in Folic Acid which will help Grandma Dotti's red blood cell production so she can start to get some strength back. I make a batch of Dandelion tea with the last Dandelion in our yard. I dig up the root, wash it thoroughly, boil some water, and let it steep for an hour. I add some honey because it doesn't always taste that good, but it's always a loving cup of good health.

"I feel good today," Grandma Dotti announces to everyone as she sips on her protein drink. "Getting a little strength back, I think."

We all, simultaneously, look up from our plates.

"That's great, Mom," my mom says, her eyes wide with excitement.

As I sit there, with three of the people that I love the most in the world, I watch them smile a genuine smile for the first time in weeks. I look over to my algebra book on the kitchen counter and look directly at Wesley's paper sticking out. At this very moment, my pluperfect heart feels the best it's felt all summer! Grandma Dotti is getting better!

After we eat dinner, I do the dishes, kiss Grandma Dotti goodbye, grab my sling bag, and I'm off to Bonnie's.

Bonnie swings open her backdoor and greets me with the biggest hug I've ever felt from her. Her hug tells me that she misses us. Our girl talk, our friendship, our getting closer summer after hot summer.

"How's everything going, Ruby? How's grandma." She asks, pulling her long black hair through a rubber band.

"Okay. Grandma had a good day today," I tell her. "I haven't seen you much this summer, Bonnie. I'm sorry. It's already July and we've barely done anything together. My fault. My grandma is so heavy on my mind, and..."

"Wesley at the same time," she interrupts.

Bonnie knows me almost better than my grandma. She knows I've fallen in love with her cousin. And even though I told myself earlier today that I wouldn't let any of my conversations with her relate to him, I've only been here five minutes and I immediately cave in. "Yeah, where is he tonight? Still working?"

"Yeah, he and Clyde had some deliveries to make, so I'm not sure when he'll be home."

Yuk. I just had an ugly feeling run throughout my entire bloodstream. I might not see him today, and I was looking forward to it.

*Don't get weak over a boy, Ruby,* I tell myself - Don't *do it!*

"Good. I know he's saving his money and that's... great."

Bonnie pulls out two wooden ladder-back chairs away from the kitchen table. "Sit down, Ru," she says, pointing to one as she sits down in the other.

I sit down in the hard wooden chair and pick at the strawberry jelly that's stuck to the seat of the chair. I feel like I'm the world's worst friend. I think I owe Bonnie a big apology for being such a best friend letdown.

"We've been friends for a long time," she begins. "True friends. So it goes without saying that we always want the best for each other. I've waited for the right guy to come along and give you the love you deserve, and guess what? He's here."

I smile and smirk at the same time.

"I'm always going to be here," she says, "walking with you to and from school, hanging out over summer vacation, and when we're 50, 60, and 70 years old, we'll do all those old lady things together. You know - dye our hair the same color blue. Help each other go to the bathroom, become grandmas at the same time. But Wes is, probably, only here until the end of the summer."

I feel something instantly pierce my heart and it hurts worse that any broken bone, stitches, ear infection or contagious rash I've ever had. "End of... Summer? Then where will he go?"

Bonnie shrugs her shoulders. "I don't know. I really don't know much. Everyone's waiting on his mom to get better so she can decide."

"His mom is sick?"

"No. Well, sort of. Not really. Kind of." Bonnie leans into me and whispers, "mentally ill," she says pointing to her forehead, "Anyway, what I'm trying to say is - spend as much time with him as you can and don't feel bad about it."

Her answer took me by surprise, and I wasn't sure how to respond to it. His mom is mentally ill and his dad has died. What a horrible thing for a family to go through, especially a 16-year old, "I have something for him," I say instead of asking more questions. "It's in my bag. I'll be right back." I grab my sling bag and run up the stairs to Wesley's bedroom.

When I walk into his room, I notice he hasn't unpacked yet. His duffle bag is still sitting on top of Jodi's dresser which makes me wonder if he's anxious to leave.

Jodi's room, I think, is the best bedroom in this house. It has a wall of windows that look out into the back yard, and on a clear fall day you can see directly into my backyard and maybe into my bright yellow kitchen. The pillows and blankets on his bed are starchy white, and the walls washed of fingerprints and dirt. The dresser shines with a glaze of polish, and I breathe in a hint of lemon.

The blankets on his bed are slightly crooked, and the only thing that lay on top of them was a pair of white crew socks. The only sound the room makes is from the alarm clock that sat on the nightstand next to his bed. It ticks softly next to the Bugs Bunny coffee cup that is filled with colorful jelly beans, which instantly reminded me of my missed cartoon date.

I walk into the attached bathroom, and it is the cleanest I have ever seen it. When Jodi lived here, she got tired of Clyde always leaving towels on the floor, his facial hair shavings in the sink and the seat on the toilet constantly up, so she stopped cleaning it and started using another bathroom in the house.

There is nothing out of place in this bathroom. His toothbrush lies neatly alongside a bottle of Old Spice deodorant, a bar of Irish Spring soap, a tube of Aqua-Fresh toothpaste and a small bottle of Listerine mouthwash. The navy blue bath towels hang perfectly straight like they have been military inspected and the faded blue shower curtain is pulled tight and lays flat.

I reach into my sling bag and pull out a big bag of chocolate candy kisses. I bought them this morning after breakfast when I went up to Checkers to get the latest issue of *Rona Barrett's Hollywood* magazine. I pull apart the crimped cellophane bag, without making too much noise, and start to sprinkle the candy kisses around his room. I put some on his dresser, some on his pillow, some on his shoes that were hidden behind the door, some on his bathroom counter, and one on top of each bar of his soap. I even lined some along the toilet tank. As I dumped the remainder of the bag on to his bed, I hear some footsteps on the staircase getting closer.

My eyes widen and lock in place as I slowly turn around.

"Hi, Ruby," Wesley says as he instantly appears.

"Hi... ah, Wes." I didn't forget his name. The frontal lobe of my brain shut off and then quickly turned back on.

He looks around the room at the random piles of candy and smiles.

"I know you've been working hard, and I thought that you might want some kisses." I say to him.

*Kiss me. Kiss me, Wes. I want you to kiss me,* was really the only thing circulating in my head.

He looks down at the pile of candy kisses on his dresser and scoops them up in his cupped hands. He leisurely walks over to me and took a hold of my wrist. He delicately places all the candy in my palm and then closes my fingers slowly on top of them. My weary heart filled up with a new batch of love as he pulls me close to him and slowly kissed me.

I'm weak all over. Every part of me.

The kiss is long. You know, the ones that lead to heavier and deeper kisses. I didn't want it to stop, but I did have to start breathing again.

"I thought about you all day," he says quietly between kisses.

"You did?"

"Yeah, I missed you. How's your grandma? Is she feeling okay?"

"Pretty good today, but I'm still working hard at getting her better," I tell him. I feel his warmth and affection run through my entire body as he continues to hold me close to him. I could have stayed there all night in that one spot.

"That's great!" he says.

*Hold me tight, kiss me long, touch me anywhere you want. I'm ready for more of you* - is all that my entire mind and body was saying to itself.

"She's gonna be alright, Ruby," he says, his voice so deep and reassuring. "I know she will."

I'm trying not to cry in front of him, which would make me feel weaker, so I change the subject.

"I loved checking your homework this morning. It made me smile."

He pauses for a minute, looked at me, and slowly said, "I love... when you smile." His thumb caressing my cheek sends another wave of warmth down my spine. "How 'bout we take off somewhere? Just me and you. Let's go somewhere."

"Sure. I'll go anywhere with..." I say, but abruptly stop talking. What embarrassing thing did I just say? I want to bury my face in his starchy white pillows and never emerge. It sounds so weak and irrational. But I'm thinking another facet of love must be moments of weakness and irrationality.

"You wanna get some ice cream?" I finally say, trying to recover.

"Yeah, then maybe we can go for a walk. To the park you like."

Not really what I feel like doing, but a smarter choice than what is floating around my head.

As we started our walk down Fenkell, we hold hands tightly. We let go only once when he took out his wallet to pay for our ice cream cones. Mine strawberry, his vanilla dipped in chocolate.

We sit down at the picnic tables in front of The Tastee Hut and kiss, lick our cones, and then kiss some more.

"Hey, look, a butterfly,' he points. "My Grandma Alice always told me that when you see a butterfly, it's to remind you to hang on to hope. Because life's struggles and changes, can sometimes turn into something beautiful. Like the transformation and struggles of a butterfly life.

"Hmmm..." I say quietly. ""Like something good may soon happen?"

"Yeah. You wanna switch cones?"

"Sure," I say, gladly making the sticky exchange as the butterfly circles around my head.

"I know these last few weeks with your grandma have been really hard for you, and I want you to know, I'm here for you. Whenever you need me."

I smile at him as his green eyes sparkle underneath the glow of the Tastee Hut Ice Cream sign.

*I love you-* almost slips out.

"I think about you a lot," he says slowly, "and I hope you know that I... really care about you. I think about you all the time, actually. I know that you're going through a tough time right now and, if you'll let me, I'd like to help you through it."

"You've already helped me, Wes. Just sitting here sharing an ice cream cone with you makes things a little better for me. You've become the best diversion for me right now."

"I was thinking that, maybe, if you can, and I

understand if you can't, maybe sometime tomorrow you can meet me at Keeler's Gym. I'll be up there all day and I was thinking...I would like to show you how to box. It's important to me, and I want to share that with you. Awhile ago I was going through a tough time and Holden's friend taught me how to box. He felt that I needed to...get some anger out. I fell in love with it, and it does help me release some pain that I still carry around. And well, I just want to help you do the same."

I've questioned all my feelings regarding Wesley, so I can stay by grandma, but for some reason, I have to be with him.

"Boxing? Sure, I'd love to learn," I finally say back to him.

"I don't want to take any time away from your grandma, so come up whenever you can."

"One o'clock okay?" I say knowing Ian will be home all day tomorrow to stay with Grandma Dotti.

"I'll look for you at one."

We take the longest way to Stoepel Park and we walk the slowest we can to get there. We kiss under every streetlight, which makes me grateful to our mayor for making sure they are all in working condition this summer. The soothing sound of a jazz band playing at the park gradually pulls us a little bit closer, but we still take our time getting there.

We walk through the dark, tree-lined tunnel in the back of the park, and when we emerge from the end, Wesley suddenly stops. Our hands, still stuck together, make it easy for him to pull me close.

As sad as my days have been this summer, it's hard for me to believe that this night could make me feel happy.

Especially, at this *exact* moment.

July 2, 1978, at 10:21pm, Wesley Henry Everett asked me the question all girls want to hear gorgeous guys like him. He asked me to be his girlfriend.

I think the jazz band was covering a Louis Armstrong song, but I can't think of which one. From a distance someone screams my name, but I don't look to see who it is. I think I feel a few raindrops fall on my head, but really, I'm not paying any attention to the weather.

"You're the most beautiful girl I've ever met, and I would love it if you were my girlfriend," he says to me.

I dug my toes into the soft green grass and then stretch them to reach Wesley's lips. I give him another sticky kiss and say, "I would love to be your girlfriend."

Hmmm...that butterfly.

When you're young, you think a lot about when you'll fall in love for the first time. As you watch your friends around you fall, and as you wait your turn, you somehow already know how wonderful it's going to feel when it happens. Love will make your world instantly perfect, and not one single thing will be wrong. Love leaves you with such a great feeling that you would never think that your heart could break apart at the exact same time it is filling up with love. Like mine is.

My grandma just *has* to get better.

My heart beats loud and fast as I lie diagonally across my bed in the dark. The night's heat is making it difficult to fall asleep, so I fidget subconsciously for an hour. I close my sleepy eyes and feel the taste of

143

Wesley's kiss still on my lips. I still feel his embrace.

As I slowly drift in and out of sleep, a summary of all that Wesley has done for me, in the short time that he's been here, vividly floats in my dreams. His diversion from the pain of my grandma's cancer is filling up the cracks of my heart. His hugs now are embedded in my soul. They have become therapeutic and medicinal to me and because of that, I feel different. Something is changing about me.

A song plays in the dark, and even though I'm not allowed to turn up my radio at night, I twist the knob, and sing along to Stevie Wonder's *Signed, Sealed, Delivered, I'm Yours.*

Yup, I'm yours! So happy I'm yours!

# HOT STUFF
♥♥♥♥♥♥♥♥♥♥♥♥♥♥♥♥♥♥♥♥♥♥♥♥♥♥♥♥♥♥♥♥♥♥♥♥♥♥♥♥

There is a certain time on a summer morning you can inhale the air, and it's the freshest, cleanest and most peaceful air of the day. That air seems to fill you up enough to pull you from your slumber and start your day with every positive thought and feeling floating throughout your body.

Or maybe it's because I woke up this morning the proud girlfriend of Wesley Everett that I'm sitting on the edge of my bed with every positive thought and feeling floating throughout my body.

I inhale another dose of peaceful morning air as I get a glimpse of myself in my bedroom mirror. My hair is tangled in my face; my pajamas hang off one shoulder and are bunched up in a very uncomfortable spot. The hair on my legs must have grown at least a half inch last night, because they now resemble a Euphorbia Canariensis Cactus. My chipped and neglected fingernails match my chipped and neglected toenails, and my never-welcome puffy face screams for attention.

But, today, I actually feel beautiful.

I'm anxious to meet Wesley at 1:00, so after my two-and-half minute shower, I rummage through my dresser drawer and pull out my gray cotton capri pants, a navy blue tank top, and I tie my white Chuck Taylors nice and tight. Hard fashion decision because there is no such thing as *cute* gym clothes, but hair resolutions are even harder. I comb out my hair for 20 minutes and daydream into my bedroom mirror.

145

I part my hair evenly and make two separate ponytails. I braid each one and then tuck the ends through the rubber band at the top of the braid to form a loop. Shaking my head with exasperation, I think - *this is as good as it's gonna get for a boxing lesson.*

It's noon when I start my walk to Keller's Gym. I look up and count the clouds that are peppered in the sky. I don't feel rain in the air, but after only four blocks, I jump on the Fenkell bus. I guess I just want to get there quicker.

It took 22 minutes.

I pull on the metal doors at Keller's Gym that are almost too heavy for me to open. The repetitive sound of punching bags in rhythmic motion, the clashing sound of weights being dropped to the floor and the squeaky and high pitched sound of rubber sneakers scuffing a dirty, but polished wood floor instantly fill my head. The dusty air makes me sneeze as I stand on my tiptoes and slightly crane my neck to look for Wesley.

"Ruby!" I hear Wesley call out. "You're early."

He's dressed in oversized black boxer shorts, and his boxing shoes are dirty and stained, with matching untied shoelaces. His smoky gray t-shirt is snug at the arms and shoulders, but loose around the waist.

Wow! He looks so gorgeous.

"Hi...am I early? Wasn't sure," I say, fidgeting with my braids.

"Damn, you look cute," he says to me as his eyes gaze into mine.

I didn't want to mention to him that my main goal

of the morning was to be the cutest girl in all of Metro Detroit, so I give him a light punch to his bicep and confidently say to him, "Thanks. Hey, I was thinking - did you ever think that maybe I already know how to box?"

"Well...," he hesitates, his smile straight and his eyes wide as he gives me an even lighter tap to my bicep. "I've seen you throw a wooden bowling ball. You have no upper body strength."

I scrunch up my face, and he laughs, then leans in and kisses me on the forehead.

I *absolutely* love when he does that.

He takes my hand, and we walk over to a worn out punching bag that's hanging in the corner of the gym. He hits it with his bare hands and it sways back and forth. I watch him crisscross his arms and lift his shirt up over his head. I inhale, but stopped suddenly in the middle of it. I'm immobile and captivated. Just like I thought. He's absolutely perfect. Everywhere.

I didn't want to stare too much, even though he's my boyfriend, but I can't look away from him. It's just like the first night I saw him. I can't, and don't want to look anywhere else. Here it is - another "Holy shit" moment.

He's thin. The only weight on his wiry body is his perfectly toned muscles. His back, chest, abdominals and his arms are perfectly sculpted. His perfectly carved chest is smooth and looks incredibly soft. The tone of his skin is perfectly even, with no marks of any kind. Except one.

He has a tattoo on his right bicep which looks fairly new. How could someone his age have a tattoo, I

147

wonder? That can't be legal.

I nonchalantly glance at his tattoo, which is a Celtic Trinity Knot, while I do a couple of fake stretches with my arms and legs.

I'm always fascinated by what people choose for a tattoo. It becomes forever a part of you, so I know there must be some heavy decision making behind them. I always find the stories attached to them very interesting because they are usually stories that connect the tattoo to love, devotion, or pride. And being Irish myself, I know that the trinity knot means life, death and rebirth. The interlocking ovals in the middle reflect an eternal life connection. It must mean something pretty important to him, which really makes him even more beautiful to me.

Wesley hands me a pair of boxing gloves, and I forcefully put them on. They are heavy and seem tight as I watch his long fingers making loops and knots on my wrists securing the gloves. As I watch him, all the thoughts in my head are going in a direction that a 15 year-old girl shouldn't go. It's normal and healthy to be thinking about them, but they're very mature thoughts, and I'm pretty sure I'm blushing.

"Got it so far?" He says to me.

"Got what?"

"The proper stance? Are you okay?"

"Oh, yeah," I say, realizing that he was talking to me, and I didn't hear a thing he said. "Yeah, just... taking it all in...okay, run it by me one more time."

"You need to start with the proper stance. I'm left handed so you should do everything the opposite of me. Stand with your legs shoulder width apart. Your

148

left foot should be a half-step in front of your right foot. Your right heel should be slightly lifted from the ground and remember – your feet *never* leave the ground."

He walks in a complete circle around me, checking my feeble attempt. "Looks good so far," he says. "Now, your hands... you need to put them about six inches in front of your gorgeous face. At eye level. Left hand in front of your right."

He wraps his arms around me from behind and alters my gloves an inch. I feel his lips near my face, which distract me. I inhale his thin coat of sweat as I throw some punches into the air. When he kisses me on the cheek, my already weak knees grow weaker.

"Keep your right elbow close to your ribcage to protect your body," he says, winking at me. "Tuck your chin in and keep your hands high and your elbows low. You need to always protect your face. I wouldn't want anyone to ever hurt it."

All the stuff I learned in karate class years ago I thought would help me today, but it hasn't. I can't remember a thing. Not one thing. I really have lost all concentration.

"Good so far," he says as he continues walking around me in circles and double checking my stance. "Now, when you punch into the bag, you want to have a loose fist - don't clench. Your fist should become more solid as you hit the bag. Three or four punches at a time. Remember your gloves start at your face and end at your face. Now hit the bag turning your fist over for a straight punch. I'll stand behind you, and I'll punch with you. We'll do it together." he says, as he puts his arms around me.

My body is constantly moving, and punch after punch is making me tired. I only stop once to wipe the sweat from my forehead. Punch, punch and punch again. My feet shuffle vigorously around, and my arms are, somehow, throwing all my body weight into the vinyl bag. The entire time I punch, Wesley coaches me on.

"Hands up. Exhale after every punch. Look straight ahead. Stay loose and relaxed. Knees slightly bent. Put your full body weight into the punch and move around lightly. Breathe. Nice and easy shots - don't reach."

After a very exhausting hour, not only am I tired, but a little frustrated that the bag hardly budged for me.

"Why didn't... this thing.... move much?" I try to say while out of breath. "I see them bouncing...around all over... the place in here. Why couldn't I...get this thing going?"

"You did great. I was getting a little nervous, actually," he says, jokingly, with a cute smirk as he unties my gloves.

"Did I resemble Joe Louis?"

"First person I thought of."

"I got some hot stuff for sure. Funny. It's... so hot in here," I say, drenched in sweat, but really it was hot everywhere. Outside, inside and especially in my head.

"Did you want to go take a shower?"

And even though my brain is sweating, and it's still not functioning properly, I'm pretty sure he *did not* mean together.

"Uhh, no. No shower... I...don't think I should...will. But go ahead. I'll watch you...wait for you, I mean."

150

He lifts one eyebrow and gives me the cutest smile. "Here, you can have my water. You might be a little dehydrated. I'll be right back," he says, handing me a sweaty water bottle.

He leans into me, softly touches my chin, and kisses my dry chapped lips.

*Is that what you're thinking - Dehydration? -* My pruney brain says.

I sit down quickly on an old rickety wooden bench close by. Well, I either sat down or my legs and spine simultaneously collapsed on me.

I drink three-quarters of the bottle almost immediately, and I think - *Is this place mentally taking me to places I didn't think I was ready to go? Has Wesley ignited something in me? His beautiful build, his soft touch, his sweet smile, his tender kiss, all have me craving more of him.*

My brain may be dehydrated at the moment, but it needs to start functioning properly and stay responsible.

"Did you check my algebra?" Wesley says, interrupting my thoughts by sliding in next to me. "I don't think I did as good this time."

"Just five wrong. Not too bad really. I did make them a little harder, but it's an easy fix," I say, as we start our walk home with our hands automatically reaching for each other and locking together.

"For you maybe," he smiles.

"Wes, I'm curious," I say, my body still feeling the side effects of boxing. "How did boxing help you?"

"Well... there was a time, not really that long ago, that all I felt inside of me was anger and pain. I was becoming a bitter and violent kid because of it. Holden seemed to be the only one that noticed so he took me to his friend Connor, who had turned his garage into a boxing ring. Connor told me that boxing will give me a release and all my anger that has built up inside of me will drain out in my sweat. It will destroy all of the tension I feel if I redirect all my pain into the punching bag."

"I understand. It makes perfect sense. The release of the Cortisol hormone."

"I was thinking about you the other day and how painful it must be for you to see your grandma so sick. Pain has a way of taking over a good heart and changing it forever, and I don't want that to happen to you. You're going to need some way to release all that your heart feels. So you don't get bitter like me."

"It is hurting me. Seeing her sick... it's tearing me in half. My heart, my life...feels horrible."

He was quiet for a minute. His eyes fixed on the sidewalk as our arms swing back and forth.

"At one time I wasn't very nice... to anyone, Ruby," he said. "I used to get into a lot of fights in school. I'd get kicked out, and then when I was at home, I just continue hurting everyone around me - my mom especially, and that just made everything worse in my life. But hate was all I felt. When Connor taught me how to throw a punch, everything changed. I found that I gradually started to feel better. All the aggression I was feeling was slowly disappearing, and at night, I would fall asleep before any bad thoughts could enter my messed-up brain. I always woke up feeling better. Not so much tension anymore."

"It was your dad. It was his death that put you in so much pain, wasn't it?"

He looked at me with sad eyes and slightly nodded.

"I was young, and I didn't know how to deal with it. No one was able to help me. I understand now why they couldn't, but... I didn't understand any of the feelings I was having. When Holden finally saw that, he stepped up with what he thought would work. And it did. Boxing worked for me."

"I'm glad you have Holden. Thanks for trying to help me today."

"I'd do anything to help my girlfriend," he says, as we stop, turn to each other, and kiss in front of the doors of my favorite library. "The what hormone?" He asks.

"The Cortisol hormone. It's the hormone that releases stress," I tell him as I throw my arms around his broad shoulders, and he grabs me at my waist. It would be the perfect time to tell him about the Oxytocin hormone, also known as the love hormone, but I'm planning on getting to that.

When we get back to my house I grab a blanket, my algebra book and a glass of strawberry lemonade, and we sit under my sycamore tree. Wesley flattens out the blanket as I toss the algebra book into one corner and nuzzle our strawberry lemonade into a flat part of the grass. He lies down, his hands behind his head, looking up at the sycamore tree and its dwindling blossoms. I watch him, his eyes smiling as he winks at me.

"Ruby?"

"Yeah?" I ask, mesmerized by the structure of his perfect everything.

"I want you to know that whenever we are together I'm the happiest I've ever been. And I hope you know, anytime you need me... for anything, I'll be there for you."

"Thanks, I'm always here for you too."

"Is there such thing as a cuddle hormone?" he asks. "Some kind of cuddle chemical?"

"There is actually," I say, smiling at his cuteness.

"Really?" he asks, surprised.

I nod my head as he sits up on his left elbow and puts his right arm around me. I fall into him, and we kiss. Long kisses, than short kisses, than more long kisses. The midday sun changes around us as we kiss for hours.

And even though I think the words "I love you" are the greatest words ever spoken, and should be the most overused words in any language, I almost make the mistake of saying them to him. They are very serious words, and maybe he's just not ready for the word and the definition attached.

"Wes, I...," I immediately stop myself from saying those three wonderful words and sit back up and fix my braids. "I think you are gorgeous in every way."

He smiles at me and says, "Yeah? Not only are *you* gorgeous in every way, but I'm pretty sure you're the best thing that's ever happened to me."

As we kiss, my brain hums the entire Etta James song *Something's Got a Hold on Me*.

Yup, Etta - love certainly does have a hold on me.

That night I had an amazing dream. Grandma Dotti and I were walking down Fenkell on our way to go shopping at the Grandland Strip Mall. She told me that her cancer was gone. Her exact words in my dream were, "Ruby, the doctor said my cancer has disappeared. It's completely gone. " She shrugged her shoulders in the dream and smiled. "But I could never leave you anyway."

That dream faded away and turned into a mixture of unimportant dreams that night.

But, dreams sometimes do come true, they always say. And this one has to!

# PLAY WITH FIRE
♥♥♥♥♥♥♥♥♥♥♥♥♥♥♥♥♥♥♥♥♥♥♥♥♥♥♥♥♥♥♥♥♥♥♥♥♥♥♥♥♥

My arms stretch long and wide in my sleep, and my feet point firm and tight, giving my left calf an instant Charlie horse. I wait for my muscle spasm to subside, make a mental note to add more dairy to my diet, and breathe in the warm morning air. I roll over, pull my cotton sheets over my head, and sleep for another thirty minutes.

Today is the Fourth of July and Jimmy Drew's party. Before Wesley and I kissed our final kiss good night last night, I asked him to come with me and Bonnie to the party. Being the great boyfriend that he is - he said he would.

I'm anxious to go, but Grandma Dotti and I have a traditional Fourth of July dinner to make. Every year we make red, white and blue layered jell-o, macaroni and potato salad, and we barbeque some hot dogs on the grill. We gut and carve up a watermelon (like you would a jack-o-lantern) and eat under the sprinkler for a nice cool down. Nothing feels more like summer than having the warm sun on my shoulders and face and my legs sprinkled with the best drinking water in the state.

After dinner I pick my very favorite dress to wear to the party. It's my cream-colored, crocheted, mini dress that Grandma Dotti and I made the summer she taught me how to crochet. And because it's so hot outside, I decide to wear my hair in a high pony and give it a wave. Another great thing about summer is today's sun gave my face a nice pink glow, which means next to no makeup is needed. I pull my favorite peace sign necklace over my high hair and let it drop at my bra. Twenty-three stitches in the bottom of my foot didn't really teach me a thing, as I make the easy decision to go barefoot.

After I do the dishes, I kiss Grandma Dotti goodbye, and I'm out the back door.

I delicately hop over the fence - careful not to show the world my favorite silky lavender underwear - and I run up to Bonnie as she lights a cigarette in her driveway.

"Wes! Come on!" she yells into the only open window in the house. "Ruby, what the hell have you done to Wes? I've never seen him like this. He's so happy. He's driving me fuckin' crazy," she says yelling at me in the nicest way. "Did you know that Jimmy is dating Roxie Sheppard? Good luck to him. She's such an ass."

I smile, as she rambles on about Jimmy and Roxy. Am I really making Wesley happy?

Under the warmth of the soft purple sky, the three of us start our seven-block walk to Jimmy's. The tenderness of Wesley's grip and his loving smile always seems to change the way my heart feels. And even though I silently struggle with the guilty feeling of leaving my grandma, my heart feels contentment right now, and content hearts come along very few times in life.

We enter Jimmy's backyard through the alley behind his house. I feel the heat from an oversized bonfire warm my face. I squint from that heat, and see the Archer sisters keeping their tradition alive by skinny dipping in Jimmy's pool. It has always been a big rumor around Harding, and as I try to force myself to look away, I find it almost impossible.

We slowly wind our way through the smoke-infested living room, and as I start to look for Jimmy, I'm a little distracted by the smell hovering over the room. Rumor number two regarding his parties verified - lots of weed. And his "amazing weed" does smell pretty good.

The Rolling Stones are playing at deafening sound and everywhere I look there are couples making out, which now verifies rumor number three (very loud music) and four (lots of making out). I've heard these rumors for years, but really, this is just a typical high school party in Detroit.

Everyone seems to be drinking, and even though I have never caved into peer pressure, I feel like drinking something I know I shouldn't.

With Wesley's arm intertwined with mine, we make our way through the kitchen, where I immediately see Jimmy standing with Cole Thompson. Cole is eating a banana like you would corn on the cob - which makes me laugh.

"Hey Ruby, my Queen, what's up? You wanna smoke a cigar with me?" Cole slurs to me.

"No thank you," I giggle. Bonnie leans into me and whispers, "That the first words I've ever heard him speak. Really? " Then she says, "I'll smoke a cigar with you!"

"Ruby you came do you have anything to drink here come with me," Jimmy says, unable to complete a sentence, as I watch Bonnie disappear with Cole.

I did want to try beer, and I know that my mom and

158

grandma always trust that I do the right thing in situations like this, but tonight, I feel like pushing the "responsibility" envelope.

"I think I want a beer," I tell Wesley, feeling that he sensed my reluctance.

"How 'bout I share one with you?" he suggests. "There are other things here besides beer if you're not comfortable."

"No. I want to try beer," I smile to him.

Wesley and I pick a spot between the living Room and kitchen, lean against the wall and snuggle up to each other immediately. We drink our beer together, which was going down pretty smoothly, and after my third one, I still haven't decided if I like the taste of it or not. The only conclusion I came up with was that the smell reminds me of Grandma Dotti's brother, Uncle Nash. Whenever he hugs me, that's what his hugs smell like.

The more I drank, the more I wanted to love Wesley. Hold him, kiss him, and touch him in places that make him feel good. I realize that I was probably getting a little drunk when Van Halen's *Feel Your Love Tonight* rang through Jimmy's enormous speakers, and I wanted them to become more of a reality.

I feel my inhibitions confidently leaving my body as my emotions grew deeper and deeper with Wesley. As we drink our ice-cold beer together, I feel that I could easily push away all my principles that go along with drinking and push things further with Wesley.

The more I drink, the more we cuddle up tight to each other, kissing long and hard. You can't help but look at couples making out. You stare at them because

159

your eyes are just drawn to them for some reason. Wesley and I were, all of a sudden, one of those couples - and it makes me so proud.

Sometimes first kisses are the best because they feel like nothing else you've ever experienced. Sometimes it's the last kiss that has more meaning. But I think it's all the kisses in between that are the most important. They are the ones that fill up your heart with love.

I love kissing him and tasting the beer on his lips. I want to tell him that I love him, but I don't know how he would respond to major words like "I love you." From what Ian has told me, guys usually don't like to deal too much with those words.

But I feel incredible inside. I feel like I could say it, so I decide to tell him.

Right after I drink just one more beer.

Wesley seems fine with our number-five-shared-beer, but I am pretty sure I am drunk. But what I do know for sure is - I should of stopped right then.

He pulls me close to him, and with his fingertips, he brushes the hair that had fallen from my messy ponytail, and gently tucks it behind my ears. He holds my chin in his hands and then he kisses me so softly that I collapse into him.

"You know you're perfect," he says to me after his tender kiss.

"I'm not, but I think my boyfriend is the most perfect part of me," I tell him with a big smile on my face.

"I love you, Ruby."

"What?" I say, surprised.

I heard him. I know what he said.

"I love you. I really do," he repeated.

"You do? I love you too, Wes. And I mean that. You mean..."

"You mean everything to me," he interrupts, "everything."

Now, there is a bedroom down the hall that is notoriously popular with the kids in our neighborhood. A lot of stories are attached to it. Three girls I know got pregnant in it. All four of the Harper brothers lost their virginity in it, and I know that there is a Polaroid camera next to a heavily stocked "condom drawer," in that room. The spacious waterbed inside seems to be a hit with the aforementioned, so because I was feeling an instantaneous amount of confidence, I decide to take Wesley's hand and guide him down the hallway to that infamous waterbed.

"Let's go somewhere...private," I tell him, pulling him down the hallway.

I close the door behind us and I pull him close to me. I'm certain my blurred consciousness was taking over. I heard about this kind of thing happening at parties all the time, but I was positive that it would *never* happen to me.

I kiss him the deepest kiss that I could produce. I've practiced it before, so I was confident that it was my very best.

I lean up against the door as the panels firmly pressed into my back. My arms wrap around his neck, and we kiss harder and deeper each time. His hands gently grab my waist, and as our kisses grow passionate, he leans into me. Every loving emotion turned on inside of me. I want more of him. My

161

irresponsibility was on the forefront.

I pull out his perfectly tucked shirt and put my hands up his back. I squeeze his taut skin as he kisses my neck. Slow kisses, then hard kisses. I unbutton his shirt, put my hands around his waist and press him close to me. I want to feel him against me.

I start to tell myself - *Be responsible, Ruby. Be responsible.* But when he slowly wiggled my dress around, and spread his fingers on my hips I lost all consciousness of the word.

"I love you, Wes. Every time I'm with you I love you more," I whisper to him.

We stop kissing and he looks at me with his gorgeous green eyes, and says, "Ruby, the greatest thing that could ever happen to me is if you were to love me."

"I do love you. I know I do."

Again, I should have stopped right then.

The room was dark, except for the backyard bonfire that glowed dimly through the window. I wanted him to take me over to the renowned waterbed and show me how much he loves me. Was I that drunk, that in love, or that irresponsible?

I'm thinking at some point soon I should start feeling bad about everything that is happening - but I don't. The more we kiss, the better I feel. I'm thinking regret would kick in sometime soon, but it hasn't.

I run my fingers down his chiseled back and up his muscular chest as he continues to kiss me on my neck, my shoulder and then back to my lips. He is such a distraction to me that I can't possibly come up with an intellectual thought if I had to.

I stand against the back of the door as his hands caress my back and waist, so gently, so softly, that it tickles. He moves my necklace around and then kisses me all the way down my shoulder and past my bra strap. I feel a little bit of my dress slide off my shoulder, but he quickly moves it back in place. His fingers poke through the holes of my crochet dress, and when he squeezes my waist, it sends a chill down my spine.

I put my hands low on his waist and notice that his boxer shorts are slightly sticking out the top of his jeans. I tuck my thumbs between the elastic of his shorts, and his lean smooth skin, and slowly move them around to the small of his back. I was getting close. I have to stop; I know I have to be responsible, but that word keeps fading quickly from my brain. As soon as it enters - it leaves.

He kisses me all around my lacey bra. I don't care that I am showing him such a private part of me. I let him touch me and kiss me anywhere he wants. I let his hands move slowly around my body, simply because I want him to. He carefully watches where he puts his hands more than I do, and he seems hesitant. I can't stop any of it. I am leaving that up to him. He feels too incredible.

Now I get it. Now I know. This is what it feels like to lose yourself with a guy you're in love with. To play with fire, and hopefully, not get burned when you push the responsibility envelope.

I don't know who it was that interrupted us, by banging on the door, but I'm grateful to them. They pounded with their fists, and then tried to open it.

Wesley lets out a sigh and puts both his hands on the back of the door by my head, and says, "We have to stop. I don't want to hurt you. I love you too much."

I smile at him because he is right. If anything were to happen on that bed behind us, I know I will regret it tomorrow. Not because I don't love him, not because I didn't want to share that part of love with him, because it should be a decision made with a clear and responsible head. And I certainly don't have that right now!

We stand there quietly for a minute or two, kissing and deliberately not moving away from each other. He delicately fixes my dress, and I skillfully fix his shirt. He helps me fix my messy hair, and we decide to let someone else have their turn in the famous waterbed room.

We walk through the living room, and outside to the raging bonfire. I feel everyone there knew exactly what we had been doing in that back bedroom. But for some reason, I feel no shame. I feel proud, a little less drunk, and a lot more in love.

I guess love also makes you unapologetic and oblivious sometimes too.

I step up on the first step of my front porch, which puts me at the same height as Wesley. I dangle the bouquet of daisies that he picked for me on our walk home, behind his head. My heart is still racing as we kiss goodnight.

"Ruby, I hope you don't think I told you that I love you at the wrong time," he says.

"Wes, what I know about love is - there is never a

wrong time."

"Things are happening fast for us I know, but I've never had anyone hit me so hard in my heart and change me like you have. That's how I know I'm in love with you. If my parents taught me anything, it is to love someone when they're yours, because you never know how long you'll have them. I don't know how long I'll be here - so I had to tell you."

Ouch. I feel my heart sting from that. He doesn't know how long he'll be here?

"I need love like anyone," I tell him, "but I *really* need it right now. And I think you understand. Wes, let's make sure we both love each other the right way. That way we never hurt each other like most people in love do."

"I promise you that."

I want to tell him that I actually loved everything about this night. Being attached to him - the cutest guy at the party, the spectacular beer kisses, and the fact that wherever he put his hands tonight, they warmed my entire body. Especially my heart. That's a feeling I have never felt before from anyone. I even love the fact that he was considerate enough to not ignore our interruption and stop kissing me when things got too heated. Something I wasn't able to do.

I know I love him because I felt it all the way from the bottom of my scarred-up foot, to the top of my disheveled hair.

I sit down on my porch step and watch him walk away. I stare at the smattering of stars that look like diamonds in the sky, and think about young love and how most people must see it. Somewhat senseless, immature, and meaningless. I suppose. But I think there's more to it.

No one can tell me that I'm not capable of loving someone at my age. When true love hits, it has a certain feel to it, and it doesn't know an age. Everyone loves the feel of it regardless of your age or maturity level.

But love has one thing in common for everyone. It's fragile. When your heart has not been damaged yet, your heart loves perfectly. If your heart gets broken, you love differently from that day on. Young love and young heartbreak set the stage for how you will love the rest of your life.

No wonder we never forget the first time we fall in love - it's the one and only time love is flawless.

# STUPID GIRL
♥♥♥♥♥♥♥♥♥♥♥♥♥♥♥♥♥♥♥♥♥♥♥♥♥♥♥♥♥♥♥♥♥♥♥♥♥♥♥

I don't feel as bad as I thought I would when I wake up the next morning. I rub my pounding temples and then close my eyes again. I smack my lips, and they stick together. I'm so parched from dehydration that I doubt I can pull myself out of bed and make it to the refrigerator for the first liquid I can find. Boiled hot dog water even sounds good right about now.

I bury my head underneath every single pillow that I have on my bed, and I pull my blankets up and over every one of them. I decide to lie there as long as I possibly can and try to transfer certain parts of last night to the back of my brain to forget.

But it simply doesn't want to budge.

It all seems a little bit dangerous to me this morning, but the dream I just had was even worse!

Beads of sweat start to form on my forehead, but I lie completely still, ignoring the world around me and decide to sweat out all the shame and embarrassment that fills my entire body.

*Why did I do the things that I did last night? I don't like the feeling of being drunk - I felt I wasn't in control of myself. And not only did I drink too much beer, which of course I'm not allowed, but I* believe *I went too far with Wesley in that back bedroom.*

All of these thoughts make me feel extremely irresponsible this morning. My head is overrun with all the incessant amount of stupid things I did, and as I continue to lie there, I wonder - Is love making me stupid?

I think it is, and I didn't think I would ever let myself get that way.

The Germane language - easy, calculus - easy. Shakespeare - easy. I've memorized the entire 1962 New York Yankees roster', including birthdays and birthplaces of all the players. I took a physics test last month, and it was so easy I thought I couldn't possibly be doing it right. Mr. Tichik told me once that I was "scary smart," and last year my geography teacher left a note for the substitute teacher that said if she had any problems - "Let Ruby Vander take over." I actually had to fill in for the last 15 minutes of class!

But today I don't feel so smart.

I was alone with my boyfriend and I let myself get a blood alcohol level that no 15 year old should have. I couldn't think of an intelligent way out of anything last night. It was like every neuron inside me malfunctioned, which makes me wonder if I've taken the responsible approach to anything this summer?

But considering everything that happened last night with Wesley, I trusted him. He didn't pressure me - it was me that wanted it more. If he didn't stop us, what would have made me stop? I don't know. I don't have an answer. Not smart.

And do I have the intelligence to help me survive all this anguish and confusion my heart is going through? That must be it - You're smart until you fall in love.

I dig my head deeper into my pillows. I think about my self-respect and how it completely left my mind and body last night. It reminds me of the time, a couple years ago, where I stood proud and demanded it.

It was at Jimmy Drew's thirteenth birthday party. We played spin the bottle in his basement, something I was nervous about from the start. And even though I don't pray, I was praying that the bottle would never point to me. Of course it did, and Curt Balfour had to spend seven minutes alone in the closet with me. Nothing happened, He talked nonstop about the basketball playoffs, and I remember I left a little disappointed that I didn't even get a kiss on the cheek. Instead I got detailed information on how The Golden State Warriors basketball team would soon be champions.

However, back at school rumors flew about Curt and me. My "seven minutes in the closet" turned into a big lying game about things that never happened. I hated the feeling it left me. I tried to end the rumors by explaining to everyone I knew, the absolute truth on what happened in the closet. No one, except Bonnie, believed me. It seemed that there was no way out of all the lies and I felt humiliated.

But today I'm not so sure that if there were rumors about Wesley and me circulating, I would feel that same humiliation. I would just hope everyone would get the "rumor" right. Yep, Wesley and I were in the back bedroom making out. Yes we were. Not going to deny it. It was wonderful, exciting and he made me feel the best I've ever felt.

Why do I think it was so wrong of us, but I can't wait to see him again so we can continue where we left off?

I'm right. Love is making me stupid.

My radio plays softly as I sit up on the edge of my

169

bed while my brain spins around. Physically, I guess, I feel okay. Mentally - Yuk.

I glare at my radio as, ironically, the song *Love Hangover* plays. I'm not at all interested in hearing Diana Ross tell me how sweet her love hangover is, when mine doesn't feel so right. I hide my head in my hands and then turn my radio completely off.

Man, I gotta stay away from Jimmy's parties.

I run my fingers through my hair. The same hair that Wesley got his fingers got caught in hours ago. It made me feel incredible that he held me so close, so intimate, so loving. But now that my head is a tad bit clearer, I wonder how he knows all the ways to make me feel so incredible. I wonder how he knows how to hold a girl and makeout with one so well. His fingers, hands, and his warm body felt so good anywhere on me that I couldn't push him away from me.

I learned a lot about Wesley last night. I may not be smart, but he is. He's so smart that he knew not to take advantage of me in my slightly drunken, and very vulnerable state. He made me feel like I was the prettiest girl at the party, and he didn't hold back his emotions with me, alone, or in front of a crowd of people he didn't know. We rarely admit it, but blatant affection is what we all really want in a relationship - obvious love.

I fall back onto my bed, and my peripheral vision catches my "Ten goals for summer vacation" list hanging from my bulletin board. I have made no attempt to do anything on them, and that's something I feel terrible about. Every year it became something that I was dedicated to do for myself to help me grow. I feel I have completely ignored it, which makes me feel stuck.

I have become so concerned with Grandma Dotti getting better, which is still most important, and too preoccupied with anything, and everything, regarding Wesley Everett, that my brain feels congested and cloudy.

I slowly get out of bed - my energy level at its all time lowest - and I'm thinking about how pickle juice sounds like the perfect thirst quencher right now. I hope my dehydration isn't noticeable to everyone in the house. Ian would pick up on it immediately. He's drank at parties, and even though he won't tell Mom, he won't like that I did.

The humid air is heavy on my face as I listen to the light rain spit on my windowsill. I grab a rubber band off my dresser and pull my hair through it. I look into the mirror and poke at my puffy eyes and cheeks.

"Gasp!! What... the... oh... my!" My dry mouth fell open and locked into place. "I have a hickey."

Big "Holy shit" moment!

I moved in closer to the mirror for a better look. I rubbed it with my thumb and then pressed on it.

"How did I get that thing?" I whisper to myself, leaning even closer to the mirror. "It's not too dark. Well, it kind of is. Wesley did kiss me more on the right side of my neck for some reason. It's not really that big," I tell myself.

"Oh, yes it is!"

I quickly dab some liquid foundation on it and then gather all my hair to the hickey side. I wrap it loosely with a hair band and grab my hairbrush from my dresser. I frantically backcomb my ponytail until it is a ratted mess, and situated it wide between my chin and clavicle. It's nothing but obvious now, a pure panic job, but I wouldn't know how to begin to explain it - especially to Mom! I should also keep my distance from Ian this morning too. He has been hanging out with Clyde a lot this week, and I'm thinking Wesley may have come up in a conversation at some point.

It's lunchtime when I finally emerge from my room. My eyes bat back and forth, the look of suspicion and guilt, as I fill a plastic cereal bowl with Quisp cereal and a little bit of milk. I watch my crispy golden saucers float to the top of my bowl, as I sit on the living room couch with my hickey facing the other direction.

After I eat, Mom – who took the day off - Grandma Dotti and I leave for her appointment with her new doctor, Dr. Marshall, an oncologist.


It already feels like it's going to be a tough day.

The car ride is short - the length of four songs on the radio. When we get to Dr. Marshall's office, I try to hum a song in my head, but can't decide on one, so I sit in the doctor's office and impatiently tap my foot on the gray paisley carpet.

"Ruby, I want you to wait here," my mom says, fumbling through her purse looking for Grandma's insurance cards.

"Why can't I come in?"

"I don't want you to. Just stay put, Ruby," she insists.

Maybe I *should* stay here. Close quarters with my mom and Grandma might force them to pay attention to my new hairstyle. But when the nurse calls out "Dotti McAuley," I'm reminded that my hickey is the smallest problem I have.

That will go away soon.

I sit in the waiting room with an elderly couple who held hands and never let go. I sit with a mother and her child, who are totally still – never moved- as their eyes frown with worry. Another older lady sits with a bandage on her thigh. Her eyes are dark and sunken. Her body bruised and drained of color.

An older man in the corner, who is sitting by himself, made my heart hurt. His body emaciated, his face skeletal, and his rangy body was so frail, I didn't know how he was able to stand. I smile at him, and he smiled back, but my body feels flushed with grief.

I bite my lip and daydream out the window. Through the window reflection, I'm reminded that my hickey has not gone away. I know it won't fall off, but I'm desperate to get it off of me now.

But, for some reason, the longer I sit there and stare at it, I talk myself into it. I kind of like having one. It's different for me. I know a lot of people sometimes associate it with something it's not, but I'm developing a love/hate relationship with it. I really can't seem to take my eyes off of it.

Until my mom sees it.

I rat out my ponytail with my hands to try and make it fuller. When the doctor's door swings open, Mom and Grandma Dotti step out. My mom inhales deeply and gives me a fake smile. That's her "I'm nervous" look. Grandma Dotti is smiling, but it's a distracted smile. Her eyes are wide, and she stuttered as she said goodbye to the nurses.

"Grandma's not responding to her medicines, Ruby," Mom tells me as I hold open the door to leave. "We have to watch her closely so she won't get any kind of infection."

"Sure... Of course," I say.

When we leave the doctor's office, I immediately step into a puddle. I follow Mom and Grandma Dotti back to the car while trying to wipe the mud from my knees. I'm agitated and distracted. I was hoping that the doctor would give her some new medicine or, even better, tell us that there are no signs of the cancer, and it's completely gone.

When we get home, I follow my mom upstairs into her bedroom.

"Mom?"

"Yeah, Ruby?"

"Have the doctors said anything to you about taking another approach to getting Grandma better? You know - different drugs or possibly a blood transfusion?"

"No, the doctors haven't talked too much about that. They would have to find someone with compatible blood and, well, the leukemia is progressing too rapidly."

"Progressing too rapidly? What does that mean?" I say as my voice escalates. "Well... I know what it means... it means no one is moving fast enough to try and help her. I will give her my blood, Ian's blood, yours, Uncle Nash, Uncle Levi. I'll ask Bonnie's family. I'll post a sign at the library and at Chicken-N-Joy looking for anyone with the same blood type. Or we can ask about a bone marrow transplant. Why hasn't anyone talked to us about that?"

"It's not that easy, Ruby. A procedure like that would be very hard on Grandma. I know you are anxious for her to get better, we all are, but they're doing what they think is best for her."

"No they're not. If it was someone in *their* family, I bet they'd move quicker. Or maybe someone they *think* is more important in this world, like the President!" I say to her in the meanest voice I had.

Raising my voice to my mom - not smart, or kind. I know she's hurting as well.

"Ruby, they are very concerned..." she says sternly.

I interrupt my mom. Something I have never done. "Concerned? Tell me, Mom, do you think that they really want to help her get better? Who so far has really tried to help her? Hasn't it been people going through the motions of doing the job they're paid to do? Or do they look at her as a sick, elderly woman, who *they think* might have lead a full life, and they are just obliged to do *something* for her. The chemo is not working for her; they can see that, so wouldn't common sense tell you to do something else? Cancer is a *huge* money maker, and it employs a lot of people. Finding a cure, or performing a procedure that could help her, might eliminate someone's job. Think of all the people in the medical field that would lose their job if they discovered a cure. Think of all the places that would shut down! The economy would go haywire, and that's really what's more important to them. They will not admit there is a cure until the next big disease comes along. Science is advancing all the time. There is a cure, and it's heartbreaking to know that they really don't care about her, and we have to sit back and watch her suffer." My eyes fill with tears.

My mom lays her purse on the bed and slowly turns around. There haven't been many times in my life that I've raised my voice to my mom. I can count them on one hand. And in those cases she would usually raise her voice back to me, stronger and firmer, and tell me to calm down. But this time she put her arms around me and hugs me tight.

It didn't help however, I feel discouraged and crushed. Really, just so heartbroken. I woke up this morning thinking I was one stupid girl, but I'm not. At almost 16 years of age - I got it. I got what life is all about it. It's all about money.

The next five days, as I watch my hickey fade, I never leave Grandma Dotti's side. I stand beside her through her bi-weekly chemotherapy treatments, and then later in those days, I hold her while she violently throws up over the toilet.

The doctors remind us that because Grandma Dotti's immune system is so weak, it's important that she doesn't catch even a slight cold, because that could make her sicker. So all week I am overly cautious. I wash my hands multiple times a day, and I seem to have a constant load of wash going. I wash blankets, towels, bed linens, and really anything that sits near her I sterilize. At night I sleep next to her in case she has to get up, or needs anything through the night.

I let her sleep as much as she wants, and I only wake her up to give her water or juice, or some lunch if she's able to eat it. Every time I've taken her temperature this week it's been perfect, which gives me hope.

When I do have to leave her, I never forget to tell her that I love her.

"Love my Ruby girl," she always tells me back.

Of course I'm thinking a lot about Wesley too. I called him yesterday, and we agreed to meet every night, at exactly 9:20, at the back fence. I commit to only ten minutes, but it is a much-needed ten minutes. Eight of it is kissing.

Tonight I run to the back fence, and my tiptoes stretch to meet him as the triangle fence wire pokes into my chest.

"Even though I miss you, I hope you understand that I need to stay with my grandma, to get her strong again, but I'm thinking about you all the time, Wes," I tell him between kisses.

"Of course I understand. It's just another reason why I love you so much. Take care of your grandma, Ruby. Oh, and...I'm sorry about the hickey. I should have known better. "

"Don't apologize. I secretly loved it, and I've come to the conclusion that I'm going to miss it."

I just finish making a big batch of vegetable soup when I realize I wasn't sure what day of the week it was. I look at the calendar that hangs on the side of the refrigerator, and figured out that it was Tuesday the eleventh of July. Just about the middle of summer.

I scoop a ladle full of soup into a big coffee mug and place it in the middle of a TV tray. I place another mug full of herbal tea next to the soup and squirt a tablespoon of honey in the middle. The other side of the soup I place a dish of plain yogurt that I mix with fresh blackberries from our backyard, and a tall glass of ice water that I stir with a pink straw.

As I carry the tray down the short hallway to Grandma Dotti's bedroom, I glance down at my tray of heavy nutrition. I purposely put extra squash in the soup for double vitamin C to nourish Grandma Dotti's immune system and protect her cells. The herbal tea with honey will kill any germ that's trying to form, and the blackberries are essential for her bone mineral tissue.

"I'm getting her better," I whisper to myself when I open her door.

"Hi, Ruby," Grandma Dotti says as she sits up in bed.

"Good nap, Grandma?"I ask, as I sit the tray down in her lap.

"Yeah, still a little tired though."

"I made you some lunch. Lots of nutrients to get your strength back."

"Ruby?" she says, sipping on her herbal tea. "You know that quilt I was embroidering a few months ago?"

"The one with all the state birds?"

"Yeah, could you finish it for me?"

"Su...re. I'll... help you with it."

I rearrange her pillows around her back and hum my favorite song of the summer. My face grimaces as I watch her struggle to drink from a straw. Her hands shake as she tries to lift the glass and direct the straw into her puckered lips. She struggles and keeps missing, which makes me feel instantly sad. I help her with her straw and brush back her thick dark hair that has now lost its curl. I don't want her to see me cry, so I cough back a few tears, and quickly rearrange her blankets, and make sure she's tucked in all the way around.

I sit at the end of her bed and gather the heavy bird quilt around my legs. The wooden embroidery hoop is tight, and the needle is stuck in the wing of New York's state bird, the Eastern bluebird. The blue embroidered thread is tangled and thin.

"It's beautiful, Grandma. I hope I don't ruin it," I gently wipe my fingers across the half finished bird as my eyes fill with tears.

"I'm not done fighting your cancer, Grandma," I whisper to myself. "I'll never give up."

I think about all the endings to the many movies Grandma Dotti and I have watched together. Our favorite movies are the ones that end where everyone is happy again. Will she defeat her cancer and have a happy ending? I will never think for one second that this sickness will end in anything but happiness. I will be patient, stay strong, and wait for our turnaround period. It should be here soon.

I sit and sew the rest of the Eastern bluebird and watch Grandma drift off to sleep. I wipe a few tears from my eyes and think of all the emotions that I've had this last month. From the day of graduation, to becoming Wesley girlfriend, to chemotherapy treatments, to highly anticipated eight minutes of kisses, to wiping my grandma's mouth from vomit. Is it possible that I'm living every emotion known to man all at the same time? When I hop the back fence into

Bonnie's yard; my heart steps into superlative love. And when I hop the fence back over to my yard, my heart steps into unbearable pain.

Not only do I not feel too smart these days, I feel selfish. Every time I leave the arms of Wesley, I walk into my house and instantly feel the pain of my sick grandma run through my soul; and at the same time I long for the moment that I can see Wesley again. Guilt weighs a ton, and it feels ugly too.

Everyone will tell you that love is the greatest feeling in the world. Wanting to be loved is really the one and only desire every human can agree on in life. Some people have love continuously in their life, some people sparingly, but everybody secretly longs to have it. This summer it fell into my lap, hit me hard, and landed directly in the middle of my heart. But I just can't enjoy love right now. I just can't.

# WILD HORSES
♥♥♥♥♥♥♥♥♥♥♥♥♥♥♥♥♥♥♥♥♥♥♥♥♥♥♥♥♥♥♥♥♥♥♥♥♥♥♥

I bake some chicken for dinner that I crisp up and sprinkle with thyme, which I read, will create new white blood cells. I mash some rutabaga and make beets and a salad with the darkest greens I could find in the garden. I made mini pumpkin pies for dessert and packed the leftovers in Mom and Ian's lunch bags. It is a heavily nutritious dinner that filled everyone up with extra vitamin C, A and K.

Grandma Dotti's temperature is good all week, so I decide that after dinner I need to see Wesley. I miss him.

I put my last dish in the cupboard, kiss Grandma Dotti goodbye, and I'm off to Bonnie's...or should I say Wesley's?

Wesley is in the driveway playing basketball with Toby, but when he sees me, he immediately abandons his attempt on teaching Toby a jump shot, and we leave for Stoepel Park.

"I stole a few things from Rosella's bedroom," he says as he pulls a jar of liquid bubbles and two plastic water guns from all three of his pockets.

He looks extra cute tonight. His hair is growing out a little, and I think he forgot to shave today. But really, when he smiles at me, I forget about all the pain in my world, and my heart instantly feels revived.

"Look, fully loaded," he says, pulling the trigger on one of the guns.

A blast of water hitting my arms, feels good from the night's heat. I grab a gun from his other pocket, and we begin to drench ourselves all the way to the park.

We sat on the grass by the swing sets, kiss, blow bubbles into the hot sticky July air, and listen to a blues band on a makeshift stage by the tennis courts.

"I have an idea," he says, standing up. "You thirsty?"

"A little thirsty."

"Are you thirsty for a lime slush?"

"I'm a lot thirsty."

"Hop on," he says, turning his back to me.

I wrap my arms around his neck, hop onto his back, and as he grabs a hold of my legs, I wrap them around him. I kiss his cheek ever tenth step, as he carries me all the way to Chicken-N-Joy.

"You know I won that water gun fight," I tell him as I watch him punch in the numbers to the security code like he's been doing it all his life.

"Ruby, your hair is soaking wet, and it's 85 degrees out. You're so cute."

I giggle as I hop off his back and watch him turn on all the buttons to the slush machine. I sit in a booth, in the dark and secluded corner, and watch Wesley fill the biggest bucket Chicken-N-Joy has for their carry-out chicken, with glowing green slush.

"That's the best looking lime slush I've ever seen," I say, laughing.

"I'll bring extra straws, we might lose some," he says. "I'll bring you my shirt too. I left it here earlier. It's cold in here."

He places the bucket of slush in front of me. I take a long sip from the drowning straw, ignoring my painful esophagus spasm, as Wesley drapes his green plaid flannel shirt over my shoulders. It feels cold on me at first, but I lean into him, and he wraps his long arms around which warm my entire body.

"I was thinking about you today as I was cutting up a stalk of celery," he says, taking a sip of slush. "Uncle Charlie had sharpened some knives, and he has just told me to be careful with them. But I was thinking about how cute it is that you're such a random celery eater... and I sliced my arm." He turns his forearm over to show me.

"Wesley! That is a really bad cut! I hope you cleaned it out. You can't let it get infected. You better keep it bandaged. Maybe go to the doctor."

"Nah, you know my Grandpa Duke never took any of his kids to the doctor. He stitched everyone up himself."

"Did he have a medical background? Some schooling?"

"Not a day," he says, and I laugh until I get hiccups.

Love from your family is usually apparent and very vital, but love from the right boyfriend should be too. My love-congested head is repeatedly telling me that Wesley's love shouldn't be important to me right now - but in fact, it is extremely important.

The next morning, I somehow remembered, in this mixed-up brain of mine, that Mom said she was going to call Dr. Marshall. So, instead of the usual family of robins waking me up outside of my bedroom window, it was my mom's soft voice on the phone that did.

I slide out of bed and delicately hang Wesley's shirt on the back of my doorknob. I peek my head around my door and eavesdrop on Mom's phone conversation.

"She's completely lost her appetite now," I hear my mom say. "Oh, okay, thank you."

She set the handset down into the base as I instantly appear behind her.

"Everything okay, Mom?"

"Yeah, I just moved Grandma's appointment up. Dr. Marshall wants to see her this morning."

"Why? Is he worried about her not eating? The days have been really hot lately, and she always loses her appetite when it's this warm."

"I'm sure that's all it is."

"Or maybe it's the chemotherapy. You know it's all chemicals."

"Does Grandma look a lot thinner to you?"

I hesitate with my answer. "Yeah...she does."

When Mom, Grandma Dotti, and I get to the doctor's office, it's the same routine. I sit in the waiting room like a child. I wish my mom would let me come in with them. I have a lot of questions for Dr. Marshall.

I have a hard time making eye contact with anyone in the waiting room today, so I pull on the string of my shorts and watch it unravel across my thigh. I pull tight on the blue string, roll it between my fingers and thumbs, and then finally look up.

An older lady sits across from me, and I smile at her. Her long strawberry blonde hair is thin and her skin is pasty white. Her face is gaunt, and her sweater hangs off her left shoulder. Her eyes sparkle, and her smile feels warm and sincere. Her smile tells me that she would never hurt a living thing. I bet she's an amazing grandma too.

184

The middle-aged man next to me sits slouched in his seat. His dark and heavy eyebrows are stuck in a glazed stare. His gangly body sits uncomfortably in his seat as I watch him fidget back and forth in his chair. His long fingers, that bear no ring, tap lightly on his boney knee. I hope he's not fighting his cancer alone. I hope he has someone in his life, maybe a sister, niece or nephew, who loves him tremendously. I wonder what he's thinking about. Or do I really want to know?

A new batch of pain hits my empathetic heart, so I quickly look down at the carpet. I bite my lip hard, but a tear still falls out onto my lap anyway.

When Mom and Grandma Dotti finally come out, I wipe my face with my palm and force a smile.

"Ruby, the doctor wants to admit Grandma Dotti into the hospital," my mom says right away.

"Why?"

"Her medicines aren't working for her, she's losing too much weight, and they're worried about her dehydrating."

As we take our quiet ride to the hospital, my exhausted brain, still thinking of the people in the waiting room, wonders if Grandma Dotti will soon start to resemble them. Or does she already, and I refuse to notice? Is her cancer spreading? Has her cancer now become terminal? Have I not taken good care of her?

My heart feels like it has completely split in half and is leaking liquid anguish throughout my entire bloodstream. I hurt all over. My blood, my muscles, my bones.

"Mom, could you turn on the radio, please?"

185

*I'm in desperate need of a good song to fill my head.*
*You're my Best Friend* comes on the radio, and I softly sing along with Queen, and think of all the times Grandma Dotti and I have sung this song together.

I wipe a tear from my cheek. But it was a tear different from the others that have come out of me today. It was a grateful tear. I know not many people can say that their Grandma is their best friends, but I can.

I realize that not only do I need extra love this summer, I need extra friendship. All these emotions that I feel today remind me that I could possibly lose the friendship that has always been the most important to me.

Room 203 at Newsted Hospital is every negative adjective I can think of. The window next to Grandma Dotti's crisp starchy bed is long with shadowy streaks. I pull the heavy blue curtains open and let out a heavy sigh as I stare into the crowded parking lot. I'm trying to remain positive, for Mom and Grandma, but it seems to be getting harder and harder for me.

I sit on the brown leather chair by the window and watch Grandma Dotti change from her yellow and brown flowered polyester short set to a gray tattered hospital gown. The nurse, who seems to be smiling a little more today, starts to attach Grandma Dotti up to an IV pole that she rolls alongside her bed. Her name tag is crooked on her pale green scrubs, so I tilt my head to read her name. Nurse Cece O.

Nurse Cece delicately situates a tray onto Grandma Dotti's lap. It has a Styrofoam cup filled with water and

186

a lonely bowl of red Jell-o. Grandma Dotti's hands shake as she lifts the Jell-o filled spoon up to her mouth. I watch it continuously fall off the spoon and back into her bowl.

"Grandma, let me help you," I say somberly.

"I'll get it, Ruby," she smiles.

I feel exhausted. I don't know if I can keep holding back these suppressed tears much longer. It pains me to sit here and watch her struggle with a simple thing like lifting a spoon. It's getting harder every day.

The announcement is made over the hospital speaker that visiting hours are over.

"Let's go, Ruby. I'll see you tomorrow, Mom," my mom says as she tucks Grandma Dotti's feet in with an extra blanket.

"I'm not leaving," I tell the both of them. "Seven miles is just too far away. I've never been that far from Grandma. I'm not going home tonight. I'm staying here," I say firmly.

"Ruby, you can't stay."

"Sure I can. Wild Horse couldn't drag me away, Mom."

"No, Ruby. You can't. Grandma needs some rest, and well, so do you. You look tired."

"I'll sleep here," I say wiggling my butt back and forth in the chair. "I'm okay."

"Not in that chair?"

"Well, yeah..."

"Ruby, you can come back tomorrow," she says firmly.

I turn to my mom and quietly say, "I'm not leaving, Mom. As much as this hurts me, this hospital, this disease - nothing could keep me away Grandma. She might need me in the middle of the night."

"Ruby, I'll be fine," Grandma Dotti interrupts. "You go home and get some sleep. You do look tired. Come by and see me in the morning. We'll have breakfast together, okay?"

I've always been a good kid, and obeyed my mom and Grandma, so as I look back and forth into their glaring eyes, I cave in to their demand.

"I'll be here first thing in the morning, Grandma," I say confidently, as I kiss her goodbye.

Discouraged by my pitiable surrendering to my mom and Grandma, I stare out the window of my mom's car in frustration. My heart hurts more today than ever, and it feels like I'm letting Grandma Dotti slip away from me.

"Mom?" I say, reluctantly turning off the radio and the wonderful Four Tops. "I'm going to get up early tomorrow and take the earliest bus I can to the hospital. I don't want Grandma to wake up alone. I don't care what visiting hours are, I don't care that I'm there before I should be,  I don't want her to wake up and see that no one is there with her. Don't worry, I'll give myself plenty of time to eat breakfast, and I'll even squeeze in some chores. But I plan on being at the hospital all day, because I'm gonna learn everything I need to so I can take care of her, and then she can come home. I'll work alongside the doctors and nurses, and together we'll beat this cancer. I know I can take better care of her than anyone at that hospital because I care about her more. I definitely love her more, and my commitment to her is stronger than any

Hippocratic Oath a doctor or nurse has have taken. Nothing will keep me away from her."

"That sounds like a lot of responsibility for you Ruby, but I know how much you love Grandma. I'll come directly from work to relieve you."

"Relieve me? No, I'll stay until visiting hours end and then I'll ride home with you instead of taking the bus home."

"I love your commitment, but I know you, Ruby. You're going to let it consume you."

"Yeah, I absolutely will."

"I think you should squeeze in some time for yourself. You're going to need a break, just like anyone. You're going to need a little diversion and some time away from the hospital. It's all very overwhelming, and I don't want you to get rundown. You're going to try and do it all, and that's what always gets you sick. Grandma will understand if you're not always there. Ian and I will be there as much as we can, so among the three of us, I doubt she will ever be alone."

I shook my head at her. "No," I simply say.

"How about you continue your sleepovers with Bonnie?" she continues. "That way I know where you are at night. I'll know your safe and not at home, alone, crying your heart out and making yourself sick. Bonnie's always been good at taking care of you."

*Taking good care of me? I know someone else that is "good at taking care of me," that resides in that house,* I think to myself. *And Mom would surely NEVER recommend that sleepover if I had told her about Wesley. Should I mention him right now, or am I too late?*

I decide, one more time, that this is not the time to mention Wesley to her.

"Okay, I'll... stay the nights there," I tell her.

I cry into my pillow as the image of Grandma Dotti sitting in her hospital gown - trying to eat a bowl of Jell-o with a needle stuck in her arm - sits in the very front of my brain. It's haunting me.

I close my tired eyes at exactly 2:22 in the morning. My dream was in one color. The color of love - red. No one was in my dream but me, which surprisingly, didn't make me feel lonely; it made me feel the power of love.

No distance, no dark days, no lonely nights, and no lapse of time will diminish your love for someone when you have the truest of love in your heart. The power that it has actually makes the love increase. I love my grandma tonight more than I have ever loved her, and I love Wesley more than I have ever loved him.

And they both seem so far away.


My alarm clock drowns out my radio and I slap it off. I slowly sit up and stare out my bedroom window. I watch my mom get into her car and leave for work. I don't know where my instant burst of energy came from, but after I watched Mom cautiously back her car down the driveway, and then quickly accelerate and disappear down Kentfield, I shower, dressed, and braided my wet hair, in just under fourteen minutes.

Before I leave for my day at the hospital, I sprint back to my bedroom and grab my favorite sweater from my closet. Even though the mid-summer days are

190

still very warm, I just about freeze at the hospital. Grandma Dotti made me my favorite sweater four Christmases ago, and it, somewhat, still fits me. It's still stark white, and incredibly soft, but the little pink crocheted flowers on it are curled up and have slightly faded.

I pull on the sleeve of my old reliable sweater, and it falls off the hanger and onto my wrist as I glance at the clock by my bed. It reads 7:30 - gotta get moving!

I quickly grab three apples from the fruit bowl that sits in the middle of the kitchen table and shine each one on my shirt. I lock the front door behind me and run to catch the Fenkell bus.

I stay true to my ritual for over a week. Every day's the same (except Mom's day off from work on Sunday). I wake up early, shower, dress, grab my sweater, wake up Ian when he's able to come, make some whole wheat toast with apple jelly, and find something to bring for Grandma Dotti to make her smile. Yesterday she enjoyed the blueberries from our yard so much that I decide to make her some strawberry shortcake for today's snack. I'll pick the strawberries from our yard right before I leave so they're nice and fresh. I always pack double of everything so Mom has something to eat when she gets to the hospital.

Ian is with me this morning, but has to leave the hospital at 3:00 to go to work, so I grab my stuffed bag, Ian locks the door behind me, and we run to catch the bus.

For spending a beautiful hot summer day in a monotonous, contaminated hospital - I had a little fun.

I try to keep up with Ian as he pushes Grandma Dotti around in a wheelchair most of the day. I push her IV pole along side of her, and even though she never questions Ian's disruptive speed and his questionable wheelies, he made me very nervous. Grandma Dotti seems a little groggy and fumbles with her tubes, that are taped on her skinny arm, most of the day, but like always, she smiles and laughs along with Ian.

Before Ian leaves for work, we delicately put Grandma Dotti back into her bed. I pull her bed sheets firm and taut, and then I walk Ian to the elevator. I hand him one of my freshly shined apples, and hug him goodbye as we wait for the doors to open.

Ian holds on to my hug longer than he ever has. They are usually very short and very awkward. But for the first time, his long skinny arms wrap around me solid and strong. I rub Ian's back and hear his breathing shake. I think he's crying.

I haven't seen Ian cry in so long. So long, that I can't remember what it was that would possibly ever make him cry. It's tough for me to see anyone cry or feel their heartbreak, but especially Ian's. I wonder if he has faced a reality that I refuse to go near?

Ian abruptly lets go, and I watch him quickly turn into the open doors of the elevator. He rubs his teary eyes and then slaps a button on the elevator panel. He gives me a quick wave and I take one step forward, but the doors close between us.

I stand there for, maybe fifteen minutes, and let my tears roll down my face. When people you love are hurting, their pain becomes your pain, and you somehow begin to hurt even more. Even when you don't think you possibly can.

I slowly walk down the hallway. I stop and look at myself in the reflection of the hallway windows. My face is smeared with tears, and my eyes puffy and red. Grandma Dotti will notice the very second she sees me, so I try, with all the strength I have, to stop my tears. I inhale, then exhale, and smile my way back to her room.

She is sleeping soundly by the time I wash my face and adjust my emotional state. I lean into her and check her breathing and then watch her chest slowly rise. I wipe my face with the sleeve of my sweater and sit down in the metal chair next to her bed. I grab the latest edition of *Rona Barrett's Gossip* and hide my face behind it. I try to read the first few pages, but instead I lay the magazine down on the bed, take hold of her hand, and listen to the peaceful sounds of her sleep.

I think about how truly important loving someone is. Not a second should be wasted on anything else. In our life together, I know she has always felt the love I have for her. She knows I appreciate her, am grateful to her, and feel honored that my young life was in her hands. Because every day - I made sure she knew. As she lies here, in pain and suffering, and all without complaint - I still feel enormous pride.

I watch her sleep for hours, hoping that she is having a beautiful dream and not feeling the horrific chemicals flowing throughout her body. I carefully caress her arm that has turned black-and-blue from the needles that are constantly stuck in her. I'm careful not to disturb them, as they look like they hurt.

I make sure that the blanket from her bed at home,

which I brought to her a couple of days ago, is snug around her bed, keeping her warm and covering her. I look up at the clock that hangs on the wall next to the ignored television. It reads 5:00. Mom should be here soon, and even though I don't want to leave, I'm thinking that today maybe a dose of Wesley will make my heart feel a little bit better than it has. When he stopped by the house a couple of nights ago, his couple dozen of kisses, lime slush, and his genuine concern about everyone in my family made my heart smile for a short while.

Nurse Cece interrupts my thoughts as she brings in a tray of food and sets it down on Grandma Dotti's tray table. I eye the pile of orangey-red spaghetti, tossed salad and side of buttery corn. My stomach gurgles. I think I forgot to eat today.

The aroma of spaghetti quickly fills the room. Grandma Dotti wakes up suddenly, and her instant confusion forces her to sit up and forget about her IV and its attachments.

She places her hand over her mouth, grimacing in pain, and fills her slender palm with bile.

"Grandma, I'm right here," I say, as I quickly grab a large plastic cup and some tissues that sit by her bedside table. She fills the cup up with more bitter acid from her stomach as I carefully clean off her hand, wipe her parched lips, and then rub her back.

My hands slowly rub up and down her vertebrae. I can feel her bones, which catches me by surprise. She sits quiet and lifeless as I feel her body jerk in pain and watch her continue to fill the plastic cup.

I have no words to comfort her. Nothing. I can only I

194

watch her disintegrating muscles tighten and then relax. I look at her dinner tray and realize that the smell of food is making her nauseous. I abandon my weak attempt to console her and move her tray out to the hallway.

The pressure felt from my entire head filling with tears has given me an instant headache, so I was ready to go when Mom got there at 5:20. I'm finding it harder and harder to hold my tears back. I feel like I'm ready to break in half.

"Mom, I'll be at Bonnie's tonight. If you need me, I'll come home," I tell her as I grab my sling bag, kiss Grandma Dotti goodbye, and I leave to catch the bus.

I cry the very second I left Grandma Dotti's room. I hold my face in my hands and cry harder as I wait for the elevator doors to open. I cry during the two minute elevator ride down, and I hold on to the metal bars because I could barely stand. My legs are weak and my body shakes. I continue crying as I go into the parking lot that connects to the bus stop. I couldn't stop.

My eyes strain to look at the hot afternoon sun that beats down on my face. I stop, turn, and look up to Grandma's window on the second floor. I find her window easily. I find it because through my teary eyes and the humid July air I see Grandma Dotti. She is waving at me while my mom is next to her untangling the tubes that look caught in her IV pole.

I wave back at my beautiful Grandma, and as I stand there, it becomes a moment in my life I know I'll never forget.

She smiles her biggest smile at me. She put her fingers up to her mouth and blows me a kiss. I blew a kiss back to her, and she pretends to grab it out of the air and tuck it into the pocket of her hospital gown. My very emotional heart remembers all of the times when I was little that she would walk me to school, and just before I would turn to go into class, I would wave goodbye, and then blow her a kiss. She would always catch my invisible kiss and then tuck it deep into the pocket of her purple cardigan sweater.

Everything about me feels broken.

I don't want to turn around and leave her. I want to stand here and blow kisses into the air all night, but I doubt that would help my crumbling heart. I turn and walk away as fast as I can to catch the bus.

My bottled-up tears are uncontrollable. I wipe them with my hand then try to think if I had ever cried this hard before. My dog bite didn't hurt this bad, my broken Humerus didn't hurt this badly. The three black eyes that I've had in my life no way have hurt this badly. And all the different types of burns and their degrees that I've had have do not come close to this pain that I feel throughout my entire body.

I climb aboard the bus and slide into the first open seat I see. I sit there as the bus driver quickly pulls away, and I admit something to myself that I haven't before. It was the very hardest thing I ever had to admit to myself in my life.

My grandma...she is dying.

Honestly, it's never been a thought that has ever entered my mind. I understand - we live, we die - I know. But admitting to yourself that someone you love so much might die someday has always sent instant pain throughout my body. So painful that you tell yourself to destroy the very thought of it instantly. So I always did. But I think reality has just taken over because I can't seem to destroy it this time.

I sit on the bus, staring out the window, crying harder and harder. I'm positive this is the hardest I have ever cried in my life. I don't care who is looking at me, and I don't care what I look like or sound like to anyone. I feel my nose starting to run, and the little makeup that I wear, I'm sure is being smeared around my face. And I just don't care. I only wipe my face when the tears start to tickle my cheek.

I pay no attention to who is boarding the bus and who is exiting. Nothing matters to me right now. I hold my face in my hands and continue to cry so hard that the bus driver asks if I was okay. I don't answer him. My heart feels inconsolable and the world around me seems oblivious at this moment. I just continued to sit and cry.

I don't focus on anything and not concerned for a second about what I'm doing or where I am going. I grab the rolled up tissue that I keep tucked in the sleeve of my sweater, and I delicately wipe my nose.

My grandma has never wanted me to ever be in any type of pain or hurt in anyway. She always told me, "All hearts get injured, Ruby, but never let the pain of that injury change how your heart loves. Always keep a loving heart."

Wesley Everett. He's what I need to keep my heart from changing.

The bus stops at the corner of Grand River Avenue and Chapel Street. I know I'm near Keeler's Gym, and I'm not sure if Wesley is even there today, but I quickly exit the bus and run my fastest down Chapel Street.

My instant batch of adrenaline swings open the big metal doors of Keeler's Gym, and I instantly start to look for Wesley.

He's there. Our eyes meet as I watch him hastily slide his boxing gloves off and throw them down on a bench next to him. Tears pour uncontrollably from my face, and I run directly to him.

His arms wrap completely around me, so tight, that I couldn't move even if I wanted to. I nestle my teary face into his chest, feeling my hyperventilating body, worn and tired.

Wesley moves his hands into my stringy hair. He spreads his fingers wide into the back of my head like he's trying to push it even closer.

"Wes, it hurts...everyday it hurts. I can't stand to see her so sick. To see her...dying." The warmth of his hugs coated my bruised heart. "I'm sorry if I bothered you," I say.

"You could never bother me. I'm glad you came here. I'm so sorry. I love you, Ruby - so much. I'm here for you; I'll always be here for you."

He put his warm hands on my face and kissed my tear-streaked cheeks.

We stand there holding each other in Keeler's Gym. I cry all the tears I have inside of me. My heart is crushed, but there is still hope for it. I know that it can still feel love, and that is something crucial for me to realize.

Love can sometimes be selfish, we're probably all guilty of that at times, but it can also be selfless at the exact time you need it to be. I would do anything to help someone I love through their saddest time, and even though things are cloudy right now in my head, I can see Wesley's trying to do that for me.

I think of the powerful words that Grandma Dotti once told me about love. She said, "Always keep your heart open to love, Ruby. Even when it's hurting. Because the truest of love will heal your heart, so it's always worth the risk."

Holding Wesley, I decide not to question "us" anymore. I'm going to hang on tight to him and nothing is going to make me let go. No guilt, of any kind, will stop me from being with him. I'm going to love him and the long or short road we have together. Nothing will pull me away from my commitment to my grandma or to him.

# AS TEARS GO BY
♥♥♥♥♥♥♥♥♥♥♥♥♥♥♥♥♥♥♥♥♥♥♥♥♥♥♥♥♥♥♥♥♥♥♥♥♥♥♥♥

Both of my eyes are puffy and sore. My left eye is almost completely swollen shut. I need to get the swelling down before I go over to Wesley's for dinner, so I find a frozen bag of peas in the freezer and gently press them on each eye. My headache is worse, so I lie on the couch, on my left side. I remember Dr. Cantrell told me that is my "healing side."

After a half hour my headache hasn't gone away and my eyes still hurt at the slightest touch. I place the bag of peas back in the freezer, grab my sling bag, stuffed my algebra book deep inside, and hop over the back fence.

I walk slowly through Bonnie's back yard, slowly through her kitchen, and even slower up the stairs to Wesley room. My mind and body - entirely exhausted.

"Hi Wes," I say, my voice dry and cracking. I watch him take the t-shirts from his duffel bag and arrange them neatly in the top dresser drawer. I hope this means he's going to stay. "You're unpacking?"

"Yeah..." he says, as he quickly abandons his laundry and turns to give me a kiss. "Are you feeling better? I'm sorry; I know that's a stupid question."

"It's not. I'm a little better... not really. It's just...that... I realized some things today. Things I've been refusing to see...and it hit me hard."

My voice breaks, and I feel myself tearing up again. I don't want to start crying again, so I abruptly take out my algebra book.

"I thought maybe we could go over some algebra,

you know, put my mind somewhere else. Plus I have a book for you. It's my favorite. My grandma used to read it to me when I was little. I thought maybe we can read it together."

I pull out my favorite book, *Oliver Twist,* by Charles Dickens, and hand it to him.

"I made you some dinner," he tells me, pointing to a tray sitting by his window.

I look over at the tray by his bedroom window. A small cup of water overflowing with purple daisies sits next to a lime slush, a plate covered with a heart-shaped napkin, and four pieces of black licorice. When I remove the napkin, the combination of fettuccini alfredo, buttered popcorn, and about a dozen marshmallows, instantly makes me smile. I hold my slush tight with both hands. I put the straw to my lips, take a big sip and then slide it into Wesley's lips to share.

"I *think* I got all your favorites," he says, kissing my instantly frozen lips.

"You did. I especially love the side of black licorice."

We take our normal spot on the roof outside of Bonnie's window, and I share all my dinner with him. I know I'm hungry, but my stomach feels completely full. We work on a little algebra, read, and kiss between paragraphs. The house and the neighborhood have suddenly become quiet. The night air is still, warm and dense, and even though the temperature is 80 plus degrees, we hold on to each other and listen to the crickets, Mr. Morgan's frog pond, and the sound of Mr. Norcross' ongoing pulsating sprinkler.

Wesley pulls his t-shirt over his head and gathers it

201

up into a ball. He folds his hands behind his head, and lies down on his spherical t-shirt pillow. He pulls me into him, and I lie by his side, listening to the softness of his beating heart.

"Wes, I'm sorry I'm keeping you up so late."

"You're not. Stay with me," he says, pulling me closer.

With his arms wrapped tightly around me, my heart feels loved. And I am in desperate need of love today. It seems that every time we are together our hearts grow closer. But tonight, Wesley shares his painful past with me and it changes us forever.

I sit up as my hair falls into my face. "Wes, how did you decide on your tattoo?" I ask him.

I rest my head back on his chest, and my fingers rub his soft skin.

"Last January Holden took me to a friend of his that does tattoos in his basement. It's illegal as hell, but Holden didn't care. He thought that if we got matching tattoos it would help us find some peace with our dad's death, and it would also honor him. He picked this Celtic symbol. It means everlasting love."

He points to the ovals that are sticking out of the circle.

"These three triskeles symbolize the three characteristics of people - mind, body and spirit. They intertwine in the middle of the circle to represent the everlasting circle of eternity. Of course when my mom found out I had gotten a tattoo, she was beyond pissed. Holden ended up telling her during a fight they had. It became their biggest fight."

"Well, I can understand your mom being mad," I tell

him. "But I do understand what Holden was trying to do for you. It's actually a really beautiful thing for the two of you to forever share. Wes, do you want to tell me about your family?"

"Yeah," he said quietly.

"If it's too hard you don't have to."

"It is, but I've wanted to tell you. I've wanting to a couple of times, but...it's hard to hear, Ruby. And the last thing I want to do is make you sad. Well, sadder. That would just be horrible of me. With everything you're going through," he pauses for a minute and then rubs his fingers up and down my arm.

"I want you to tell me so I can help you," I assure him.

"I was ten years old when my dad died. It was the end of March, and I remember it was cold with a little bit of snow on the ground. Holden had to pick me up from school every day because my mom didn't want me walking home alone. I remember that I was excited about getting 100% on my spelling test. It was the first time that entire school year. My dad and I had been working on getting my grades up, and I knew he was home that day. I ran home with the test clutched in my fist to show him. I ran up the driveway."

He hesitates, but then continues.

"I ran in the front door and...my dad was lying on the living room floor completely still. I somehow knew that he was dead, I don't know how, but I did. I just felt it. And for some reason, I still went up to him. His entire body was covered in blood. There were stab wounds all over him. I stood over him and counted. Seventeen. His eyes...and mouth were open. He wasn't breathing. The door slammed behind me, and when it did, it was the first time I felt scared. I called out for my mom, even though I knew she was at work. There was blood everywhere. I remember I got mad that there was blood on my brand new shoes that I had left under the couch.

Holden grabbed me and dragged me out onto the front porch. He kept screaming the same thing over and over. 'What the fuck! What the fuck!' That's not unusual for him to say, but he sounded different. It didn't sound like his voice. He ran back in the house, locked the screen door, and told me to stay outside. I heard him call the police. He was quiet, but frantic at the same time. I think I heard him cry. I've never heard Holden cry. I tried to go back in the house because, for some reason, I thought I could revive my dad. I pulled on the door so hard that I bent the frame. I shouted into the living room for Holden to check his pulse and give him mouth-to-mouth, but all I heard was him giving the police our address and telling them to hurry. I stood on the front porch in the cold and listened to the sirens get closer. That's when I got really scared. I realized they were coming to my house, and I started to shake. I don't know who notified my mom, she was at work. When someone dropped her off in our driveway, she ran into the house, hysterical. I had never seen her like that before. She was screaming so loudly that the neighbors were outside staring at our house from their porches. It made me feel embarrassed. The police would walk in and out of the house, passing me each time, and never saying a word. Different cars would come and go within the hours I was out there, and still no one said one word to me. They barely looked my way."

I sit up, take a hold of his hands, and squeeze them tight."

"It's strange," he says, "but every time I hear the sound of a zipper, I think of when the police zipped up the body bag they put him in. That's weird, huh? That I would think of that?"

"No, not at all," I say, my heart aching for him.

"I remember two really big guys carried him out of our house, right in front of me, into a dirty red van without even asking me to turn around. I was dying inside. Right there on my front porch."

He stops talking for a minute, stares at the night sky, and then continues.

"I don't remember much more about that night. We stayed at a shelter for a couple days. I remember a small funeral. Bonnie was there. I remember that she and Clyde got in trouble for something they did in another viewing room. And she put gum in my hair. I remember that too. I didn't go up to the casket at all. That's something I think I'll regret someday. Some guy in an ugly plaid suit kept talking to us about 're-creation' and every time he did, I quietly told him to shut up."

His eyes fill with tears, so I lean in to kiss him.

"That's it," he says. "That's the day my world, my heart, and everything else about me changed."

"Who killed your dad, Wes?"

"We don't know. My mom went back and forth to the police station for a while, and they never gave her any kind of answers. At first they made a promise to us that they would find the killer, but there was no forced entry into the house or witnesses. They really have no evidence of any kind. Nothing. My mom gave up. She gave up on everything. She stopped leaving the house, and then she lost her job. And... everything else. But, that's what heartbreak does. It makes you want to forget about everything around you even though...you shouldn't."

"I...can imagine," I tell him as I wipe a tear from my cheek.

"She stopped paying attention to us, and we needed her. Holden went to school on occasion, but I never finished that year. That's the year I flunked, so I decided to just stay in my room for a while. Hide, you know. And it felt so good to hide. I stayed there until the end of summer, but it was just so comfortable to hide that...I never fully emerged. Not until this summer, actually."

"I'm glad your mom let you come here to live." I say, with slight excitement in my voice.

"Well, my mom lost the house; she let it go into foreclosure. She tried as long as she could to pay the mortgage, but it just got too hard for her with no job. I hate that house anyway. I hope I never go anywhere near it. And you know something that's weird? Since that day...the day I found my dad...I was never able to walk through the front door. I went through the back door every day after that. Strange."

"Not strange at all," I tell him.

"We had no money. We barely ever had anything to eat, which was another thing that made Holden angry all the time. My Grandma Alice would bring us food sometimes. Cold sandwiches."

"You know, Wes, your family is entitled to Social Security benefits from the state of Ohio. Money to help you."

"My Uncle Jason tried to help my mom with that, but I guess she never followed through on anything. Something else that frustrated everybody."

I don't want to interrupt him too much. I'm thinking that maybe him sharing this painful part of his life with me would somehow help him start to heal. There are different ways to heal yourself, and you have to do what is exactly right for you. Sometimes to verbalize your deepest emotions brings peace, and sometimes it's a tattoo in memoriam.

He takes a big swallow of our shared slush and continues.

"When I went back to school that next fall, all the work they gave me seemed too hard, and I just couldn't concentrate. I was in so much pain, Ruby! I remember my entire body hurt. I would throw up for no reason. I wasn't sick. It was pain that I'd never experienced before. I started getting into a lot of fights in school, and I'd get kicked out. I was relying on my mom to help me, but she couldn't because she was hurting just as badly. Holden was the only one who could see that things were getting out of control. That's when he talked to me about boxing. He said it would help me with the anger I had built up. But it made my mom even madder. She didn't like that my dad had done some boxing; he had hurt some people too, so she definitely didn't want me to start. But... she wasn't doing anything to help me...she just wasn't able to. Holden was all I had. But he was a mess himself. He got thrown in jail - more than once. Got some girl, he barely knew, pregnant. He'd disappear for a few days, and we never knew where he was. When he dropped out of school, that's when my mom forced him to join the Army. And...I think he was glad to go."

"I bet you miss him," I say, trying to sound strong for him.

"Yeah, I do. But he needs help. Help my mom and I couldn't give him."

"How is your mom, now?" I ask him, knowing of his estrangement from her.

"My mom...my mom is sick. I know that Bonnie told you that she didn't want me, and that's why I'm here, but it's not that," he says, shaking his head in annoyance. "That's just another smart ass answer from her. It's... it's just been hard for my mom to take care of everyone, and she was just not mentally strong. So right now.... she's in a mental hospital."

"Wes, I'm so sorry."

"Ruby, I'm worried about her. Life got too tough for her and she...got sick. Mentally sick. My dad's death hurt her so badly that she let go of everything important in her life - her job, our house, all her friends... me and Holden. Everyone tried to help her, but she pushed them away. I was doing it too, I guess. Her sadness turned to depression and, she stopped taking care of herself. It got so bad that it was starting to scare me. I was afraid that when I came home from school, she wouldn't be there...or worse. I might find her....I tried to help her the best I could - but she wouldn't let me. And I admit - that hurt me more than her not being able to take care of me and Holden. I tried. I tried everything. I told her that I'd take care of all of us. I had planned on getting a job after school and pay for everything, but she said that admitting herself into the hospital was the best thing to do for everyone."

"She's right, Wes," I interrupt. "It's a very courageous thing to do."

"I am proud of her for that. I guess I shouldn't be upset with her anymore that she asked Aunt Lauren if I could live here for the summer."

"The first step is always the hardest they say, but she's on her way."

"She promised me she would try and get better, and she just ...has to, Ruby. She has to get mentally strong again. And most important - happy again."

"She will. She'll do it for you and Holden."

"I don't know, Ruby, I would tell her everyday that I loved her, but she acted like she didn't care."

"But she did. She loves you enough to send you here, to a safe and loving home. And she loves Holden enough to enlist him in the Army, which will help him."

"He seems happier. I talked to him yesterday."

"You did? That's great!"

"I told him all about you and how happy you make me, but now I need to tell my mom. I need to tell her how much I like living here. How much I've healed. I need to tell her about you, and how much I love you. But I can't. She's in isolation. My grandma Alice is the only one who can talk to her. No one else is allowed for some stupid reason. All I know is that...she is getting better, and when she is released, the doctors will help her find a job and a new place to live. That just can't be anywhere - it has to be here, so I can be with you. That sounds selfish of me, but don't I have a say in my life?"

"You do. Of course, you do."

I have a lot more answers floating around my head than that one, but I can't say them out loud. Mine are way more selfish than anything he's thinking. I can't keep him away from his mom, but I can't let him go either. And I know how life works when you're forced to say goodbye to someone. That person leaves, and the spot that they had in your heart sometimes fades - then disappears. If he leaves me, like Grandma Dotti, I'm afraid that he'll fade from my life.

I feel a tear trickle down my cheek and quickly roll down my neck.

"I didn't mean to make you cry," he tells me. "I'm supposed to be making you feel better tonight," he says to me, as he reaches over and wipes the tears from my puffy cheeks.

I hold on to his hand, kiss it and give him a sad smile.

"I'm going to help you and your family in every way I know how," I tell him, sounding my strongest of the day. "I've studied forensic science, so I'll learn all about your dad's case and I'll do whatever it takes to solve it."

He laughs softly, "Of course you've studied forensics science. How is it that you keep me falling deeper and deeper in love with you every time that I'm with you?"

"Wes, I will help heal your broken heart any way I can."

"You already have," he says with a crooked smile. "You know, Ruby there was a time that I was pretty convinced that I would never love *anything* ever again in my life. Finding my dad dead...well... it did things to my brain. To my heart. Even when Holden kept telling me to never shut down my heart. He kept saying, 'Don't plant that bitter seed in your heart; the one that destroys everything that dad taught you. Because if you do, he will be completely eliminated from your life - never to have existed.' So I must have somehow listened to him because I fell in love with you, and it has been the easiest thing I've ever done. You've erased the pain in my heart and made it feel the greatest it's ever felt. I understand the 're-creation' part that the man in the ugly plaid suit was talking about the day of my dad's funeral. People you love leave you, and new love enters your life. They don't replace the old, they just create new love. And you have to let yourself do that because that's the only way we all survive heartbreak."

He looks up at me and gives me a slow wink that makes my stomach twinge and my heart skip around. I rest my head on his shoulder as his fingers get lost in my hair.

"I'm so glad my parents taught me what love is," he says, kissing me softly, "because I can't imagine having you in my life and not being able to love you, to hold you, to kiss you, and to feel you hold me."

Wrapped in his arms, I think about our re-creation of love and how the hole that has formed in each of our hearts is filling up.

"Ruby, you know what I've learned?"

"What, Wes?"

"When someone you love dies, everyone expects you to find a way to get over them. But I learned that you really shouldn't. You can never erase the mark that they left on your heart - especially when they take up most of it. It's impossible to do. So you should never try to get over them. Instead, do the opposite and honor them every day. I try to make my dad proud every day, and I know that you will make your grandma proud every day. I already know that about you."

"She's has left the deepest mark on my heart."

"You know, I still rely on my dad every day for something. I think about him, and I think about what he would do, and he somehow answers me."

"Yeah, I believe that," I say, as I blink away more tears.

"Someday your heart will feel better, Ruby. A lot of people love you, and someday your heart will feel different. Falling in love with you this summer made me realize that."

"As hard as life can get, and as tough as it is, Wes, I've learned this summer that when you feel your heart filling up with pain, it's important that you still see love."

"I know I'm not as smart as you," he says to me, "but I know what I feel, and it doesn't matter how old we are. I know that all I want to do is love you in all the ways I know how."

"Wes, I do think you're smart. I think you're very smart. Some people think that being smart is based on the level of education you have, but that's not true.

Smart people figure out what matters most in life, and that is love. Love as much as you can, because it's the only thing in life that really matters. Wes, I want you to stay here, but I understand if you can't. And, I was thinking, when you're ready, if you want, you can talk to a counselor at Redford when school starts. You should never feel ashamed of anything that's happened to you in your life, especially what your heart feels. Maybe I can go with you," I put my head down and stare into my lap, "I might need to."

"We'll go together," he says, softly rubbing my back.

It's 2:18 when we climb back in to the house from the roof. We kiss in the dark hallway, and he watches me go into Bonnie's bedroom.

I cautiously climb into bed, trying not to wake a sleeping Bonnie. I lie there next to her, completely still, and listen to the radio she left on for me. I listen to Al Green sing me a song that I immediately decide will be Wesley's and my song. I move my lips and sing along to *Let's Stay Together*.

I can't fall asleep. My brain is overloaded and doesn't seem to want to shut down for the night. Wesley is circulating in it and I already miss his touch. My body feels paralyzed, and my arms feel empty without him in them.

I think about how terrified he must have been as he walked into his house and found his dad dead on the floor. That's something that had to have left him severely damaged. I think of Holden and his mom, the dearest people left in his life, and how he's been forced to live without the both of them this summer. I think about when they both come back for him, and worry that he will start his new life somewhere else. Somewhere maybe far from me. Wesley knows all the feelings that I'm going through right now. He knows what it feels like to lose someone you love so much - someone who has influenced your life so deeply, that it's become crucial that they are always around to continue. Someone you're positive you can't live without.

I take a deep breath and say to myself in the dark, "I need him."

Experiences like he went through change people for life. You can go either way. Shut off your heart and die inside, or leave your heart open for someone to come along, love you and fill the tremendous void.

"He needs me too."

There are very few things that I do in my life that I do not have an explanation for. What I've just decided to do is one of them.

I slowly get up and walk out of Bonnie's bedroom. I creep as quietly as I can down the hall to Wesley's room, and I carefully choose the least creaky floorboards.

His door is slightly open so I push it a little wider and step quietly into his room. He is sitting up in his bed, his arms folded behind his head and his blankets in a small pile next to him. I shut his door behind me, and I lock it. I tiptoe over to him.

"I just heard a song that made me think of you," I whisper to him. "Let's make sure that we always stay together - somehow," I tell him. "No matter what. Loving you forever is exactly what I want...."

He reaches out his arms and pulls me on top of him.

"It's what I want more than anything in my life, Ruby," he whispers in my ear, as his one hand slides low on my back and the other is instantly lost in my tangled hair.

We hold on to each other and let our hands slide all around our warm bodies. Wesley delicately shifts my bra and underwear around, and I do the same to his loosely fitted boxer shorts. I touch all of him and he touched all of me. We kiss harder than we have ever kissed as our lips press deeper into each other. This is where love feels so good.

I just can't stop. He's always the one who stops us. We kiss until I can't breathe anymore
e. I think this is what it feels like to be drowning in a pool of water. Everything that I think is wrong - feels right. Even the dangerous stuff. But knowing that, I decide that this is exactly where I want to spend my summer nights. And no apologies this time, because I need it. I need this extra love in my life.

"I love you so much, Ruby," he whispers in my ear.

"Everything's going to be alright, Wes. I'm always going to show you how much I love you. Everyone will see, and then you'll be able to stay here, where you belong." I tell him.

Right now I want him to feel the love that I have in my heart for him, because no one ever knows how long they have someone.

We fall asleep holding each other until the sun comes up - which was only a few hours later. I don't think I slept for very long because I soon hear the birds chirping and feel the morning sun on my face.

Wesley looks gorgeous lying there next to me. His face so sleepy, so peaceful, that I don't want to wake him. I carefully slip out of his arms, kiss him goodbye, and then walk silently through the house and back home to my unsullied bed.

This morning, as I realize my grandma is slipping away from me, I also realize that Wesley has slipped it. That's how love works sometimes. It can sneak up on you when you least expect it, and your wounded heart can get a chance to survive without tremendous damage. I need that right now so desperately, because the love I have for my grandma is just too big a loss for me.

Today I cried every tear that I had stored in my body. Really, that's all I did was cry today. But as the tears go by in your life, something always takes its place - something bigger, and something essential to your life. Today, for me, it was strength.

# I GOT THE BLUES
♥♥♥♥♥♥♥♥♥♥♥♥♥♥♥♥♥♥♥♥♥♥♥♥♥♥♥♥♥♥♥♥♥♥♥♥♥

Ian has to work early today, so I wake him up after I am done with my shower. I grab my sling bag and make a mental list of things to take to Grandma Dotti at the hospital.

From her bedroom I take her favorite embroidered pillow that the two of us made together in the summer of 1975. Also, from her room, I take the beautiful sapphire sunflower sun catcher that has hung in her window ever since Ian made it for her on Mother's Day of 1972. I make a mental note to stop at Checkers on my way to the hospital to pick up some ginger-flavored hard candy, too. I think that the candy will help settle Grandma Dotti's tender stomach so she won't throw anything up today. I shout a quick goodbye to Ian from another room and head out the door.

After stopping at Checkers, I am the only one who boards the bus when it arrives fifteen minutes late. I quickly pick my spot behind the bus driver. I sit quietly and hug my sling bag that hugs my paper bag, that cradles my crisp new magazine and new bag of candy.

I immediately start to think about Wesley. I have trust in young love, and I believe in love at first sight. I root for, support, and believe in *Romeo and Juliet's* fictional love for each other, as well as all the other great love stories in literature.

I wonder what will happen to us.

Wesley says he loves me now, but will he end up breaking my heart, or will he continue to love me and strengthen that wavering heart of mine? People change as they get older - life forces that on you. I want him to be the one who heals my broken heart. But if he re-breaks it, I'll never be the same. Damage to any heart always remains; the pain lessons, but it never leaves you entirely.

I usually smile at everyone who boards the bus, but today, as I listen to the bus driver methodically do his job, I sit sullenly and stare out the window at the inflated gray clouds. All these thoughts in my head about love, death, and all the destroying it can do, have left my heart feeling my lowest ever.

When I'm down, I think, like everyone, that life feels negative. Your heartache and confusion surface and it's hard to move around it all. I usually think about two things when life knocks me down - The Vietnam War and my dad.

Derek Scott Vander is my dad. Born sometime in the spring; is a salesman of something; has one sister and six brothers; likes to smoke Pall Mall cigarettes and drink Dewar's scotch. And while married to my mom, he had lots of girlfriends, and hardly ever lived with us. That's all I know about him.

Strangely, I miss him today. I think somehow he would be able to help me through my sadness.

"What's wrong, Honey? You look so sad," a lady in the aisle across from me says, interrupting my thoughts. Her pretty blue eyes match her denim bell bottom jumper that, for a second, made me smile.

"I got the blues," I half heartedly tell her glaring back out the window, "in every shade."

"You need to change those blues to yellow," she tells me fidgeting in her seat.

218

I disregard her words instantly and try to shake all my sad thoughts out of my head, because I know that no words, of any kind, can pull me out of my heart paralysis. The only thing I can muster up is, "I'll try."

Grandma Dotti is sleeping when I get up to her room, so I pull the crammed, and now wrinkled, pillow from my bulging bag and lay it next to her. I check her feet again and make sure they're covered with her quilt from home, and I re-tuck her in all the way around. I hang Ian's sun catcher in the window - The same window that I looked into just yesterday from the parking lot, and cried a thousand tears. I take the ginger-flavored candies from my bag and neatly stack them next to her on her nightstand.

I watch her sleep as I play with the corners of the magazines that I plan on reading to her later today. Despite all the medical equipment attached to her, she looks peaceful, like Wesley did when I left him just a few hours ago. I wiggle into the gray leather hospital chair until I'm comfortable, and I stare out at the drizzly sky.

I think of her job as a nanny before she married Grandpa Kip, and the family she loved and took care of before us. I think about everyone's admiration for her, and all the health issues she's conquered over the years. I love that she still cooks from scratch, sews mostly everything by hand, hangs her clothes out on the clothesline to dry, reads every night before she goes to sleep, and I love her dedication to raising Mom and Ian so perfectly. She's such a rare and beautiful person. I couldn't possibly love her anymore than I do.

My eyes feel heavy. I fight to stay awake, in case Grandma Dotti needs me, but I soon cave in. I softy sing to myself *I Wish It Would Rain,* as my eyes slowly close. In my dream I am standing beside the great David Ruffin, making myself the sixth Temptation, and wondering why rain, like tears, is associated with sadness.

Rain and tears work the same. They cleanse our earth and our soul. They sometimes bring relief or hope, and sometimes a fresh and beautiful change. I really should stop holding back my tears, because they are helping me through my most difficult change. My emotions are a big part of who I am, and if it's natural for me to cry, then I absolutely should.

Cry when I need to, listen to all my favorite music as much as I can, and let Wesley's love continue to fill my heart - that's the only way I'm going to survive this summer.

I'm not sure what woke me up, but Grandma Dotti was watching me sleep when I opened my eyes. She smiles at me, and usually that makes me smile, but not today. I can't even pull out a fake one. For some reason my glowering mood is not changing.

I give her the ginger candy, some raisins, and a small jar of peanut butter with whole wheat crackers. A dose of iron and protein, I'm thinking. She keeps them all down, and she is alert and sharp when we critique the latest edition of *Rona Barrett's Hollywood* magazine.

It's amazing to me that she doesn't complain about anything. All the tubes sticking out of her tiny, beaten body must hurt, and certainly have to be uncomfortable for her, but she smiles through it all.

I help her go to the bathroom and then untangle her tubes. When I help her back in bed, she asks me a question that I was hoping to avoid.

"Ruby, how are your summer goals coming along? Have you written any new songs that you can sing to me?"

I didn't want to tell her that I've not attempted anything on my list, but I've never lied to her, and I'm certainly not going to start now. So I tell her the truth - The truth and a little more.

"Not yet, Grandma. I've had a little writer's block, I guess. I try to put some things down on paper, but I can't seem to do it."

"Don't stop writing Ruby, no matter what. It's important now more than ever that you do."

"Yeah...I'm sure I'll get a few things down...before summer ends," I pause for a minute or two. "And...I have a boyfriend now. His name is Wesley. Wesley Everett. He's Bonnie's cousin. He's just here for the summer. Then he'll probably go back to Ohio... or somewhere... to be with his mom. You'll really love him, Grandma. He's cute, sweet, and funny, and it sounds like he has a wonderful family. I love him, and he loves me. I feel good when I'm with him. He makes me feel loved... just like you always have. And I was thinking that when you come home, we can have a barbeque with Bonnie's family. You can meet him, and maybe his mom and brother too. You know, every time I see Wesley, he asks about you."

She takes both my hands and squeezes them. "Anyone with such a beautiful and loving heart like you have should always feel loved. You deserve love,

Ruby."

"Anything that is beautiful about me is because of you," I tell her, as I look down at the floor.

I want to say so much more, but I know it will make her cry. Anytime I tell her how much she means to me, her eyes fill with tears, and she always says, "You mean that much to me too, Ruby, but times that by a million." So instead I say, "You sure are getting a lot of get-well cards. Ian counted - thirty-three."

Grandma Dotti crunches on her candy throughout the day and keeps both her breakfast and lunch down. We spend most of the rainy day catching up on all our magazines, and even though I feel sad today, I end up having a good day with her. Days like today make me confident that she can get stronger and possibly come home.

It's 5:00 when Mom arrives. Just minutes later Uncle Nash & Uncle Levi, and their wives Aunt Marie and Aunt Carlie, also come to visit. They have been to visit a lot lately.

I say my goodbyes to everyone, kiss Grandma Dotti, remind Mom that I will be home later tonight, and run to catch the bus.

The bus ride seems long today, the mesmerizing sound of the swishing wiper blades almost makes me fall asleep again. And even though I was anxious to get home, I gather my things and kindly let the other people on the bus exit in front of me. I am purposely the last one off.

I wave goodbye to the bus driver and watch him cautiously head east on Fenkell. I look up at the dark viridian sky, and a few raindrops hit my nose. I squint my eyes and then open them to see Wesley sitting on the steps of the Fenkell Dry Cleaners with a lime slush by his side. I immediately sit on his lap, and we kiss. He holds me tight as I nuzzle into him. The rain suddenly grows stronger, but we sit unaffected by the increased downpour. We continue to kiss, and his hands caress my back, my leg, my arm, and my face. My skin grows increasingly clammy, my hair inelegantly damp, and my clothes stick uncomfortably to me. But kissing in the rain with the one you love - Heart therapy.

Wesley helps me change from my wet clothes to another favorite summer dress of mine. It is slate blue with royal blue daisies. For dinner I heat up some rutabaga pasties that Grandma Dotti and I made in the spring and had stockpiled in the freezer. When the dishes are clean, and two loads of laundry folded and put away, we leave to go shoot pool.

"Ruby, tomorrow's my Grandma Alice's birthday," he tells me, with his arms wrapped around me helping me adjust my pool cue. "I'm going to see her, and I was wondering if you'd like to go with me. I told her about you, and she wants to meet you."

He turns, faces me, and says, "But... I understand if it's not a good time. Being with your grandma is the most important thing right now, so I totally understand if you can't."

The tone in his voice is different – it's very serious.

"You know Wes that is really sweet... and considerate. I would love to meet your Grandma Alice, really," I tell him, as I wiggle our cue sticks next to each other into a wooden cue rack.

"You know, Ruby, the last thing my mom said to me before she went to the hospital was, 'Go find happiness, Wes.' And I have. My Grandma Alice will see that's it's because of you, and she'll tell my mom. I know she will. It will help my mom get better, and it will help me stay here, at Aunt Lauren's, so we can be together. I want our new life to be here in Detroit, so I can be with you."

"Anything that will help your mom get better, Wes, we'll do together."

Before our final kiss goodnight, we decide that we'll meet in the hospital parking lot at 5:00 tomorrow. That's right around the time Mom gets there. I hate this feeling of sneaking around and not being totally honest with my mom. I should have told her about him from the beginning, because now I think I'm in too deep with him. If I tell her now, I know it would end all sleepovers at Bonnie's, which honestly, are the only thing that makes me happy right now. I don't want to give them up. I can't. I'm not strong enough yet.

I climb into bed and look out at the indigo moon and make a wish. On hot summer nights like tonight, I sometimes sleep with nothing on. But tonight I put on Wesley's flannel shirt so I can feel him near me.

I never get around to checking Wesley's algebra paper. I decide that I am done teaching him something that he will probably never need. Instead, together we can continue to teach each other the most important thing in life - how to let love into your tender heart. And that really is the most important thing to teach anyone, *ever,* in this world.

The next day at the hospital, while Grandma Dotti sleeps, I ask Nurse Cece to show me how all the medical equipment works. She shows me how to check all her vitals, change her IV bags, check her needles, and what all the buttons on the infusion pump mean. I already feel confident that I can take care of her when she comes home.

When Mom arrives, I do a quick makeover in the hospital bathroom. I comb my hair, brush my teeth, dab a little Wild Cherry *Lip Lickers* on my slightly chapped lips, grab my sling bag, kiss Grandma Dotti goodbye, and hurry down the elevator to meet Wesley in the parking lot.

I see him almost right away, but what puzzles confuses me, is that he is leaning up against Jodi's 1968, steel blue Mustang. I run to greet him and give him my biggest kiss.

"Is this Jodi's car?" I ask him, a little confused.

"Yup."

"Where's Jodi?" I say, looking around for her.

"At home."

"Why... isn't she here? I don't understand why Jodi's car is here, and she's not."

"I asked her if I could borrow it, and she said yes."

"But you don't have a license."

"That doesn't mean I can't drive."

I laugh a *very* nervous laugh.

"Wes, you can't drive this car around. It's against the

225

law," I say, trying hard to sound serious. "We could get in some serious trouble," I add.

"No, I won't, and I can't worry about things that might never happen. Plus, I have Holden driver's license memorized. Come on, hop in. We got a good hours' ride."

I reluctantly get in, glance up to Grandma Dotti's hospital room, and sigh in relief that neither Mom or Grandma Dotti is looking out of the window today. How in the world would I begin to explain this one to Mom?

Love *is* making me stupid - and it's making me crazy!

Even though Wesley drives with just one hand on the wheel, I think he is a really good driver. He drives the speed limit, never goes over, and always uses his turn signal. I'm pretty nervous the whole ride, but I feel, maybe for the first time in my life - adventurous.

I constantly play with the radio dial and with the straw from the lime slush that Wesley and I share. We sing love songs back and forth to each other, and even though we arrived safely, I still looked around for a police car.

We pull into a small neighborhood of multicolored houses that are all connected by their garages. Wesley parks the car in the driveway of a tiny periwinkle house encircled with powder blue hydrangea bushes. He pulls out two bouquets of flowers from the backseat and hands me one. With a quick kiss on the cheek, he says, "I forgot to give this to you. Damn, I'm slipping as a boyfriend."

My "thank you" was cut short when Grandma Alice

immediately stepped out onto the front porch and gives us a wave.

"She is so cute," I say softly as we both step out of the car.

"Wesley, are you old enough to drive?" she shouts.

"I was sixteen last November, Grandma," he says, his eyes opening wide as we meet Grandma Alice on her porch. "I'm better at it than Clyde, and he's had his license for almost a year. Aunt Lauren won't even let him use her car! Grandma, this is Ruby, and Ruby, this is my Grandma Alice."

"Hello, Grandma Alice. It's nice to meet you. Happy Birthday," I nervously say.

"Oh, thank you, Honey. Wesley is right, you are a beautiful girl," she tells me.

"Thank you."

We walk through the pristine house that smells heavily of lavender. Wesley stops once to fill the pockets of his jeans with butterscotch and peppermint candy. We sit on her back porch, under a wooden ceiling fan that hums softly and has a slight wobble. Grandma Alice's soft white hair matches her soft white cotton dress, and her stark white tennis shoes.

We talk for over an hour, sipping on pink lemonade and barbeque potato chips. I have my best manners on as I sit still and listen closely to all Grandma Alice's stories about Wesley and his family.

"Are you still mad at me for the bad haircut?" she says with a wink and a smile. "Where's your hat, by the way. You told me you were never taking it off."

"I had it on Bonnie's cat for awhile. Clipped it on with a hair thing," he says, motioning his hands, "Then

227

I had it tucked over a picture of Elvis that Aunt Lauren has on her dresser in her bedroom. Last time I saw it, it was on a cactus in the living room."

Listening to the two of them laugh together makes me miss my grandma. Instead of feeling hopeful, my emotions shift. I feel the darkest blue.

"You okay, Ruby?" Wesley says to me, instantly picking up my gloom.

"Yeah, just thinking...that's all."

"Grandma, Ruby is Bonnie's best friend. She lives in the house directly behind her."

"The house with the beautiful flower gardens?"

"Yes...thank you. That's my house," I quietly say. A house that seems so far away to me right now.

"Wes, how are you sleeping? How are your night terrors?" Grandma Alice asks him, which immediately makes me curious.

"I'm sleeping good Grandma. I don't have them anymore," he says quietly, as he looks down at his shoes. "Grandma, how's Mom?"

"She's doing a lot better."

"Good. When will you talk to her next? I want her to know that I'm really happy living at Aunt Lauren's, and I want to stay."

"I talked to her last Friday, Honey. She said she was working hard on getting the two of you back home to Toledo," she tells him affectionately.

Wesley looks at me for a just a short second.

"But I don't want to go back there, Grandma," he says, sounding strong. "I don't want to go back to Toledo. Before Mom went into the hospital, she told me to go find happiness. I have. It's in Detroit with

228

Ruby. Grandma, Ruby has helped me in so many ways, and I want to be with her. Tell Mom that for me. Tell her I found my happiness, because it will change everything."

I look away at some pictures on the wall and act like I didn't hear much of the conversation. I can't interfere with their decision on where they should live.

"I'll tell her, Honey, but your mom will want to stay near your dad's grave."

"I don't understand why she would. Anything that is attached to his death was the thing that was breaking us apart as a family. Holden's gone from that house, and he's happier. I'm gone, and I'm happier. Help me, Grandma. Help me convince Mom that distancing ourselves from everything in Toledo is exactly what we need to help us all be happy again. And most importantly... healthy again."

"I will, Wes. But your mom...she was so ill, for so long. We need to support her decision, whatever that may be."

"I know. I have, but Holden and I were not healthy either. You're my only hope, Grandma. She'll listen to you."

I look down at the floor like I'm searching for something. And I guess I am. It's something we all look for. A solution to make everyone happy - in his family and in mine.

I don't want to cry and ruin Grandma Alice's birthday, so I ask about the pictures that hang on the wall in her hallway. I know it's such a girlfriend thing to do, but I know that the cute little boy with the black eye is a little Wesley, and I want to get a better look.

"Here's my favorite of all the older kids," Grandma Alice says, walking over to a row of pictures displayed on a bookshelf.

"Christmas, 1967. Jodi, Clyde, Bonnie, Holden, and Wesley all sitting under my Christmas tree in matching pajamas. Isn't that cute?"

"It's adorable," I smile at Wesley, and he winks at me.

"Look at this picture. Wesley with no teeth. And Bonnie, I don't know what she had done to her hair that year, but what a mess," Grandma Alice says, her eyes frowning. "Here's Holden's army picture."

"Wow!" I say. "He looks so much like Wesley."

"Wesley's first day of kindergarten," she says, pointing to another picture. "Look at that smile."

I stare at that smile. Not only was I thinking that he has been adorable at every stage of his life, but I was also thinking that, having a little Wesley at some time later in my life, would fill my heart with additional love. A son that looks just like him could possibly displace the hurt that my heart feels today. I want to go to college and have a career, so that little Wesley can be proud of me, but it's the first time I have ever remotely thought about being a mom. That sounds like love certification to me.

Wesley interrupts my thoughts, "Look at Clyde's newborn picture. *Not* a cute baby."

"Here's Kristine and Phil's wedding picture - Wes's parents," Grandma Alice whispers. "Such a sad story. Phil was a great man. Didn't deserve an end like that."

I feel instantly flushed. I stare soberly at the picture.

230

His dad has on a paisley shirt that represents all colors of blue. His crocheted navy-blue tie was thick, wide and spectacular. His long blond hair covering his eyes looked to be the same as Wesley's hair color. So handsome.

His mom wore daisies in her long brown hair that had a slight curl at the end. I instantly fell in love with her chunky beaded necklace that matched her beautiful turquoise eyes. They both looked so happy in the picture that I almost started to cry.

It's 8:20 when we decide to leave. I'm quiet on the ride home, because my heart is filled with a lot of different things. Being around Grandma Alice makes me think about how much I truly love my grandma, and how much I'm going to miss her.

We stop at a little restaurant off the expressway. Wesley gets a plate of waffles that he put entirely too much syrup on, and I get a grilled cheese sandwich with the greatest, glowing, chartreuse dill pickle I've ever seen. We share a large chocolate milkshake and load all the quarters we have into the jukebox.

"Your Grandma Alice is sweet, Wes," I say to him as he dips a forkful of waffle into his river of syrup. "I love the pictures of you and your family. You look like your dad. I love your parents' wedding picture. Your mom...so beautiful, your dad - so handsome. I'm glad your mom is better. Wes, do you have night terrors? I know what they are. I know they're related to trauma."

He was quiet for a minute. "I did," he finally says.

"You did? You don't anymore?"

"No. Not anymore."

"That's great. I know they can be pretty bad."

"Yeah, I'm good. I had then for awhile, but now I don't have them anymore. They stopped. They stopped..." he says looking up from his empty plate. "When I moved in with Aunt Lauren and Uncle Charlie. When I met you."

"That might be just a coincidence. You left a place that was very traumatic for you."

"I don't know. I started having them after my dad died, almost right away. I'd wake up in the middle of the night in a panic. I didn't know where I was. I was confused. I'd wake up in a sweat, and my heart would be beating so fast that I couldn't breathe, which made me even more nervous. My Uncle Jason took me to the doctor, and they said I was having them because I had post-traumatic stress disorder or something like that. I never took the medicine they gave me. I sold it at school. I had the tremors up until recently, but now... I don't have them anymore. Ruby, I think that the love I feel for you, and the love I feel back is so strong that it's dissolved my heaviest pain. Mentally, I feel the happiest I've ever felt, because my heart feels loved - something that I was missing." He reached over and slides his hands down my arms. "Are you sure that you're in love with me?"

"Am I sure? I'm positive. I've never been more positive about anything ever in my life than about how much I love you. I know we're young, and to the world what we have is not yet love. It's something less than love. And I know a lot of people question love for some reason. But I don't. I learned at an early age that this world is cynical, and that's a negative way to be. I think I'm responsible and mature enough to know how to love someone. Because... my grandma taught me how."

"How could you fall in love with such a broken kid?"

"You're not broken. Broken people sometimes feel that they need to give up on love, life, and everything else, and that's not you. And, well, even if you were broken...I'd fix you," I say to him, kicking off my sandals, and curling my bare feet on top of his sneakers.

He has one elbow on the table as his fingers spread wide into his messy hair.

"Thanks for loving me and for letting me love you back," he affectionately says.

The soft blonde hair on his toned arms, that I never want to let go of me, is smooth, but masculine. His face, soft with a serious stare, is the most gorgeous I have ever seen him look. It makes my heart feel instantly weak and immediately makes me think of my "hickey night," I loved every part of that night, and that certainly doesn't sound responsible or mature.

"I'm glad that everyone is on their way to getting better in your family, Wes, honestly I am. And I love your fight to stay here." I take a deep breath and think of my mom, Ian, and my long and bumpy road to recovery, that has not yet begun.

Wesley takes both of my hands and holds them tight.

"When someone changes your heart like you have mine, I know to never let go. My life has a chance now. A chance for what it deserves. My heart feels incredible when I wake up, and I sleep better knowing that you love me.

When you're in my arms at night, I feel a closeness to

you that I never experienced before. And it's not for any other reason that I want to hold you when I sleep."

We walk home from Jodi's after Wesley delivers her car back to her. I feel a little vulnerable, so Wesley and I sneak up to his room and snuggle into his bed.

Before we fell asleep, Wesley whispered in my ear, "I can't believe *you* happened to me."

"I love being yours, and right now your love is saving the most important part of me - my heart. Thanks, Wes," I whisper back to him as I immediately fall asleep.

Even though I know driving with my boyfriend in a car that he's not legally able to drive, and falling asleep next to him at night seem irresponsible at our age, I don't feel that emotion. But what I do feel is when you love someone - really love someone - you should feel no regrets. Even if the rest of the world thinks you should. Yes, you have to be responsible, but never regretful.

Because as I watch my grandma fighting for her life, her chances with of all of life's most glorious things - are over. She is nearing the end of her one and only shot at the life she was given, and all the love in it.

The heart that she has forever told me to listen to - is telling me to not live a regretful life. So I won't. Not in any way.

# AIN'T TOO PROUD TO BEG
♥♥♥♥♥♥♥♥♥♥♥♥♥♥♥♥♥♥♥♥♥♥♥♥♥♥♥♥♥♥♥♥♥♥♥♥♥♥

The next two weeks stay pretty much the same. Every day I stick to my same regimented schedule that I have set for myself. After I reluctantly slip myself away from the tangled and resplendent arms of Wesley every morning, I hop the fence back home, shower, eat a small breakfast, wake up Ian when he's able to come, and pack my bag with everything I think I'll need for my day at the hospital.

Some days I pack it with some kale salads that I load with onion, which is good for the blood, or maybe some sliced apples that I sprinkle with dry wheat germ. Some days I make some cookies, homemade applesauce, oatmeal bars or blueberry bread. Maybe just make up a big bowl of cranberries or dried papaya slices for everyone. Other times I gather a handful of blackberries or raspberries from our yard or some pears from one of Mr. Hardy's pear trees that hangs over our fence. A couple of times I pack Grandma Dotti's favorite candy bars or some sunflower seeds, grapes, leftover pie from dinner the night before, and of course, more ginger flavored candies, which seem to help Grandma Dotti's tender stomach.

I never forgot to pack our *Rona Barrett* magazines and *The Detroit Free Press,* and I always remember to bring her a fresh bouquet of flowers from our yard to brighten up her room. Today I have a bowl of elderberries and some spinach salads. I grab my button-up sweater and run to catch the bus.

I arrive at the hospital every morning just before

Grandma Dotti wakes up. Some days she wants to go for walks around the hospital, and other days just lie in bed and rest. Some days she feels good, some days not so good. I do whatever she wants because every day she seems a little bit weaker.

Sometimes I sit with her and read our horoscopes from the newspaper, even though I don't believe in astrological fortune. Or I color in, and then read her the comic strips, never forgetting her favorite, *The Lockhorns*.

I always read the weather forecast for the week to her, and always give her the rundown on the latest baseball scores. We read together or play gin rummy. Sometimes I just sit with her and watch her sleep, hoping that she isn't dreaming of anything scary. Some days I take a nap along with her.

When I do nap, I dream heavily. So many dreams and so many feelings are running through my head at once. I wake up and instantly feel a difference in myself. My heart seems to be getting a little bitter and resentful. I feel the lack of empathy from other people hitting me hard. I usually don't let myself get that way; I've always felt that I could tolerate apathy in a polite way, but it doesn't seem like I am able to control that these days. There are times when I leave the hospital and go to Keeler's Gym with Wesley and hit the punching bag. As I vent my anger into the bag, it seems to give me a small sense of relief at the pain and unfairness of the world. Good or bad, whatever I release into the punching bag seems to give me the revitalization that I need to continue on in my life, when really, I just want to curl up in Wesley's arms and hide from everything. I also find that the days I box, I'm so tired at night that I fall asleep so fast that my brain doesn't have time to tell my heart to cry.

Every day I wait for my mom until five o'clock. I kiss Grandma Dotti goodbye, and then I catch the bus home to Wesley. And every night these last two weeks Wesley is waiting for me at the bus stop with a lime slush.

Wesley and I take long walks together that usually end at Stoepel Park. Sometimes we go to the movies or just stay home and watch a movie together with Clyde and Bonnie. We sometimes make dinner together, and I always remember to save Mom and Ian plates for when they get home from the hospital. We played Skee-ball one night, which was the first time I actually beat Wesley at anything. We sometimes play basketball and pepper ball, and the night he taught me how to play poker, I taught him how to make pizza from scratch and cook it on a barbeque. We picnic a lot with leftover chicken from Chicken-N-Joy and all the cookies that we bake together. Most nights we end up out on the roof outside Bonnie's window until two or three in the morning, and only Bonnie knows that we're out there.

And I noticed something: Wesley is no longer smoking.

The night Wesley taught me how to drive was not as scary as I thought it would be. I sat on his lap as we drove around the block a few times in his Uncle Charlie's car. I'm surprised I didn't hit anything (well, I *almost* hit Clyde) because, even though Wesley was very dedicated and very serious, I giggled the entire time he was teaching me.

When we are together, anywhere, Wesley deliberately makes it obvious to everyone around us that we're a couple. He either holds my hand, or wraps his arms around my waist and holds me close to him. He's never afraid to randomly kiss me either. It makes me think that he's proud of me, but in actuality, I know I'm more proud of him.

Sometimes he comes up from behind me, like when I'm really concentrating on something, and he'll kiss me the most romantic kiss ever. He'll slowly gather my hair from my neck, move it to the other side, and kiss my neck so softly that I shiver and tense up at the same time.

It's true what they say about hugs, kisses and displays of affection. They're one of the greatest things in life and sometimes it makes all the difference in someone's world.

Last Thursday was one of the hottest nights we've had this summer. It became my favorite summer night ever in my life. The night never cooled off, so Wesley and I went pool hopping. I was nervous to go, mainly because of my (lack of) swimming ability, but I dusted off my hardly-ever-worn bathing suit, and followed Wesley as we snuck down the desolate alleys of Detroit and into the backyards of our neighbors with pools. I, of course, clearly reluctant and nervous, was relieved that Wesley sensed my apprehension and never let go of me. I've developed a feeling with him this summer that is the same as the one I've always had with my Grandma Dotti. They both help me find my courage and make me feel proud of myself.

That same night was the night I taught Wesley how to slow dance. Back at my house, I put on my favorite slow dance song *Sleep Walk,* and he held me tight as the passionate sound of Santo & Johnny overflowed in my living room. With our old antique fan droning beside us, I put my arms around his neck and my fingers played with the back of his hair. His hands gently cradled the small of my back and, forehead to forehead, lip to lip, I truly felt loved from my head to my toes. His kisses were tender and soft as we slowly moved in the dark, our bodies wittingly stuck together, kissing in slow motion in the hot August night. It was the living definition of a romantic summer night. Slow dancing in the summer night's heat with the guy you love is a beautiful part of life. Romance and love - It's what every girl dreams of.

One night, up in Wesley's bedroom, as I discreetly watched him change from his swim trunks to his shorts, I sewed a button onto one of his shirts. I listened to him sing the cutest songs to me, which made me laugh an honest laugh. Something I don't remember doing in awhile. My rush of guilt quickly subsided as I watched him comb his hair in his bathroom mirror, and I listened to him sing me the song that has always been connected to my heart. He sang *Ruby Tuesday* in its entirety.

"I love that song," he says, as I let my eyes fill with happy tears.

I never thought that anyone could ever sing that song better than the incredible Mick Jagger - but I was wrong.

Every night we hold each other tight. We whisper "I

love you" over and over until I fall asleep. His kisses make my heart turn the most fragile it's ever been. I want to whisper in his ear - *Please don't leave. Don't move away from me. I'm begging you to stay here. Please don't go anywhere, Wes, please.*

But I know I can't. Instead, I lie next to him and stay awake just a little bit longer than him, so I can watch him drift off to sleep.

Every night during these last two weeks I've grown to love Wesley Everett more and more. I feel grateful that he distracts my heart from the everyday pain it feels. He takes me away from it by trying his hardest to fill me with momentary happiness. Every day I thank him for making me as happy as I possibly can be.

"Now that I'm happy, it will always be easier for me to make sure that you're happy too," he tells me.

My nights are spent in the arms of pure love and happiness. I am absolutely in love with him, and the love I feel from him when we're together, is the greatest feeling anyone could ever experience. I know I'm lucky I have it right now. When he repeatedly tells me the four greatest words I've ever heard, "Ruby, I love you," my world feels *almost* perfect. The confidence that has grown inside me these last two months with Wesley makes all my thoughts of my grandma seem hopeful. I feel positive that she will beat the leukemia, come home and everything will be like it was before she got sick. I'll be at my happiest. I'll smile more, I'll laugh more, and I'll love deeper than ever. When he holds me I feel audacious and fearless, like the world and its problems seem conquerable.

I wake up every day with my new-found confidence

and carry it with me all day. And every night Wesley mentally takes me away to a healthier and happier place.

Temporarily anyways.

Because things start to change.

As you grow up, you sometimes feel your life changing. But sometimes you don't. And sometimes it's simply because you don't want to.

And sadly, the biggest change in my life was about to happen.

Ian and I arrive at the hospital at 8:22 and we quietly sneak into Grandma Dotti's room. She is sitting up in bed while nurse Cece places an oxygen mask over her face. Grandma Dotti fidgets with the straps and then reaches for my hand.

"Why...is she wearing an oxygen mask?" I ask nurse Cece.

"She's having some difficulty breathing, and we want to make sure she keeps a normal oxygen level," she tells Ian and me. I feel instantly agitated by her answer, and I'm sure she could detect it.

"Sure," I say firmly. I look to Ian. His hands are in his pockets, his body is still, his head is down and his face is hidden.

While Grandma Dotti sleeps on and off throughout the day, Ian and I take turns crying in the hallway. I sit in the chair next to her bed and talk quietly to her even though I know she's sound asleep. The repetitive sounds from all the machines in the room would make it hard for her to hear me.

I whisper to her, "Promise me you'll keep waking up every morning. If there is a 'other side' don't go to it. If

241

there is a light that shines on you, don't look in its direction. Turn around and stay here with us. If you see Grandpa Kip in your dreams, don't go over to him. Wake up and see me next to you. I love you, Grandma, and I can't live my life without you in it. You mean too much to me. Promise me. I'm begging you to promise me."

Later that day I let Ian have some time alone with Grandma Dotti. I wander around the hospital with no direction, oblivious to everything and everyone around me. My heart physically hurts, so I clutch the pocket of my shirt and then hug myself tight. I don't know what to do to help Mom, Ian, and especially Grandma Dotti.

I've always seemed to come up with an answer when it's time to help someone. But now I can't. I've struggled every day this summer with that, and I have nothing left inside of me to help the person I love the most in this world.

As early as fourth grade the kids in my class would shove one of their failed papers in my face and ask me how to fix it. I would look at it for a minute, and I would fix it for them. My math teacher last year asked me how to do a certain trigonometry problem. I figured it out, and then I had to explain it to the class. When Bonnie's dad, Nigel, came to visit last Easter, he couldn't get his car started. For some reason, I figured out that it was his alternator. I don't know how I knew, but I did. I've never failed a test at school in my life, but now I feel I've failed the biggest one possible. I don't know how to save the most vital thing to my family - our life with Grandma Dotti.

I lean up against the wall outside her room. I slowly

slide down, sit on the floor in the hallway with my head in my lap, and cry.

I'm alone, until a man with an elongated mop slowly sways by me, whistling an unrecognizable song. I start to talk quietly into my hands. I'm begging someone, anyone, to save her.

I quietly repeat to myself, "Please don't take her from us. Please. Someone save her. Please. I need someone to save her. I'm begging. Please. I'll do anything, so please. Please."

"I ain't too proud to beg, honey. Neither should you be. You go right on; I know they must be worth it to you," the man with the mop tells me, as he glides by and continues his whistle.

I smile at his sweet sentiment, but continue to whisper to myself, "Please save her life. Please," I cry.

I am still sitting on the hospital floor an hour later. I'm so physically tired that I can't get up. I feel like I just went twelve rounds with Muhammad Ali, and I know that no one here really cares about my heartbreak or my grandma's fight. My heartbreak is not unique.

My dark thoughts are interrupted by the sound of high-heels rhythmically hitting the tile floor. It's a sound that I've listened for and recognized all summer long, so I know right away that it's 5:00 and my mom is here.

I look up at her, my eyes full of tears, and my face, red and streaked. She doesn't say anything, but helps me up off the floor and hugs me tight.

There are different kinds of hugs in this world, and this one felt different from what I usually get from her.

I haven't felt this kind of hug from my mom since her friend Maggie was killed in a car accident a couple of years ago. I knew how much pain Mom was in, because my heart was aching too. I babysat for Maggie's little kids, Ronnie and Gray. They were just too young to lose their mom. She was only 27. That day, as I cried for my little friends, and my mom cried for her friend, she gave me a hug so tight that it made me feel her own grief and devastation. I got that exact same hug today. It's the kind of hug that makes you feel worse instead of better.

"What are we going to do without her, Ruby?" my mom says, as her voice breaks and her tears fall into my hair.

I hardly ever see my mom cry, so whenever I do, it just makes me cry harder. "I don't know. I just don't know," I say, blinking my tears onto her shoulder.

"I know this has been really hard on you, and I haven't been able to help you through it. I can't. I don't know how, Ruby. I tried to protect your heart from being hurt, but...I just couldn't this time."

"My heart...it hurts so bad, Mom. I don't believe that it will ever stop hurting."

*Keep protecting my heart, Wesley Everett. Stay. You're the hope I need,* my brain reminds me.

We hold on to each other, trying to find the right words of comfort, but there are none. There never is.

It's beyond horrible to watch someone in your family dying, but to also watch the rest of your family's hearts break is equally as crushing. I've never wanted to see my mom or Ian cry over anything in life, so their pain just makes everything intensified. This pain is the deepest I've ever felt.

Pain that I learn will *never, ever* go away.

It's a little before 6:00 when I pack up my things to leave. Ian and Mom are staying until visiting hours are over. I've had cramps all day, and really just want to go home.

Through Grandma Dotti's oxygen mask I see sadness in her eyes. She hasn't smiled at all today. Has she given up her fight, I wonder? Can she feel herself dying? The last thing I want is for her to feel fear.

I kiss Grandma Dotti softly on her cheek and leave for the bus stop. But as I make my way down the hallway, past the front desk, to the elevator, and out the revolving doors of Newsted Hospital, I repeat to myself. "Please keep fighting, Grandma. I refuse to let you go, so don't give up. I'm begging you, please," I repeat over and over.

On the bus ride home I realize that I haven't had anything to eat all day. My stomach growls and my cramps intensify, as I look in my sling bag for a snack and a tissue to wipe my wet blurry eyes. I can't find either one, but I come across a folded piece of paper. I quit looking for the snack and the tissue, and open up the unexpected paper.

I recognize Wesley's handwriting immediately. It looks like he made a handmade crossword puzzle. There are some crooked squares that are all attached and some questions at the bottom of the paper.

1 across- The first time Wes saw Ruby it was ____ at first sight

1 down- Wes Everett is truly in ____ with Ruby Vander

2 across- Wes and Ruby will be forever in ____ with each other

2 down- I____ to be with Ruby, she's the greatest person in the world to me

3 across- Wes + Ruby =____

3 down- What is Wes's heart full of for Ruby?

I hope you and your grandma had a good day together

I love you, Wes

Love *is* always the answer.

I fold the paper back up using the same creases and squeeze it in my hand. I hold it up to my damp face and kiss it knowing that Wesley touched it.

I am the first one off the bus today, as I forget all my manners and etiquette and start to look for Wesley right away.

And just like every day for the last two weeks, Wesley is standing by the bus stop waiting for me. He instantly gives me a hug and a kiss, and wipes away my messy tears with the bottom of his shirt.

Today, along with the lime slush, he also has a chicken sandwich for me. I eat it immediately, barely offering him a bite.

"I've decided to stay at the hospital as long as I can, Wes. I need to. I know you understand." I tell him.

"Of course I do. That's where you should be. You know I'll be wherever you need me."

I don't think about my fake marriage in third grade to Christopher Chavez too much anymore, or all the "boyfriends" in my head, like Cole Thompson and Franco King. I don't give much thought to my imaginary "baseball player" boyfriend, Jason Thompson, or my pretend "rock star" boyfriend to Steven Tyler. Because really, they have faded because of my love for Wesley, who's turned out to be the very best boyfriend for me.

There are people who come into your life, and you just know you'll always love them. And it's because of the depth of the mark that they leave on your heart. It does not matter when they arrive, or how long they stay. It doesn't matter why or how they leave you. Just listen to your heart, because it's constantly telling you who those people are.

For the next week, I spend every day, all day, in the hospital. I still bring Grandma Dotti some snacks, fresh flowers, and our magazines to read, but they all lie next to her bed ignored. Grandma Dotti is getting worse by the day, and there are no good days anymore.

On Thursday her doctor moved her to the intensive care unit of the hospital. I have never spent much time in any hospital until this summer, and I have only seen the intensive care unit depicted on TV. It takes only seconds to realize what a devastating place it is.

I'm told there are no flowers allowed in the ICU, so I strategically place my freshly picked bouquet of cosmos on a desk in the hallway, directly in Grandma

Dotti's view, hoping it will be the first thing she sees when she wakes up.

The nurses had left her sun catcher in her old room, but it is later collected and given to me. There is no window to hang the sun catcher on, so I carefully tuck it into my bag to take home. Ian should have it.

Grandma Dotti is still wearing her oxygen mask and is now hooked up to a kidney dialysis machine. Filtering her blood is a good idea, but she now has a Port-A-Cath planted in her chest that looks so incredibly painful that I instantly start to cry when I see it. I notice too that she has a new needle taped to her arm. My eyes follow the fresh tube that it's attached to, and from her IV pole hangs a bag of morphine. I stare into the drip chamber.

*Morphine. What's next? What else will they pump into her, now, 70 pound body?*

I look around the room and wonder if any one of these machines is actually helping her, or are they all slowly killing her. All this medication intravenously dripping into her frail body, and not one is able to kill the cancer. All this medicine that I once trusted has done nothing for her except make her sicker and now make death certain.

I stare at the bag filled with the chemotherapy, almost looking past it. I realize that's the one that is killing her. That's the one that's made her sicker, filled her entire body with poison and left her unable to fight. She was nowhere near this sick before she started it. It is too powerful of a drug for her, and it's going to stop her heart.

My heart feels dead. My brain is not able to respond

248

to anything in the room. I realize that is what devastation does to you.

I sit paralyzed.

It's getting harder to hold Grandma Dotti's hand and stay close to her considering all that she's hooked up to, but I wiggle myself onto her bed and gently hold her thin, bruised hand. I kiss it and softly rub it as she sleeps.

I talk quietly to myself, but speak Grandma Dotti. "Did you get to do everything that you wanted to in life and fulfill all your dreams? Is there someplace that you always wanted to go and never made it there? Because I can still try to get you there. If they ever make a fourth version of *A Star is Born,* who will go see it with me? I've seen all three with you and watching it, and singing along, will never feel the same without you next to me. How will I be able to make a daisy chain from the flowers in our yard and wear them in my hair ever again? It will remind me too much of our summers together. What about Thanksgiving? We get up early every year and let Mom and Ian sleep in while we get the turkey ready. We make a giant batch of hot chocolate as we all watch the Thanksgiving Day Parade and start our Christmas wish lists. I can't do any of that without you. How will Mom, Ian and I be able to hang your handmade Christmas ornaments up on the tree? It will just be too hard to do. What about the gumdrops cakes we make for everyone at Christmas? I doubt I'll ever be able to eat one again. And what about our trip to Ireland that we're saving for?"

I think about how hard her birthday will be to celebrate, and I try to think of the last gift I gave to her. I think it was a Betty Crocker cookbook. What was the last gift she gave to me? I think it was the ostrich print pajamas at Christmas.

I pull my prevalent wet tissue from the sleeve of my sweater and wipe away my salty tears.

"There are still so many things that we still need to do together. You have to stay here with us so you can see Ian get married and travel the world like he wants to. Collect all the postcards he's promised to send you. You'll never see me grow into the person I want to be. I want to be so much for you. You'll never be able to hold my children, watch them grow, or make them sweaters, and ostrich print pajamas like you've done for me. It pains me too much to think that my children will never know the beautiful part of my life that was you."

I dab my eyes with what's left of my tattered tissue.

"I guess these days ahead are when families say their goodbyes to each other. But I can't, and I won't."

I remember Grandma Dotti told me once that life is about holding on to all of the things that you love. I have all that is love in my grandma, so I'm never letting go. That would mean I'm giving up.

My tear-soaked eyes look up and see Mom and Ian.

"You know it's the chemo," I say. "We trusted it and it... it didn't help her. It made her worse. I'm going to take her off of it. I know how."

"It's too late," Ian says, sadly.

"No it's not, Ian," I cry.

"Ruby, I've talked to the doctors about that," Mom interrupts. "Come with me and Ian. I want to talk to the both of you in private. Let Grandma sleep."

We walk down the hall to an empty room. It's quiet in this part of the building, except for the sound of ventilators that echo through the hallway. A slight buzzing sound from another room is almost soothing.

My mom's eyes are heavy and her skin is pale, which tells me that she was probably crying on the way here. I watch a tear rolls down her pretty face and land on her shoe.

"The doctors told me this morning that there's nothing more they can do for Grandma," my mom says, as her voice begins to shake. "The best thing is to keep her comfortable. They told me that her organs will start shutting down soon. It won't be too much longer, and...she'll...be gone."

She hides her hands in her face and starts to cry. Ian wraps his arms around her and then pulls me in. We hold on to each other and cry until our eyes are swollen and our voices hoarse.

I'm broken inside.

The next day when I get to Grandma Dotti's room I notice right away – yet another tube attached to her. This one runs up her nose and down her throat. I'm careful not to wake her, but I listen for her breathing, kiss her cheek, and then brush back what's left of her thin hair. I arrange it slightly to cover her newest bald spot.

The chemotherapy has not destroyed what it set out to do. Instead it has destroyed every other part of her. Her hair, her skin, her immune system, her organs and next - her heart. Her fight is over. She's almost gone.

I sit on her bed, holding her hand, and think of all

the times that I'm in another part of the house and she calls out for me. Her melodic sweet voice singing out my name, "*Ruby? Ruby?*"

I'm never going to hear that again. I am going to miss that so badly. I squeeze my eyes shut and let my tears roll down my face and onto my lap.

Not only will I miss the sound of her voice, but I will miss her guidance, her touch, her laugh, her smile, and her love. I will miss everything about our life together.

I think of the very last thing she ate. It was zucchini bread on Monday. I remember it was the very first thing she ever taught me how to bake. I was four years old and we picked the biggest zucchini from our garden and made a couple of loaves. Just like Wesley and I did last Sunday.

The last movie we watched together was *From Here to Eternity*. Just like my love for her - to eternity.

I think this is where some families secretly hope that their loved one will pass to end all their suffering, but not me. I'll remain selfish.

"Remember, Grandma, don't give up," I whisper to her. "I'm not giving up, so neither can you. I won't, and I hope you understand."

Grandma Dotti seems content, as I continue to watch her sleep. She has all the right in the world to complain, but she hasn't - not once. I believed she tried to smile every day of her life, because she was happy and she always had hope. Two things we should all carry in our heart at all times - happiness and hope.

Today I feel that no grandchild has ever loved their grandmother more than I loved her, and I also know that death will never change that. Nothing changes love that strong.

Grandma Dotti slowly wakes up and subconsciously fixes the big piece of tape that holds the tube in her nose in place. I notice her hands shaking. She has trouble sitting up, so I help her.

There is nothing left of her petite frame, as I see for the first time, her bones protruding from her aged skin. She is literally skin and bones, and nothing but a skeletal shell. I try to breathe, but it feels like someone just punched, kicked and stomped on my stomach.

Her soiled hospital gown is hanging off her wasted body and I can clearly see her clavicle lifting up before the rest of her as I help her sit up straight.

"Morning, Grandma," I say. She looks at me with her big brown eyes as I gently move the thin pieces of hair that have fallen around her face.

"Ruby. I was just... having a dream... about us."

"You were?" I say, smiling through my tears.

"We were...picking tomatoes to can. I was telling you...don't forget to can...them...for winter."

"I won't. Of course I won't forget."

She struggles with every word and at a whisper tells me so sweetly, "I love you...and...and your mom... and Ian... you're my...everything. All...anyone wants ... is love. And...because of you three...I had so...much. Don't forget, Ruby...to love all your life...because that's the... only thing... that heals... a broken heart. You... stay brave...Ruby."

"I'm not brave at all," I say as I begin to cry harder.

"You are...It's something that... we..." she hesitates, and her eyes well with tears. "We did...together this summer. Got brave."

"My heart," I say, looking up at the dark ceiling. "It is in so...so much pain, Grandma."

"But...love, Ruby... outweighs...pain and fear. And...I know... you have an incredible... amount of love... in your heart."

"Because you put it there," I tell her.

She smiles at me, and even though I wouldn't admit it, I knew it was probably the last smile I would ever see from her.

"You know, you can't leave me," I say. "What about our trip to Ireland? We still have to go. I was saving my money so we could spend the night in a castle. It was going to be a surprise. I can't go without you."

"You have to. Every place... you go...think of me... I'll be there. Keep me...with you."

I give her a slight nod. "Always listen to my heart. It's what you've always told me. My heart that you're so much a part of. I'll listen for you because that's where you'll always be."

She tried to squeeze my hand, but there was no strength. The hand that would pull me to kindergarten and back home. The hand that would drag me down Kentfield to catch the Fenkell bus. The hand that held my chin and wiped my many tears away. The hand that soothed me all the days I've been sick. The hand that blew invisible kisses to me all of my life. A hand that held on to so much of my life.

The hand that I now have to let go of.

"Ruby...let yourself...be happy again."

"Life hurts too bad right now for me to be happy, Grandma."

"Forgive. Don't let it... take over a...beautiful heart."

My tears stop. I think it's because I ran out.

"No one has ever loved their grandma more than I love you," I tell her proudly.

"And isn't it... wonderful...that I felt that...everyday... of my life with you."

She stares at me. Her eyes sunken and lost, almost like she was taking one last look. I stare back.

"Ruby... can you do something... for me?"

"I'll do anything for you."

"I want to... go home ... I want to ... be at home...when..."

"I'll get you home, Grandma," I interrupt. "I promise, I'll get you home," I say firmly.

I sit, emotionless, and hug her. I'm chilled. I'm exhausted. My heart is in pieces. But I'm still not letting go of her. I'm still hanging on.

I nibble on an egg salad sandwich that falls apart in my hands. Stale bread or dry eggs - not sure. I watch Grandma Dotti drift off to sleep and think about all the ways I could get her home. The ride home may be tough, but I'll remind Mom to drive, at least, twenty miles an hour under the speed limit, and take the smoother side streets home.

I'll clean out Grandma's bedroom as soon as I get home tonight, and tomorrow, I'll make plans to rent some hospital equipment. I will put the sun catcher back in her bedroom window, and she'll have flowers in her room every day again. I'll read her favorite book, *Gone with the Wind,* to her and, we'll move the TV into her room so we can continue to watch all our favorite movies and TV shows together. I can help administer all her medicines. I remember everything nurse Cece taught me, and I have no doubt that I can do it all.

I can get a part time job at night to help pay for the medical bills and the higher electricity bill we're sure to have. I'm sure Bonnie's parents will hire me, knowing my situation, and that way I could steal a little time with Wesley too. I'll need him to make me smile.

It's a great idea for her to come home. Home to the house that Grandpa Kip bought for her years ago, where she raised Mom, Ian and me. A home that she's made beautiful from the core of the basement to our outward fences. If she's gonna die, I want it to be at home with us, a place where she feels safe. That way she won't leave this world scared.

So with all my new plans circulating in my head, I decide I will go home, as soon as Mom gets here, and start to rearrange Grandma Dotti's bedroom. I'm tired, and my body feels drained of energy right now, but once I get home, I'm sure my energy level will increase. I won't cry myself to sleep like I have most of these summer nights - I have way too much to do.

Mom arrives from work at 5:15. I run my well-thought-out plan by her. I even drew a drawing of the house on a hospital napkin so she can get a visual, but she ignores my plans and barely glances at the napkin.

"Ruby, I'm going to stay here with Grandma tonight. I just don't want to leave her."

"Oh, of course, Mom. I would stay with you, but...well, I got a lot to do tonight. See, it's all here on the napkin," I say as I move the napkin closer to my very distracted mom.

"Ruby, why don't you go home and get some sleep. You need it. You look tired, and I don't want you to get run down."

"You keep saying that, but I have too much to do," I say hastily, as I grab my sling bag. Grandma Dotti has never asked me for anything, ever in her life, and I promised I'd get her home - so I will. I just need to turn on some elbow grease so I can get her home by noon tomorrow.

I run to catch the bus, but before I push my way through the revolving doors of Newsted Hospital, I stop by the information desk and gather up all the pamphlets I can about homecare. It doesn't look too hard, but it doesn't matter. I'm committed to doing it.

I nestle into my seat on the bus, and when I closed my eyes to rest them, I must have gone under because the next thing I know I was being awakened by the bus driver.

"Miss Ruby? Miss Ruby? I believe this is your stop," he says, looking at me through the long rectangle mirror above his head.

"Oh...thank you," I say disoriented. "I would have ridden this bus though all of Detroit tonight," I mumbled. "But that just may have been the rejuvenating nap I needed to get me through the next few hours. Thanks, Mr. Benson!"

I run down Kentfield, onto my porch, and then swing open the front door. I throw my sling bag in the living room chair, wiggle out of my sweater, and kick my sandals off into the hallway. I notice that Ian forgot to do the dishes, so I wash them real quick and dry them even quicker. I throw a load of reds into the washing machine because they are smelling up the laundry room. I mop up the kitchen floor too, because I notice it had multiple sticky spots when I walked on it with my bare feet.

I go to my room and turn on my radio. I sit on my bed and stare down at the floor and sing along with Janis Joplin to *Piece of my Heart*.

I'm tired. My body feels sore. I think I'll lie down for just a quick minute and take a cat nap.

But when my head hit the pillow, I started dreaming right away. I remember that my dreams were about Grandma Dotti. I was thinking that her heart might feel somewhat content tonight knowing that Mom, Ian and I have "love" in our life right now. Mom has Reed, Ian has Patty, and I have Wesley. Everyone knows that you love at different levels, which is the greatness of love, and no one could ever take the place of the love we all have for Grandma Dotti. But some loves that come your way you have to pay close attention to. If it feels perfect, take hold of it if you can.

# TIME WAITS FOR NO ONE
♥♥♥♥♥♥♥♥♥♥♥♥♥♥♥♥♥♥♥♥♥♥♥♥♥♥♥♥♥♥♥♥♥♥♥♥♥♥♥♥♥♥

I changed dreams a few times during my nap. My first dream was about how fast this summer has gone. I wish I could go back and do things differently, but outside of the chemo refusal, what would I do different?

They say there is no cure for cancer, and even though I disagree, I didn't come up with the cure or the answer to my grandma's suffering. If I could back up my summer, it would mean that I would have to watch Grandma Dotti, Mom, and Ian suffer all over again, and I just couldn't do that to them. It might also mean that Wesley may not have come into my life the way he did. I can't go back. We never can.

My second dream was about my love for summer. It has always been the best part of my life, but summer vacation was different for me this year. It's already the middle of August, which means summer is almost over, and sadly, I haven't even begun to start it.

No late night walks with Bonnie through the neighborhood. No playing Frisbee in the middle of her street so we can get a glimpse of the very muscular Nordstrom boys as they work on their cars - with their shirts off - in their driveway. No watching Clyde illegally open the fire hydrant in front of his house so all the kids in the neighborhood can cool off with the street's most powerful sprinkler. No jumping on the many bikes that neglectfully lay on Bonnie's front yard to chase the police cars or fire trucks that are moving into our neighborhood. No hanging out on Fenkell just to get free bags of potato chips from the drunken patrons who frequent The Five Deuces Bar. No ordering pizza from Vio's just so Bonnie can flirt with their delivery boy, Eddie. And no bike rides past Marvin Gaye's house, or up to The Egg and I restaurant so Bonnie and I can get free pop and french fries from our friend, Bruno, who works there. No Friday night, eagerly anticipated, dinners at Scotty Simpson's Fish and Chips, which everyone I know agrees is the best Fish and Chips in Detroit. No family vacation anywhere, no annual trip to Cedar Point, and no bad sunburns that end up giving you the perfect tan.

But one thing I did have this summer, that all the girls I know long to have, is a summer romance. My bewildered and tender heart somehow let love in, and it found its way to the very middle of it. Wesley Everett somehow landed directly there as the pain from my grandma's cancer made it unravel uncontrollably.

I miss him. I haven't seen him in over a week, and I miss his warm blanket hugs that instantly change everything about me.

I'm sleeping hard, but I don't think for very long, when I hear someone in the background of my dream, shout my name.

My nearly comatose body slowly wakes up.

"Ruby? Ruby?"

I gradually stand up. "Ruby, Ruby," I hear again, and it's coming from outside.

I push my pink chenille curtains aside, and see Wesley sitting on Clyde's bike right outside my bedroom window.

"Wesley, what are you doing here?" I ask.

"I just wanted to see you tonight. To see if you're alright."

It's such a hard question to answer when your heart is hurting so much, so I don't answer him.

"Ian was just over and...," he hesitates, "he said you were home and...well, he said things aren't too good. I just wanted to check and make sure you're okay."

"Hang on," I say, "I'll be right out."

It takes me about ten minutes to get "right out" because I want to change into something nicer than my dirty hospital clothes. The nights have gotten much cooler this week, so I threw on some blue jean capri pants, and Ian's red and gray "Redford Huskies" sweatshirt that he gave me the other day.

I check my hair and face in the mirror - not much I can do with either disaster - so I hastily run a comb through my hair and let it fall where it may. I grab a bottle of Faygo Rock & Rye pop from the refrigerator, and then hurry out the front door to meet him. My body is weak, beyond tired, so I fall in to him. He holds me tight and supports my frail and exhausted body.

We curl up together on the porch swing. He is quiet, but he kisses me softly and tenderly.

"Do you want to go somewhere?" he says to me.

"Right now?"

"Sure...you know it's only 8:00?"

"It is?" I ask, "Sure, I guess we can do something."

"Let's go to Edgewater," he says, getting up and jumping on Clyde's bike. "Hop on the handlebars."

"Edgewater? You want to go to an amusement park this late at night?"

"Sure, I wanna play some of those carnival games,

261

and I know how much you love deep-fried anything and.... I just want to be with you tonight, Ruby."

I squint my eyes at him. Something feels different, but while half my brain is on sleep mode, the other half is very conscious that I want to be with him.

"Couldn't get the car tonight?" I giggle, as I situate my butt onto Clyde's rickety steel handlebars.

"I tried. I did call Jodi, but her line was busy," he says, as he starts to pedal away.

It's a summer night that reminds you that fall is fast approaching. It's crisp and cool on your face. It's a reminder that there are probably just a few warm days left of summer. School will start soon, and summer memories will begin to fade.

Fade for most, but not for me this year. This summer will never fade from me.

I wiggle my uncomfortable butt between the handlebars, and I watch the northwest part of Detroit slowly pass me by. I sing a medley of all my favorite Motown songs to Wesley, as he pedals down Fenkell.

I watch a young couple holding hands while smiling at the diamond ring on her finger. I see a very pregnant woman waiting for the bus, and reading a book about childbirth. All anticipating what their tomorrow might bring.

I see some kids race their bikes down the street, eager to get home before the street lights come on, to avoid a punishment. I see people pumping gas, washing their car, mowing their lawns and taking their trash to the curb, all because they're obligated to.

I also watch a small group of people in a hurry to get a seat at Daly's Coney Island, and a crowd gathering in line at the Redford Theater. I see people walking in and out of the Redford library with piles of books in their hands. All doing the simple things in life to make them happy.

Anticipating the next day, doing the things I'm obligated to do, trying to make myself happy - was the hardest part of my summer.

We get to Edgewater, and I inhale the glorious aroma of amusement park food. It's serious decision-making when you have to choose between fried pickles and fried clam strips.

"Ruby?" Wes says, interrupting my resolution. "There is one thing I want to do before we leave."

"Sure, what is it?"

"I want to get a picture of us from one of those photo booths. Just in case."

"Just in case...of what?" I ask.

"I don't know, just in case... I gotta move again. I want a picture of you...while I'm gone. I don't have one."

"Are you moving, Wes?" He said nothing. "You are... aren't you?"

He puts his head down and says, "Ruby, I'm not really sure what's going to happen in the next week or two, but I want you to know that I'm doing all I can to stay here with you. Even though nothing seems to be working. But I won't give up."

My legs feel like they will collapse beneath me. My torso suddenly racked with a dull aching pain. My arms, lifeless.

"You have to go, Wes. You have to go where your

mom wants you to go. She still knows what's best for you."

"What if that place doesn't make me happy?"

"We're not in total control of what happens to us right now. Our parents are. And it's about sacrifice. Think about your mom, her happiness, and her struggle."

"I do. Every day."

"I know you do, but there are a lot of times in life where we have to sacrifice our own happiness for the people we love. Let go of what makes us happy, and take the chance that maybe something else will come along and save our heart. Kids our age are forced to do it all the time, because we're old enough to maybe know what we want, but still too young to really have it. Sometimes your sacrifice will take you somewhere else you're meant to be."

"Do you really think that I'm 'meant to be' somewhere else besides where I am now?"

"Of course I don't," I say, as the cries from the rollercoaster screams behind us.

He takes a hold of my hands. He squeezes them tight. "Ruby, the other day I was thinking about what to get you for your birthday, and for our first Christmas together. I was thinking that we could get each other a Christmas ornament every year we are together. And when we are together for, say, 40 years, we would have a tree that summarizes our life together."

"That's so sweet."

"And I don't want to be anywhere except next to you on *my* birthday. I want to kiss you at midnight on New

Year's Eve, and on Valentine's Day: well, I have a lot of plans for our first Valentine's Day together."

"I want all of that too, but this means that your mom's getting better. And that's great," I say, trying to sound happy for him, which of course I am.

"She is better."

"When will she be released?

"I don't know yet. The hospital has given her a few options on where we can go, but she hasn't decided on any one place just yet. She wants to consider Holden and his life after the Army. But, it will all be decided soon. Really soon."

I try not to stand there with a look of pure shock and devastation; after all, I knew this day would come. But all of my life, my expressions, and what my heart feels, have been hard to hide. I just slowly nod my head.

"Sure, I understand," I say, almost unable to breathe. "Wes, it's important that you be with your mom. She needs you, and you need her." And even though my heart is really hurting, I really do mean that.

"Yeah, but I need you too. You're just as important to me, Ruby. This summer you helped me in the greatest way possible. You loved me and let me love you back. You've changed my life. You changed my heart. You're the one person I love the most in the world, and I'm not going to walk away from it. Not when it makes me this happy. Happiness that I wanted and deserved for so long. I'm just so frustrated that no one really listened to me. I talked to Holden, my grandma, Aunt Lauren, even my uncle Jason. I talked to them about my mom coming here to live. I think she'll be happy living here. It's frustrating," he says, wiping his face with his hands. "I won't give up, no matter where my mom chooses to live. I'll steal a car to get back to you if I have to," he says pressing his forehead into mine, trying to make me laugh. "I promise I'll come back to you."

"This is where it starts to hurt, then fall apart, and then fade away. Isn't it, Wes?"

"No. Never."

"We have young love. Which to most people is love that is not strong enough to survive anything. Wes, you're gonna move away, and I'll stay here. We'll grow away from each other, and other people come into our lives. I'll see you only when you visit Bonnie. The love that we have for each other will gradually dissolve, and we'll both go on to love someone else."

"No, because that's not what either one of us wants, so we won't let that happen," he tells me as his eyes well with tears. "Ruby, when someone has the greatest kind of love in their heart, they make sure that they do everything to keep it there. They know to never let it go. Never give up on it. I know you know that, because I watched you do it this summer with your grandma, and it was the most beautiful thing I've ever seen."

I look to the ground and nod a sad yes.

"I don't want to live without you, so I won't," he tells me.

We take our picture in the photo booth and I force myself to smile. We share both, fried pickles and fried clam strips, and I try to enjoy them. At the Carnival games, I try to tease Wesley, as he tries to win me a giant stuffed animal at the basketball hoops, but my heart just isn't in it. It is distracted.

"You know these things are rigged. They're impossible to win, Wes," I say, as he easily wins me a giant stuffed banana.

"Thanks, Wes. I think I'll name him...Reginald. Reginald the banana."

As much as Wesley has tried to make me smile tonight, my grandma is still heavy on my mind. As much as he has preoccupied my heart this summer, she has never left my thoughts for even one second.

Her struggling, miles away from me, with tubes down her throat that connect her to drugs that have poisoned her, and shortened her life, has never left my mind for one second. But I was also constantly aware these last two months, that in the midst of all my heartache, Wesley saved my heart this summer.

Now he, like my grandma, is more than likely just days away from leaving me.

But standing there, I feel a wave of selfishness come over me. Why am I here? Why am I not at home cleaning out Grandma Dotti's bedroom? All I meant to do was take a quick nap, and here I am contemplating a snow cone or cotton candy.

It's because my emotional resilience is completely gone. I'm so tired.

A couple of raindrops start to fall. I hop back on the handlebars of Clyde's bike and Wesley starts to pedal home.

I strategically hold on to Reginald the banana, so he won't drag on the ground or get in the way of Wesley's view. The sounds of Edgewater Park fade behind me as I say a quiet goodbye until next summer.

Sitting on the handlebars I inhale one of the last nights of this summer. I pull on the sleeve cuffs of my sweatshirt and my fingers hold them tight. Every block or two Wesley would lean into me and kiss me on my cheek, as he pedaled back home. More than ever, I need every one of his kisses.

As long as I can remember I've wished on stars, and tonight, I send out my biggest wish into the galaxy. I know it's unrealistic, but I'm still hanging on to hope.

*I know that time waits for no one, and it sometimes moves faster than we can keep up with. There is no way you can stop time, but my wish tonight, is for everything to stay the same. Freeze this night. Keep my grandma with me. Don't let her die. Keep Wes here with me. Somehow. Please.*

When night falls we set our alarms for a specific time and we do what we need to, to get through to the next day because we are compelled to get there. We continue to live our lives like we're suppose to and it doesn't matter how much pain your heart is in. When the sun comes up tomorrow that official starts a brand new day. We're forced to throw ourselves into it and make the very best of it, no matter what our situation.

Sometimes - impossible.

Change is tough. I might not always live here in Detroit, something might change that. But I already know that my house on Kentfield will always be the best place I have ever lived.

Edgewater will be gone someday too. It will become archaic, torn down, and replaced with something the mayor thinks we need instead. But nothing will change all the fun Ian, Wesley, all my childhood friends, and I have had there.

I imagine a time when Checkers, Harding, Redford, and even my house will look different or possibly torn down as well. But they will stand in my heart, solid and giant.

I think if you continue to love everything you have in your life, before, during, and after things change, your memories will always be great ones, and great memories will always keep you happy.

Just one more thing Grandma Dotti taught me.

*"Keep me in this night,"* I whisper to the brightest star in the sky.

Wesley and I cuddle up together on my front porch swing, and finish our Rock & Rye pop we left there. I lie my head in his lap, as his sleepy eyes look down at me.

"You know a true test of love is the level of pain your heart feels when that person you love is leaving you," I sleepily tell him. "The pain is enormous. And right now, both sides of my heart are in so much pain. Thank you, Wes. Thank you for taking care of me this summer. It's been the worst time of my life, and you tried so hard to fix my broken heart - when you have your own to fix. Thanks for letting me cry on your shoulder too, and for all the ways that you loved me...." My eyes close, and I instantly dream.

"How old were Romeo and Juliet again, I forgot?" I think I heard him say.

The sun is coming up when Wesley carries me into my house. He gently lays me down on the couch, places Grandma Dotti's unfinished bird quilt on top of me, and whispers in my ear, "I love you, Ruby."

He kisses me good-bye, and leaves.

The very early morning breeze from the open living room window made the curtains dance around. The cool air softly caresses my face. The feeling of peace completely fills my body as I fall deeper into sleep.

My dreams are vivid, and I sleep hard without any movement. A couple of times I thought I heard someone call my name.

No one did, but the voice sounded soft and sweet, loving and kind. It sounded like my grandma.

# SHATTERED

I wake up abruptly the next morning because my body starts to shake. My heart races, and I instantly panic. I inhale, and then slowly exhale. I try to calm myself down by lying still on the couch, but I quickly realize that it was the dreadful thought, somewhere at the end of my dream that has stifled me numb.

Something's different. Something doesn't feel right. I close my eyes.

*I'm begging, please. No.*

I slowly get up from the couch and I leave the blanket and pillows where they fall. I skip the majority of my morning routine and dress the fastest I ever have. I grab my sling bag, but forget to pack anything inside of it. I don't comb my hair or even stop to eat breakfast. And instead of walking out the front door to get the Fenkell bus, I walk out the back door.

I run through the back yard, take one leap over the fence, and head straight for Bonnie's back door.

It's quiet in the house; I'm not sure if anyone is up or not because I don't stop to notice. I run up the steps, taking two at a time, and run directly into Wesley's room. I open his bedroom door and look directly at his bed.

I feel my heart sink to the bottom of my stomach.

"What's wrong, Ruby?" Wesley says, immediately sitting up and pulling his tattered gold blanket off his legs.

I am out of breath. I can barely speak.

"I...I thought you... left. I just thought...you were gone, Wes. But, it's...not you. It's not you who's gone."

"Ruby, are you okay? You don't look so good."

I nod. "Yeah, I mean. No. I was just...dreaming, I guess...You're here. You're still here. It's not you.

I have to... go. I have to get to my grandma. Something's wrong. Something doesn't feel right to me, Wes," I turn to walk away; my eyes instantly drown in tears.

"Ruby, wait!" he says, as he gets up from his bed and grabs for my hand.

I feel like I ran a never-ending marathon. My sleep-deprived eyes keep filling with tears...I fight to keep breathing.

"Let me hold you for a minute, I'm worried about you," he says, wrapping his arms around me tighter than ever.

With my speech slow and labored, I tell him, "Stay here with me, Wes. Don't go. Forget everything I said last night. I can't sacrifice you or anything right now, I'm too selfish. Make this your home for good. Please don't go with your mom. Move her here. It doesn't matter, you just can't go. I can't lose you and my grandma both. It's just too much."

I quickly realize how horrible I sound. How dare I keep him from his mom who needs him. How dare I beg for my dying Grandma to keep fighting for a life that she is no longer able to live. How selfish of me to want to keep them both here for me. I stand with my face buried in my hands.

"I'm doing everything I can to stay," he tells me.

"I'm sorry...," I say, as I keep my face hidden in my hands. "I'm sorry, Wes. I'm just really tired and emotionally...exhausted."

"Don't; don't ever apologize for loving someone, Ruby. I told you that I'm coming back to you, and I'm going to keep that promise."

"Wes, I woke up this morning in a panic. I was dreaming of something, I don't remember what anymore, but something just didn't feel right. Something is... missing...besides my hope and strength. I know they are now completely gone from me. And I have this feeling that... something terrible has happened. So I ran here in a panic. I'm going to miss you and my grandma. I love you both so much. I know that I sound selfish. I don't want you to leave and live anywhere besides here, near me. I've been begging for my grandma to hang on even though I know she's suffering. That's wrong of me, I know that. It's just...I can't let either one of you go. I can't do it. I'm not able to say goodbye to either one of you."

"Ruby, you're not selfish or weak at all. You have to have an incredible amount of strength to face what you have every day this summer. Every day, Ruby. Every day this summer I watched you grow stronger, more selfless and more beautiful. And I've seen your confidence grow since I met you, and attached to that is so much more. Try to remember that I'm the least of your worries, because I know that if I do go anywhere, I'll never stay away long. *I've* already decided that for myself."

My eyes sting with tears. He puts his hands on my face and kisses my forehead.

"I know this is hard for you to hear," he continues, "but your grandma has put up the best fight she could, and it was all because of the love she has for you, your mom, and Ian. She's been hanging on to all of you, too. When life ends, love certainly does not.  My dad told me that love plants itself, and you're the only one that can keep it growing inside of you. And you will. Our love is planted, and it will grow to be everlasting, just like the love you have for your grandma, and I have for my dad."

We stand in the middle of his room holding each other, and like he has so many times this summer, he kisses my tears away. In the comfort of his arms, I feel a tear from him hit my shoulder, so I squeeze him tighter.

"I have to go, Wes."

"You want me to come with you today? I will be by your side all day. I'll never leave it."

"No. Thank you, though," I tell him.

He follows me downstairs and through the kitchen. He sticks a strawberry Pop Tart in my empty sling bag, and we walk through his back yard.

"Let me at least walk you to the bus stop," he says.

"No, go back to bed. Get some sleep," I tell him.  "I forgot my sweater, anyways, and I can't remember where I put it."

I hop over the fence and turned to him.

"Wes, remember yesterday I said that when you sacrifice your own happiness in life, something else might come along and save your heart?" He nodded slowly. "Well, I want you to be the one who saves my heart."

Then he says something that I know I will think about every day of my life.

"Ruby, you and I are going to have the greatest love

of all time."

And through my clouded brain, devastating pain and heartbreak, I knew he was right.

When I went through my back door and into the kitchen, Ian, who I thought had already left for work, was talking on the phone. His eyes squint, his face frowns as he slowly hangs up the receiver.

"Mom wants us at the hospital, Ruby, right away," he tells me, his voice expressionless.

I don't ask why, but I knew. Again, like so many times this summer, I couldn't bring myself to admit that anything bad was going to happen to Grandma Dotti.

Ian called the bowling alley to let them know that he wouldn't be in as I look for my sweater. Then we run our fastest down Kentfield to catch the bus.

As long as I live, this day will always remain in the front of my brain, and never transfer to the back.

Ian and I get up to Grandma Dotti's room in the intensive care unit at exactly 7:30. Mom is next to her, holding her hand and softly crying. No lights were on in the room.

"She's was calling for you, Ruby," My mom says, wiping her eyes with a tissue. "All morning she called for you. She wanted you to hold her hand. It was just about a half hour ago that she slipped into a coma. The nurses tell me she's starting to shut down. Come over here and hold her hand," she says Ian and me. "They told me that she can hear us, so I've been talking to her all morning."

Ian and I don't answer. We say nothing as we stare

at Grandma Dotti through our teary eyes.

Grandma Dotti's right eye is closed, and her left eye, slightly open. Her mouth droops down on one side. Her skin is ashen, and what's left of her hair, a tangled mess. Her breathing is sporadic, and her chest, filled with tubes, fights to inflate.

*Why didn't I get her home? I promised I would.*

I feel absolutely grief-stricken.

I slowly sit down on the right side of the bed and place her hand in mine, while Ian held the other. I want to think of something to say to her that will help her leave this world knowing how much I truly loved her. But, really, that's what our life together was for. Your time with someone should never be wasted on anything else, other than showing them how much you love them and how much they mean to you.

"Grandma...it's Ruby," I say to her, my voice shaking. "I'm going to stay right here with you. I'm not going to leave your side." I squeeze her hand and kiss it.

"I want you to know that you will always be with me. Whatever I do and wherever I go. Every day of my life. You hold the deepest spot in my heart, and I promise you... I will think of you every day."

I stumble through my words because I start to cry. I put my hand on her right cheek. I watch a tear rolled down her face. Not just one - I counted. There were seven.

She can hear me.

I think that moment was the biggest, deepest and most pain I've ever felt in my life. I'm watching the person I love the most fight to stay with me, but really, they know they are already gone.

"You are truly the most beautiful...," I tell her as I start to cry harder. "And I will make you proud."

I try to remember all the things she used to tell me when I was scared or hurt, but my brain was just not functioning.

"I love you," are the only words I can come up with. Three simple words that mean so incredibly much to everyone I know. Three simple words that became life-changing words with Wesley and me this summer, and sadly, the final words my grandma will ever hear me say to her.

Uncle Levi, Aunt Marie, Uncle Nash and Aunt Carlie stay at the hospital with us, and we all take turns holding her hand throughout the day, and into the night, until the sun comes up the next morning.

I watch her struggle to hang on to the last moments of her life, and I remember my own words to Wesley just two days before. Words that I've always thought were hard to hear, but sometimes necessary.

*"Sacrificing our own happiness for the people we love - Let go of what makes us happy and take the chance that something else will come along and save our heart - Sometimes sacrifice will take you somewhere else you're meant to be."* Is that what I said?

As devastated as my heart is, it's time for me to stop fighting against my own words, and start to listen to them.

I step out into the hallway and lean against the wall as tears pour down my face.

I say quietly to myself, "I fought to hang on to you, and now I fight to let go. But don't you fight anymore,

Grandma. Let go. You have to...let go."

And just two months after Grandma Dotti's cancer diagnosis, I sit in her hospital bed, cradle her in my arms, and listen for her very last breath.

It was 7:08 am - August 18, 1978. It was a sunny, but cool Friday morning when Grandma Dotti died in my arms.

A doctor came in and pronounced her dead. I heard someone say that the cause of death was heart failure.

Heart failure. Her heart never failed me once.

We spend the next couple of hours at the hospital. I continue to cry as my body shakes with pain. I throw up twice in the bathroom, and Ian is there to help me up off the floor each time. He wipes my red and swollen face with his shirt tail, and we hug the biggest hugs of our lives.

I hold Grandma Dotti one last time, and I kiss her goodbye. Her destroyed body is already returning to the fetal position, as two nurses wheel her to the basement morgue.

I wonder if she is able to see our devastation and feel all the hurt in our hearts. I wondered if she is rising above us, and free from pain. No more tears for her to cry, no worry in her eyes, no pain, no harm in anyway.

My heart feels shattered in pieces. I feel it no longer sits slightly tilted to the left inside my chest.

I pull my sweater tight around me, and sit in the vinyl chair in the intensive care unit. I double over and continue to cry. I remember what Grandma Dotti told me once when I was a little girl. She said that when Grandpa Kip died, she thought for sure that most of her heart died with him.

"I never thought my heart would feel the same again," she told me. "But, your mom came back home with you and Ian, and that tender part of my heart fixed itself. My life with you, Ruby, is what healed my broken heart. Love sometimes feels distant, but true love is always close by."

Now I know why Wesley's was really here this summer.


Mom signs some hospital papers as I gather up Grandma Dotti's belongings and place them in a thick plastic hospital bag. Still in tears, Aunt Marie and Aunt Carlie hug and kiss us all goodbye. Uncle Levi and Uncle Nash hugs are so tight that it hurt my back.

We leave to go home and no one speaks in the car.

When Mom pulls up in the driveway I barely wait for her to turn the car off. I go directly to my bedroom and fall into my bed. I lie completely still for hours, staring at the ceiling. Lying there I noticed my "Ten goals for summer vacation" hanging on the corkboard by my bed. Nothing even attempted, as the dedication diminished week by week.

Grandma Dotti can never teach me to darn my socks. I never signed up for karate or swim lessons, and I know I never will. I didn't get ready for the track team and have lost complete interest in joining. I wrote not one song, I never got to sew any teddy bears for the kids at the hospital, I never once made it to the library, and I never had the chance to change my bedroom. All those things I thought would help me grow and make Grandma Dotti proud of me will never be done for her.

Every part of my body is in pain. I lie face down in my pillow. I haven't turned on the radio or listened to any music in two days. And even though music has always found some way to soothe me, it won't tonight. Nothing will. This night is the first time in my life that I don't listen to music.

As I slowly drift off to sleep and I think I hear Bonnie's voice. Am I dreaming, or has she come over? Is Wesley with her?

I must have fallen into a deeper sleep because my dream suddenly turned black. I have no recollection of a dream that night.

# OUT OF TIME
♥♥♥♥♥♥♥♥♥♥♥♥♥♥♥♥♥♥♥♥♥♥♥♥♥♥♥♥♥♥♥♥♥♥♥♥

Mom let me sleep in, but she seemed anxious to take Ian and me shopping for some new clothes. She said I needed a new dress and mentioned that the sweater I was wearing to the hospital every day seemed too small for me, so we should pick up a new one. After she forced us to eat breakfast, we left for the mall.

I repeatedly said "No thank you" to the new sweater every time my mom brought it up, but I did get a new dress that I really do love. The beautiful black chiffon dress that fell just above my knees had an empire waist and a keyhole neckline. Mom thought it might be a little too "mature" for me, but I talked her into it, because the very second I tried it on I felt instantly pretty.

Ian picks out a new pair of shoes, and he purposely picked the ugliest socks Sears Department Store sold. He tells me that they would make Grandma Dotti laugh. Mom buys Ian a new tie too, even though he said he had no plans to ever wear it.

It seems everything she bought was black: even the short and layered wig for Grandma Dotti to wear in her casket. Mom asks me more than once if I like it, but I don't answer her. I find myself wanting to get Grandma Dotti's opinion on it first. I wonder if she would be receptive to wearing it, or embarrassed.

I hold the wig bag in my hand, and even though my disoriented heart couldn't answer my mom, I know it will look really cute on her.

We drive back and forth to King's Funeral Home,

which I find strange, because it's at the end of our street. Ian always begged to come here on Halloween night when we were younger. He thought it would be extra creepy to nosey around the rooms.

But not today. We both sit quietly with Mom as she picks out prayer cards that didn't make sense, flower arrangements that all looked the same, casket colors that seemed dull and ordinary, and even an ugly concrete vault to put the casket into. Mom tries to include me on every decision, but I sit aloof and agree with everything she says just so we could leave and go home. And even though it sounds like the entire funeral is planned, we still leave with a handful of funeral home brochures.

Mom takes us out to eat directly after, even though Ian and I tell her we aren't hungry.

I order a salad and some chicken noodle soup. I pick at my salad and over stir my soup.

While we're eating, Mom talks to us about funeral home rules and funeral manners, reminding us what to say to everyone.

"We're almost 16 and 17 years old, Mom," Ian says. "We know, but I think everyone will understand if we don't want to talk."

"Oh, Ruby, Bonnie came by last night, while you were sleeping." she says to me, ignoring Ian.

My eyes slowly move away from my salad and directly into my mom's dark and heavily eye-shadowed eyelids.

"She did?"

"Yeah, with her cousin, Wesley."

My heart instantly begins to race. "That was nice of

them. To stop by," I say, rearranging the tomatoes on my salad as I stumble through my words.

"It was. Wesley had a few interesting things to say."

From the corner of my eye, I notice Ian staring at me, completely still and suddenly ignoring his roast beef sandwich.

"He did? Ian, could you pass me the salt?"

I don't even use salt, but I quickly decide to concentrate on my soup, which was still way too hot to eat, and hope the subject will change. I figure me not saying anything told her everything I've been meaning to tell her all summer.

My mom has always held a door open for me to talk to her about boys, and any level of relationship I might have with them, but it was Grandma Dotti whom I would always share that with. And even though I've done the math relating to my parents' wedding day and Ian's birth (which were exactly seven months apart), and I know she'd understand the feelings of a young girl in love, I just don't feel I'm ready to share any details with her right now.

But as I sit there, enthralled with my soup, for the first time this summer I felt an unrecognizable strength come over me. I feel I could defend myself about anything my mom would ask me regarding Wesley, but at the same time, show her the respect that she deserves.

"He sure thinks highly of you, Ruby," she continued.

"Honestly, Mom, I don't know what I would have done without him this summer. He was wonderful to me, and I'm grateful that I met him. I fell in love with him. It didn't seem like the appropriate thing to do,

283

but it turns out...it was."

As I purposely smash my cracker pack and wait for my mom to start her round of questions, all I could do was sit there and think of Wesley. My mind wandered to all the nights this summer that we would kiss for hours at a time, and how dangerous it could have gotten. I think about how deep and passionate our make-out sessions had become. The softer the kiss, the more my heart raced. I was thinking about how we would fall asleep almost every night this summer, in our underwear, tangled in each other's arms. I think about the hickey I had, and the ones I *almost* had, which pushed the "irresponsible and dangerous" button over and over again. I was thinking about how much I miss him right now.

"He sure is adorable," she says.

"Yeah, he is...in every way," I say, certain that I'm now blushing.

"You deserve it. And thanks, Ruby, for taking care of the house this summer. The yard looks great, and I noticed you even paid a couple of the utilities bills last month. Thanks for stepping up and helping me. I depended on you a lot this summer..." she says as her voice shakes, "and you came through every time. I'm sure it was hard for you, knowing what lay ahead, and I'm glad your heart was able to find love at such a difficult time."

I look at my mom, and she smiles at me. I feel her trust. I breathe out a heavy sigh before I took my first bite of my French dressing-soaked salad.

When we get home, I go straight to my bedroom again and cry myself to sleep. I doubt I got a good night's sleep because the next day, I woke up angry.

Today is the viewing for Grandma Dotti. I absolutely dread walking in the funeral home and seeing her in a pine box. I want these next two days to be over with so badly, but when they are over, I'll never see my grandma ever again. Our life together will have officially come to an end, and I can't stand how that makes me feel. I should hang on to these last two days and somehow find a way to make the best of them. But how can I when I'm mad at everything in this entire world. I'm even mad at Grandma Dotti. I'm mad at her because she did the one thing I never thought she'd do. She broke my heart.

Did she hear me when I told her to "let go," on the morning she died? Because all summer I begged for her to do the opposite. Why did she listen to the thing I really didn't mean? My heart feels violent, so I decide not to smile at all today.

Because I tossed and turned all night, my face is puffy, and my head is pounding. I look and feel horrible. After a quick breakfast of pancakes, which I barely ate, we take our ten second ride to the funeral home.

It's so dark inside King's Funeral Home that I almost trip up the stairs. I walk around in the dark and peek into each room. There are four individual rooms and every one of them is filled with mix-matched furniture. It smells like a combination of flowers and furniture polish wherever I walk, and I faintly hear some gloomy music that makes me instantly depressed. It looks like Grandma Dotti was the only one that died this week in our neighborhood. She's here all alone.

285

Room number two (the one I purposely avoided looking in) has a sign above a doorway. It reads "Dolores Rosalie McAuley." No one ever called her that. She was Dotti to everyone. Dolores sounds so impersonal. I stare at the sign and try to think of a way I could rearrange all the letters without anyone noticing. There are no T's up there. Hmmm, can't do it.

Grandma Dotti would be disappointed in me for even remotely having that thought in my head, so I decide against it.

I step into room number two, then accidentally catch a glimpse of Grandma Dotti in her casket. I instantly look away, gasp, and clutch my chest. Something just shot directly through my heart. I think it was a giant piece of agony. I can barely breathe.

Uncle Levi and Uncle Nash are directly behind us with their entire family, and I have already forgotten all my "funeral manners" as I can barely force a smile to greet them. They hug us, and are super nice to us, but I'm not breaking. No smiles.

Mom wants Ian and me to go up to the casket and see how nice Grandma Dotti looks in her favorite dress and new wig. I don't want to, but Ian forcibly takes my hand and pulls me closer.

I try not to look directly at her and instead look at her casket and the flowers surrounding it. But standing there I felt agitated and restless inside. All the planning Mom tried to include me in, are now, all of the sudden, important to me.

*Is that pillow soft enough? Why didn't Mom pick her pink polyester short set and her bright yellow sneakers*

286

*instead of her pink coat dress for her to wear? It's made of wool, and it looks too warm. What shoes does she have on anyway? What about a bra? She always wore one particular bra with that dress. What about nylons? She always wore them with a dress. Why this casket? There were others that seemed nicer. And baby's breath and roses? Everyone has that.*

All this damage to my heart has made its way into my brain and caused it to malfunction. I'm nothing but negative. I have to somehow get through this day. I can't let grief take control of me. It will disappoint the people who need me. Again, Grandma Dotti would be disappointed in me for being so critical.

"Grandma would love everything you picked for her," I say to my mom. "It's all perfect."

Ian and I hold hands tightly as I force myself to look directly at Grandma Dotti lying in her satin-lined coffin. Her bruised and bony hands are folded high on her chest, and they look hard and cold. I hate that her lips and eyes are sewn shut, and I wonder if she would feel okay about having a little more blush on her cheeks than usual. Her skin has surprisingly good color and her wig, which is more natural looking than I first thought, is adjusted perfectly.

She looks beautiful.

The rest of the day is spent greeting neighbors, friends, relatives, some I didn't know I had, and a lot of Moms co-workers. Our mailman, Mr. Russell, came with the man who drives the fruit and vegetable truck. His name, I found out is Joe DiMaggio.

Ian and I stay close to each other as people come up

to us all day, telling stories about Grandma Dotti that continue to make us proud of her. Even though I force a smile, and I'm still mad at the world, everyone is very loving to us.

Grandma's cousin's tell Ian and me what great looking kids we are, how Grandma Dotti would brag about us, and how important Mom, Ian and I were to her. I take a lot of deep breaths, and wonder how I'm surviving this day.

Ian and I are talking to our neighbor, Mrs. Morgan, when I notice Mom greeting a tall man with a short awkward hug. He has on glasses, slicked back blonde hair, and a very expensive looking suit. This must be Reed. Mom makes her way over to us and introduces him. It's him. I look him over from head to toe.

He seems nice, but my new bad attitude wants to immediately tell him that I like things at home just the way they are, so he shouldn't try to change anything. I don't say it out loud, but I'm thinking it pretty loudly.

I look to the front of the room at Grandma Dotti; she wouldn't like these judgmental thoughts that are going through my head, and I know better. So, I try to adjust my attitude by forcing out, "It's nice to meet you, Reed."

He's nice to me and Ian, but directs most of his questions to me.

"Ruby Tuesday. I love your name. Your mom tells me music is a hobby of yours. Do you like the Rolling Stones and their song *Ruby Tuesday*?"

"I do," I quietly tell him, as I think about Wesley singing that song to me just nights ago. "I love it, actually."

Mrs. Morgan interrupts, "So, Reed, what is it you do for a living?"

Good question, Mrs. Morgan.

"Psychologist," he proudly says.

Psychologist? That instantly makes me think about Wesley and my pledge to help him with the pain from his mom and dad. I daydream and start to think about when I will see him again. I called him a couple of times yesterday and he wasn't home. I left a message with Toby who said he didn't know where Wesley was. I hope he's not left yet. Not today.

But just then, at that exact moment, something in my erratic brain tells me to turn around. When I do, I see Wesley right away. I can't believe he's here!

I don't hear anymore of anyone's conversation. I say a quick, "Excuse me," and I just about push people out of my way to get to him.

He is wearing black dress pants and black shoes with a dark jade colored dress shirt. He looks so handsome, and I'm so happy to see him, that a genuine smile comes out of me for the first time in days. He wraps his arms completely around me and kisses me a long solid kiss which instantly makes me feel better. Bonnie is there too with her entire family. She steps in and breaks up my much-needed affection.

"He's been bugging me all day to get here, but he can wait," she says, as tears instantly fill her eyes. We hug a gigantic hug that almost made me fall over, and I feel her cry on my shoulder. That, of course, made me cry. Hugs from Bonnie's family always feel sincere and genuine.

Wesley stays by my side the rest of the night. He

only left once to bring me a cup of water, and a napkin filled with four cookies: chocolate chip, snickerdoodle, Fudge Striped and a Windmill. He hugs and kisses me periodically, which surprises me. Most guys are afraid to show any type of affection in front of their girlfriends' families. I love that he breaks all of life's insignificant rules - He did all summer.

Okay, Wesley brought my smile back, but I'm still angry. Angry that Grandma Dotti would suffer so much at the end of her life. And I'm hurt. Hurt because she was the love of my life, and now she's gone.

It was dusk when Wesley walked me home. After he kissed me goodbye and disappeared down the street, my pisser mood came back. Tomorrow is the funeral. A day for final goodbyes. I am almost out of time with her.

I walk slowly into the house and down the dark hallway to my room. I slip into my ostrich print pajamas and pile my hair high on top of my head. I lie still on top of my bed and think about everyone who came to see Grandma Dotti today. So much love in the room and I'm glad that my broken heart could see it.

After an hour, I heard my mom knock on my door.

"Ruby, do you want to be pallbearer tomorrow?" she asks, standing in my doorway. "Ian said he would, but do you think you can do it?"

I think about Grandma Dotti right away, and can almost hear her say that the casket will be too heavy for me to carry. She'd say that I'll hurt myself and wreck my shoes. But she would also be very proud that Ian and I carried her to her final resting place.

"Absolutely, Mom. Of course I will," I say quietly.

"Great. Try and get a good night's sleep. Tomorrow will be a tough day," she says, closing my door.

But I don't go to sleep right away. I decide to stay up a little bit longer and write Grandma Dotti a note to place with her in her casket. A thank you note. A thank you that will remain with her forever, because if there's anyone in my life that I've been most thankful for - it's her.

Grandma Dotti taught me how to write thank-you letters, but I really don't know how to even begin this one. She always said when you're stuck; talk about the weather.

*Grandma Dotti,*

*The sky was pretty this morning. Every cloud was heart shaped, and the temperature was your favorite ~ double 7's*

I tap my pen on the paper for a minute or two, close my eyes, and think hard about my next words. I place my hand over my aching heart, and suddenly, all the love that my grandma had embedded into it, began to fill me up again. The words start to pour out of me quicker than I can write them down.

I start by thanking her for all that she has taught me, and I make a promise to her that I will teach my children everything that she worked so hard to instill in me.

*The greatest thing you taught me in life is love. And because of you, I know how to feel love and how to fill a heart*

291

*with love.*

I tell her that I hope every day of her life with me she felt appreciated, admired, cherished and deeply loved, because she was.

*You were in every way the most beautiful person in our world. You added beauty to everyone's lives by being exactly what your heart told you to be. Most people can't do that. You did it perfectly.*

I write that even though I'm glad she's not in pain anymore, I begged for her to hold on and stay here with us, because I know that I will miss her so incredibly much.

*I couldn't bear to let you go. I love you, Grandma, and I found it impossible to let go of our life together. I loved every second that we shared and the beautiful feeling that was attached to it. Thanks for making what's meant to be the best time of my life, truly, the best time of my life.*

I thank her for sharing her home with Mom and Ian and me, and I thank her for teaching me how to forgive, but to also stand strong. To never judge and to always keep an empathic heart. To treat everyone the same, with respect, but make sure you get it in return. Always work hard at everything you do, and find laughter in as many places in your life as you possibly can.

*I hope as I grow older, I will be just like you.*

As I continue to write, a tear from my cheek falls onto the paper and leaves a watermark. I decide not to get a new piece of paper, but to draw a heart around it.

*A tear of mine - because you're worth every tear I'll ever cry.*

I wipe my face from tears, and like so many times this summer, nothing stops them from flowing. I pick up my pen and try to finish.

*This letter will always be a part of me that remains with you, and I have a part of you that will always remain with me. I have a piece of your heart and soul attached to my own. And because you are planted so deep in my heart and soul, you will never leave me. And for that, I am truly fortunate and forever grateful.*

I put the paper up to my lips and give it a kiss.

*I kiss this paper and will place it by your heart. It's my last kiss to you, but not my last act of love for you. I will listen to you from the core of my heart and hope that whatever decisions I make in life would have made you proud of me. I will always remember the true love that sits close by, and know that it's what I'll need to fix the tender part of my heart.*

It is a hard letter to finish, but after picking and choosing the right words, I end it. My hand shakes as I finish.

*I will still go on to learn a lot of things in my life, but life's most important lesson I was lucky to have learned from you long ago. You taught me that all the things that you truly love in life will live inside of your heart forever because true love never dies. And because it lasts forever, you'll always feel it. My heart may be broken today, but it still feels love, which makes true love the most amazing thing in this life. Thank you, Grandma, for giving me an amazing life.*

I'll forever love you, Ruby Tuesday

I could have gone on to say so many more things, but I had to stop writing. I couldn't see through my tears.

# MISS YOU
♥♥♥♥♥♥♥♥♥♥♥♥♥♥♥♥♥♥♥♥♥♥♥♥♥♥♥♥♥♥♥♥♥♥♥♥♥♥♥♥

I was hoping the weather would be nice today. I checked with Grandma Dotti's favorite weatherman when I woke up, and he said it will be a "perfectly grand day."

As I begin to dress for my grandma's funeral, I notice that my favorite white lacey bra feels like it's digging into my armpit. My breasts feel snug in my bra as I gently pull on the surrounding lace to readjust it. As I continue, my butt feels very uncomfortably in my underwear, and my nylons that fit me in June, instantly feel firm and tight. I rip them the very second I try to wiggle them on. I already know that my feet are going to hurt all day because my black patent leather sandals, the same ones that I wore two months ago at graduation, are all of the sudden to small, which makes me desperately want to go barefoot.

I weigh myself on the bathroom scale, which reads five pounds more than it did in June. And in the bathroom mirror, I notice a slight muscle tone to my arms and a flatter stomach.

As I rummage through my jewelry box, I decide to wear a diamond necklace that Grandma Dotti gave to me on my thirteenth birthday. Today it seems to sparkle more than ever. When I stick a matching barrette in my hair, I notice that my hair seems slightly longer and fuller. Also, the lighter streaks that I put in last spring have all faded.

The other day when I reached for a book that sits on the top shelf of my closet, I didn't need to get on my tiptoes as much. It seemed easier to reach, which makes me think that I may have grown a possible inch or two.

I really have grown this summer.

And grow I did. In every way possible.

I sit down on the edge of my bed and glance over to my summer goals list - Summer goals that I wasn't sure I would reach when I set out to achieve them in June. But really, I have.

Learning responsibility for myself, and the people I love, did not come from learning the importance of swimming. It came from getting myself up every morning to take care of my family and our home, because my mom needed me to. I had to show her I was responsible and that she could always depend on me, especially in serious situations. I kept myself safe, and religiously got myself back and forth to the hospital everyday so I could be by my grandma's side, because she also depended on me. And responsibility came every night as I pushed the meaning of the word with my boyfriend. Every day and every night this summer it was tested.

My self-defense came in the form of boxing and not karate. Thanks to Wesley, I feel that I can defend myself against anyone who would harm me - mentally or physically. As boxing was giving me my much-needed physical strength, it was, unbeknownst to me, giving me emotional strength as well. I'm not sure when it all hit my brain, but I do feel mentally stronger today.

I never learned how to darn my socks, so my recreation did not come from learning that skill.

Oddly, it came when I fell in love with Wesley. I recreated the very best thing in life through him. I re-created love. I will always miss my grandma's love, and nothing will replace it, but this summer I learned how to salvage love by letting my heart love again. It's not something you think you can do when your heart is in pain, but I did it - and I'm glad I did. Holey socks are usually destined for the garbage, but think again before you give up on anything that's valuable to you. Just re-create it in another way. This summer, Wesley, was my holey sock.

I didn't write any songs this summer. Not one. But that's okay, because even though I put my writing aside, I still stayed true to my heart and listened to what it was telling me. It was telling me to stay close to my grandma, but also stay close to Wesley. The destiny my heart was leading to was that while one side of my heart was suffering an irremediable break, the other side was staying fused together. My heart was telling me to continue to love because it's the most important thing in life. I'm so glad I listened to it because falling in love was the only happiness I had this summer.

My continuous goal to read the entire encyclopedia was put on hold. However, I learned things these last few months that are not in any encyclopedia. It doesn't say anywhere in any encyclopedia how to keep living as a part of you is dying. I've never read that when you're about to lose an enormous amount of love in your life, you still have to strive for happiness. Which is not easy. I've never read from any book the importance of holding on to true love and never letting it go. But I learned this summer the most important thing in anyone's life. Hold true love tight and never let it go - no matter what the outcome.

My plan for adventure to build courage his summer did not come from hitchhiking with Bonnie. Instead, I went on multiple adventures with Wesley - adventures that my heart never thought it would go on at 15 ½ years old. And in those adventures my heart actually did find courage. You have to have courage to fall in love. You have to have courage to watch someone you love die. And you have to have courage to get in a car and let your boyfriend illegally drive you 70 miles from your home and out of your comfort zone. It's scary, it's hard, and sometimes irresponsible to venture into unknown territory, but Helen Keller once wrote - "Life is either a daring adventure, or nothing." And I found out this summer how very true that is.

Extending myself to help someone in need did not come from volunteering to teach a blind child in my neighborhood how to read. It was a little different this summer. I extended myself to the most important person in my life - my grandma. I tried to set my emotions aside as I did the one thing that I absolutely never thought I could do and that was watching my grandma with her biggest struggle in life. But by doing that I grew more compassionate. I learned that it's okay to show your emotions and never push them aside. I learned that you never need to hide your tears because they are a true sign of how much you love. I stand proud behind every tear I cried this summer because every day this summer, despite my heartbreak, empathy and compassion grew in my heart, and I never let anything else (like hate) take over.

I look around my bedroom. My determination to work on something I'm not good at, so I could practice patience, surfaced in another way. Instead of painting my room this summer, I became determined to get my grandma better. My patience was tested every day, every hour, and every second by hanging on to hope that she would recover. I waited for all her medicines to do their job. I waited for her blood to get healthy. I waited for her body to heal. And even though the obvious stared me in the face, I never gave up. Determination means to never give up even if you know you just might fail. And without you realizing, you someday look back and see that you had patience after all.

My commitment to sew teddy bears for sick children at the hospital never happened either. Instead of working on my frustration, by dedicating my time to help comfort a scared child, my dedication turned out to be comforting my own frightened Grandma. Watching her die was more than frustrating to me, but I absolutely had to be by her side. It was the last bit of happiness I could give her. Turning your back on difficult things, running away from pain and death because it hurts, or makes you uncomfortable, are all easy to do. But true love is strong, and every day I stayed loyal to my grandma. It forced my frustration to turn into something else. Dedication. It became bigger than any frustration I have ever felt, as it always should, with someone you love so much.

My goal to join the track team, and compete in front of people, I thought was my biggest fear. It wasn't. My biggest fear is *everyone*'s biggest fear - Death. Everyday this summer I watched my grandma move closer to it. I don't know how I lived through it, it's still all a blur to me, but my fear was somehow set aside, and the strength I didn't know I had, persistently appeared. Some people walk through life not knowing that they have any amount of strength inside of them and it's never used, used the wrong way, or used too late. One day this summer I found it, I used it, and it forever sits in the front of my brain so I can remember how important it is to me every day of my life. Win or lose life's struggles, we gain something. This summer I faced fear and gained strength.

Life can sometimes have a peculiar way of sneaking in all the things that you need to help you grow up and be the person you're destined to be. I really did grow this summer after all, because today I do feel a little more responsible, physically and mentally stronger, creative, true to my heart, smarter, courageous, compassionate, patient, dedicated, and one step closer to fearless - just like I set out to do.


We get to the funeral home at exactly 9:00. Mom, Ian, and I sit directly in front of Grandma Dotti on a small couch with two wing chairs at each end. I sink deep into the couch cushions and listen to people slowly start to file in behind me.

Some of them are laughing, and I wonder - why? Some of them are coughing and I wonder - what from? Some of them are praying, and I wonder - why bother?

From somewhere in the room, the regularly played sad music starts. I should request, *Hallelujah, I Love*

*Her So,* just one last time.

Mr. King stands up by Grandma Dotti and starts to talk to the crowded room. Grandma Dotti would be mad at me because my manners have suddenly disappeared. I'm not paying attention to anything he's saying. I kick my tight sandals on and off my feet, I've not looked up once to acknowledge anyone in the room, and I sit still and stare down at the floor and readjust the daisies that I stuck in my hair before I left the house.

My mom takes a hold of my hand with force, and squeezes it as we watch everyone line up to say their final goodbyes to Grandma Dotti. My eyes fill with tears, but I never take my eyes off my grandma.

Uncle Levi, Uncle Nash, Aunt Marie and Aunt Carlie are the last to say goodbye. They stand over Grandma and wipe their tears into their embroidered handkerchiefs.

Ian goes up next. He walks slowly up to the casket and tucks a picture into Grandma Dotti's folded hands. It's a picture from our vacation to New York City two summers ago. The picture is of the four of us standing proudly with the Statue of Liberty behind us. It was our favorite vacation.

"Say goodbye, Ruby," he tells me, his eyes teary and bloodshot.

My hands shake as I place my letter by her heart, and the prettiest red rose I could find from our yard, by her hands

I hug her one last time, and whisper in her ear, "I'll never say goodbye, Grandma, because I know you'll never leave me. I'll always love you so much."

I breakdown in tears and cry on her shoulder - a shoulder I have cried on so many times, and always let go with a smile on my face. But now - never again.

My mom stays with her the longest. I couldn't hear what she was saying to Grandma, but her voice shook, and Uncle Nash had to hold her up. I'm sure whatever it was would have shattered my heart even more. The seven of us stand by Grandma Dotti, and hold on to each other, as Mr. King closes the lid of the casket.

Heart - pulverized.

And just when I thought I was out of tears, they begin to pour out. I wonder if there will be a day when I will stop crying?

The ride to the cemetery seems long. Uncle Levi drove in Mom's car, and Ian counts the cars that follow behind us.  It was thirty-nine - including us. Grandma Dotti would be humbled by that.

Everyone keeps telling me that the casket isn't too heavy for me, but I struggled with it. Besides Ian and me as pallbearers, Mom has asked Uncle Nash, Uncle Levi, and two of Grandma Dotti's favorite cousins, R.J. and Bernard. My heart aches to see grown men cry, or to hear heavy crying in the distance, as I struggle to carry Grandma Dotti to the hollowed out ground next to Grandpa Kip.

Grandma Dotti always told me on my toughest days, "Always be strong on the outside, but remain soft on the inside." So I kept repeating it in my head as tears continue to roll down my cheeks.

*Strong on the outside...strong on the outside...*

We carry Grandma Dotti up a grassy crest next to a

barren lilac bush, and we gently place her down onto the lowering device. Mr. King places his hand on the casket and says a prayer that made me cry harder.

R.J. and Bernard, their eyes red from crying, both give me a hug. Uncle Levi and Uncle Nash each place a rose on the top of her casket - an admirable and beautiful symbol of love from the two people who have loved her the longest.

I think about how proud Grandma Dotti would be of Ian and me as pallbearers, and how strong Mom has been through all of this. I've seen her cry a lot these last few weeks, but she seems to pick herself up and recover strong.

I stand there looking at Grandma Dotti's casket, knowing that she's in there. She will be put deep in the ground and will someday be just dust and bones. How do you continue to survive in this world knowing that is what becomes of the one you love?

I feel a sharp pain in my stomach, which makes me almost double over. I feel panic run from my head to my toes, and I instantly feel like I'm going to throw up. This must be what grief feels like as it hits your stomach on its way to filling your entire body. I look around to see if there's a place where I can discreetly vomit, but instead I see Bonnie with all her family. Then I see Wesley.

They all run over to me and shower me with hugs and kisses that feel warm and loving. Jodi and Bonnie cry harder than I have ever seen them cry. I give Clyde a hug and kiss on his cheek as he wiped his red and swollen eyes. My hug from Wesley feels so good that I have a hard time letting him go. Knowing that, he holds me tight and softly caresses my back.

"Your grandma would be really proud of you today, Ruby," he says to me, as I notice a little redness in his eyes too.

"Thanks for being here. It must have been hard for you to come today. Is this the first funeral that you've been to since your dad's?"

"Yeah," he nods slowly, "and it was hard, but I'd do anything for you."

"Living without her will be the hardest thing I'll ever have to do, Wes. But I do continue to feel her presence. " I tell him, my voice gravelly and a little hoarse.

"Ruby, you're a huge part of who your grandma was. Whatever you choose to do in life, it will all be done through her, so you're never going to live without her. She will be with you every day, and with every decision that you make. Ruby, you told me once that she has taught you the most things in life. This summer she may have taught you about grief and loss, but she also taught you how to be brave. You'll feel her next when your heart starts to heal and then starts to revive itself. And every day, everyone who knows you will get to see her. Someday when you have children...they'll see her."

"Re-creation. Just like the man in the ugly plaid suit told you at your dad's funeral," I tell him.

"Yeah, re-creation," he smiles.

Wesley holds me close. His hands hug my waist as we stare down at Grandma Dotti's grave and listen to everyone's last final sentiments to her.

"Goodbye, Dotti. Rest in Peace."

"I love you, Dot."

"Always and forever in my heart, Dotti."

"I'll never forget you, my beautiful friend."

I give them all a half-hearted smile and whisper to myself, "I already miss you, Grandma."

As I stand there and cry heavier and thicker tears, I realize that not only could I not say goodbye to her, but she couldn't say goodbye to me either. I guess she also knew there was no reason to ever say goodbye to someone who will never leave you.

Wesley gives me a kiss on my salty cheek, and I smile for the first time that day, as we walk back to my mom's car. Ian wanted to be the last one to leave the cemetery so he, Patty and R.J. stay behind. I make Wesley ride in the backseat with me on the way back to my house, and I rest my weary head on his tear-stained shoulder.

Even though there is already a lot of food at our house when we got home, neighbors continue to bring more throughout the day. Mom somehow finds room for everything on the picnic table in the backyard.

My stomach growls as I stand over some chocolate caramel cake, a giant antipasto salad, and some very cheesy-looking lasagna. I m not really interested in eating, but Wesley makes us each a plate, and we sit down to eat it.

We share some really good meatballs and some bitter grape drink. He even makes me laugh about how sour it is. We watch my back door swing open and closed as people continuously walk in and out of our house, dropping off envelopes to my mom.

We listen as Uncle Nash and Uncle Levi tell stories about Grandma Dotti, which makes everyone laugh, but makes my heart ache. I find it too hard to listen to them, so I move to the other side of the yard.

It was good to hear Mom and Ian laugh, I guess.

Wesley and I hold hands as we walk around the yard. I quietly sing to myself, a song that has been in my head all day - *Misty Blue*, by Dorothy Moore. I sing it over and over again.

I introduce Wesley to everyone I know, and they all tell us that we make a cute couple. That makes him smile, which shows off his dimples that I love so much.

Everywhere Wesley and I went in the yard, I couldn't help but see Grandma Dotti. I see her fighting with the clothesline poles when our heavy wet blankets are being pulled to the ground. I can see her with her big shovel turning over the dirt in the spring to get ready to plant our seedlings. I see her watering the flowers that takeover the yard every summer, and I see her with her garden shears cutting flowers into bouquets that sit all around our house.

"The tomatoes...I have to pick them. There's so many," I say rearranging the weighty vines.

"Maybe you can teach me how to can those tomatoes," Wesley says. "That way I can make you some pizza."

I smile, "I will. I definitely will."

We walk around to the front of the house, and I pull on some spindly flowers that brush up against me. I tuck them into the pocket of Wesley's shirt, and we kiss. We sit on the front porch step, and I see Grandma Dotti once again.

I see her standing at the end of the driveway waiting for me to turn the corner from school. I see her face in the living room window as she laughs at the snowman I made for her. I smile as I see her race-walk to catch up to the fruit and vegetable truck that she waited all day for yet, somehow, it passed her by.

This morning, when I dried a few breakfast dishes, I dried them with a towel that she had embroidered. Mom doesn't know yet, but I took four of them and hid them in a box in my bedroom closet. That way, I will have them wherever I go in life - College, an apartment of my own, or a house with maybe a husband and children. My heart will always miss her, but everywhere in my life, I will see her. And I won't let that ever change.

Keeping great people living in your heart, and cherished memories alive, is sometimes a lot of work. Life forces you to change, and there will always be people coming in and out of your life. But it is always worth it because this world evolves from that, and I won't let "The great Dotti McAuley" ever leave this earth.

Mom interrupted my thoughts. "Ruby, I want you to meet one of your cousins. You are both the same age and both love music. Her name is Karen."

Karen smiled a warm and loving smile. One that told me we were instant friends.

"Hi Ruby," she says, "I wanted to tell you that your grandma crocheted me a sweater years ago. I was going to wear it today, but it doesn't fit me anymore. I love it so much that I'm going to save it if I have a little girl someday."

Hearing that warmed my heart. Karen and I exchange phone numbers, and aside from being cousins, I just know she'll become one of my very best friends. Re-creation once again.

Mom has stayed close to Reed today. It reminds me of my important commitment to introducing Wesley to Reed. I don't want to surprise-attack Wesley, but I stand strong on helping him. I'm going to make it happen because that's what you do in life. You take care of the people you love. Grandma Dotti taught me that too.

That night, before we kiss our final kiss good night, Wesley tells me something that puts a big smile on my face on this very sad day. Something I didn't think I would be able to do today.

"I'm sorry, Ruby. I'm sorry that your heart is broken. Losing someone you love is the hardest part of life, but I will promise you that I'm going to show you the best part of life."

"You've already shown me the best part of life. This summer my heart was breaking apart, and you did so much to keep it filled with love. You made sure I felt love every day, and there is nothing more beautiful than that. The best part of life is love, and it never left my heart for one second because of you. Thank you, Wes. I will always love you. I will always love us."

# TELL ME (YOU'RE COMING BACK)
♥♥♥♥♥♥♥♥♥♥♥♥♥♥♥♥♥♥♥♥♥♥♥♥♥♥♥♥♥♥♥♥♥♥♥♥♥♥♥

The last weeks of summer vacation are always the hardest to get through. It seems like the dreaded "first day of school butterflies" have already begun to gather in your stomach. Anxiety and excitement sit there at the very top of it, twisted in a big heavy knot. You begin to sleep differently as your nervous tension goes into overload. The air and sun feel and smell different, and you're forced to leave behind - what sometimes is- the best times of your life.

These crisp mornings and cool nights remind me that summer, and my days with Wesley, are sadly dwindling away.

After breakfast, I help Mom write out funeral thank-you cards, but it became too emotional for me. I had to excuse myself twice before I just quit all together. So I sat on the front porch swing, by myself, munching on a celery stick and sipping a glass of strawberry lemonade.

For some reason Kentfield was unusually busy today. I smile and wave to everyone who is driving or walking by my house, and they all smile and wave back, but as busy as my street is, I feel empty inside. I sit down on the curb at the end of our driveway and wait for Wesley to get off work.

He got off at 6:00 and he was at my house at 6:10. His hands are full of bags of food, but he immediately grabs my hand, and we start to walk to Stoepel Park. We take our usual spot on the lawn - at the end of the tree-lined tunnel where the grass is the plushest.

I arrange our bucket of chicken, a bag of sugar cookies, and our shared lime slush into the freshly cut grass.

I sit completely still and try to prepare myself for the second round of words that I have dreaded all summer.

"Ruby, I wanted to tell you that I saw my mom the other day, and I talked to her this morning," he said quietly, his eyes fixed on the grass between us.

"That's great," *I meant it.* "How is she?"

"She's a lot better."

"Wes, that's great news." *I meant that too.*

"I'm leaving next Sunday. She's being released from the hospital, and we're going to live with my Uncle Jason back in Toledo until she gets a job. When she gets some money saved, she'll decide on a place for us to live."

I thought I'd burst into tears, but I surprised myself. Instead, I sit there and feel just a little bit more strength and hope fill up inside of me.

"I understand, Wes. Let's take care of your mom first." *I really meant that.*

"I'm so discouraged," he says with his one hand rubbing his forehead. "I've been trying so hard...no one listened to me. Holden and my mom have found what they needed to make them happy, and I supported that. But, I've found what makes me happy, and no one seems to want to let me have it."

"I'll let you have it. I'm not going to stop being your girlfriend. I'll continue to love you here, or 70 miles away. You know, Wes, you can still continue to love someone who's not with you every day. It's one of the many things I learned this summer, and now it's my

310

promise to you. There are a lot of promises made in love, and I've never made one that I didn't keep. My grandma taught me how important that is in life. Wes, make sure your mom is okay first, and the next time we're together, I know we'll be stronger and love even deeper." *That - I meant the most.*

We never get to our leftover chicken or our bag of sugar cookies. We push our lime slush aside and, instead, we lie on the grass with my head on his chest, and his arms wrapped around me tight.

Wesley quits Chicken-N-Joy so we can spend our last week together. Mr. Smith graciously lets him.

"I'm a man in love myself," he told Wesley, "Go be with Ruby."

We try to spend every second of our days together. We box at Keller's gym in the morning and then walk, or sometimes drive all over Detroit. At night, I make Wes, my mom, and Ian, hearty and nutritious dinners with equally hearty and nutritious desserts.

Wesley bought my family a tree to plant in memory of Grandma Dotti, so we plant it deep into the back yard. I hang heart-shaped balloons on the spindly branches and secure the base with all the heart-shaped rocks I could find in the alleys of Detroit.

We make some homemade jam for his mom and mine, and we can a bunch of tomatoes for our future dinners together.

One day we took the bus into the city, and spent the day on the Detroit River and at a Tiger's baseball game. We went Feather Bowling again, and on the way home we stopped at a pet store and Wesley bought me a goldfish to keep me company while he's gone. We named him Funky Claude. Everything we did this week felt good for my heart.

There haven't been any sleepovers this week. Mom has put some stipulations on my nights spent at Bonnie's house. A wise Mom decision, knowing what I know, but Wesley and I still hold each other late into the night, and we push my curfew right to the very second. He kisses my hurt away like he did all summer, and there is still no other place I want to be at night except wrapped in the comfort of his arms.

I still cry myself to sleep every night. Some of my tears are for Wesley, because I already know I'm going to miss him, and some of them are for Grandma Dotti, because I still continue to miss her every second of my day.

Every night, since Grandma Dotti died, I wake up in the middle of an indistinct dream. My eyes are crusted shut from the tears that formed while I slept. I sit up in bed and stare into the pitch black darkness of my room, and gently wipe my eyes so I can see the stillness of the night. My heart is always in too much pain to go back to sleep, but I somehow do.

The house is quieter since Grandma Dotti left, and I collapse into that silence every night. I cry hard. I cry until my stomach hurts.

"Letting go hurts," I tell the walls around me, "and it hurts worse when you're forced to do it."

Labor Day weekend always feels burdensome. It means summer is officially over, snow will fall in a couple of months, and the holidays will rapidly appear in succession. And then a new year which will bring more change.

More change.

Saturday night Bonnie and her family have a barbeque for Wesley. They cook steaks on the grill, roasted corn, potato wedges and fried green peppers. Bonnie makes Wesley his favorite cake - chocolate with cream cheese frosting - and we all "toast" Wesley with big mugs of A&W root beer.

I try to stay positive, as I sit at the barbeque and watch him force a smile around everyone who loves him. I try to smile myself, but when you're mourning as bad as I am, it's next to impossible.

Our dreaded last night together is here. I hide my sadness once more, and try to be strong as I can while I help Wesley pack. I sit down on his bed and fold his tee shirts neatly into his duffel bag, as I watch him gather up everything on the top of his dresser. I want to stay the night tonight, and I know he wants me to, so we try to think of a way that we can, but we come up with nothing short of a lie.

When I stop and think about him leaving, I really can't stand the pain of what the next day will bring. It's just like when Grandma Dotti was sick. It's the same exact feeling.

"I have a gift for you. I made you a tape of all the songs that touched my heart this summer. Hopefully, they will remind you of me. Oh, and I bought you a new flannel shirt, because... well, I stole your other one. This one has a hood attached, so it will keep you a little bit warmer."

I wrote the mushiest love letter, in the history of love letters, and I stuck it in the inside pocket. I know

I'll always love him, so it doesn't matter when he finds it.

"I got you something, too." Wesley says, pulling open the top drawer of his dresser. He takes out a long silver necklace and glides it over my head.

From the necklace hangs a chunky marble heart with two silver letters – an "R" and a "W".
"Thanks...Wes, I love it." I say, breathless.

Later that evening I listen to the quiet ticking of the clock that sits next to Wesley's bed as, I watch him fall asleep. I gave him all the love in my heart tonight, so I fight with myself about whether I should stay wrapped up his arms, and later take my punishment from my mom, or leave to go home to my own bed.

I curl my hands into his chest, and he pulls me closer. His sleepy eyes slowly open, and as I watch him immediately fall back to sleep, I think about the greatest feeling in the world. Love. This very moment feels so comforting to my heart that I don't want it to ever end. The open windows above Wesley's bed send a calm and soothing breeze down my spine. The strength and comfort of Wesley's arms make me feel secure, content and at peace. It feels medicinal.

As much as I realize that the death of someone you love so incredibly much is something that you never get over, I'm reminded that the only remedy for that broken love is more love.

Whether you fall in love with baseball, marshmallows, a 1964 GTO, a painting by Vincent van Gogh, or the cute boy who lives in the house behind you, you have to lean on love in life's most painful times. This summer, music also let me feel love. I felt it even though I was drowning in the pain of heartbreak, and I know it will continue to shape me and guide me into my adult years.

I don't want this night to ever end, and I don't want tomorrow to come, but all summer I was reminded that this is something I just can't avoid.

I want to whisper to Wesley, *"Come back to me, Wes. Do whatever you have to do, and then tell me you're coming back to me."*

But I can't. I have to let him go. I have to give up another piece of my heart. It's always the chance you take with love.

I wiggle out of his tight grip and quietly slip out of Wesley's bed without waking him. I look at his tattoo which now looks more beautiful to me than ever. Everlasting Love. I understand that more than ever now. I'm sure when some people grow older, they may regret their tattoo choice, but I doubt Wesley Everett will, or ever should.

I slip my t-shirt over my head and step into my shorts. I take a piece of paper from my sling bag, and write Wesley a note.

*Wes,*

*I'll always remember the impact this summer had on my heart. I'll remember all the tears I cried, and all the pain I felt. But mostly, I'll remember the love that reigned in my heart through it all. As I realize that saying goodbye is not something that I can do, I also realize how very lucky that makes me. I'm lucky that I have so much love in my life that makes saying goodbye so hard. I'm lucky that I had a grandma that loved me as much as she did. I'm lucky that you came into my life and loved me as much as you have. And I'm lucky that I know I have had the truest of love embedded into my heart. The kind of love that won't fade away, it won't die; it stays strong and committed, and will forever remain a part of who I am.*

*Thank you for loving me in my darkest hour. I will always love you for that, and so much more.*

*Ruby Tuesday*

I place the note on his dresser, tiptoe out of his room, and quietly shut his door behind me.

I walk softly, but swiftly down the stairs, through the kitchen, and out the back door before Wesley has the chance to notice I am gone.

I hop the fence into my yard, quietly slip through the back door, and then sneak down the hallway to my bedroom.

I never fall asleep. I snuggle in between my cotton sheets and my heavy polyester blanket and listened to the crickets outside my window.

The morning sky is beautiful. I watch the sun slowly

316

rise above the trees. It is marbled purple, one of the prettiest skies I have ever seen. Detroit is surprisingly serene this Sunday morning, so I lie still on my bed and listen to the typical sounds of a Sunday morning in Detroit. I listened to the family of robins chirping on the ruby colored rosebush outside my window. A dog barking loudly at a distance distracts me for a minute, but the sound of our paperboy, Leonard, propelling the extra plump Sunday newspaper on to our front porch pulls me away. I watch the neighbors across the street pile into their paneled station wagon and leave for church.

When I hear my mom sauntering down the stairs and into the kitchen, I sit up on the edge of my bed.

It isn't until I smell the wonderful scent of bacon and eggs, from the Hardy's house moving through the open windows of my house, that I join my mom in the kitchen.

"Mom, I think I'll go to the library today," I tell her as I watch her pour a small pile of sugar into her light beige coffee. "I haven't been all summer. I saw Mrs. Mulroney the other day, and she asked me where I've been. I've missed going up there."

"Sure, but do you need anything for school? I see that you went over your schedule. Maybe when you get back we'll go get you a couple new outfits, maybe a new sweater, and a new pair of shoes. You really need a new sweater, Ruby. The one you wore to the hospital everyday is too small."

"Sure, I guess we can do that, but I really don't want a new sweater."

"Ruby, sit down."

"Okay," I say quietly, as I slide back the yellow vinyl kitchen chair and slowly sit sideways in it.

"I was going through Grandma's hospital bag. I forgot the nurses had given it to us, but anyway, I found this."

She pulls from the pocket of her pale green robe a small tattered envelope. I recognize Grandma Dotti's handwriting on the front of the envelope immediately.

"You don't have to read it right now." she says, her eyes filling with tears.

I slowly take it from her. I stare at Grandma Dotti's writing on the envelope.

*Ruby*

I usually devour my favorite breakfast cereal of Quisp, but this morning it takes me a lot longer to eat it.

After I take my bowl of cereal to the sink, I pick up my envelope from the table, and slowly walk back to my bedroom. I sit on my bed and stare emotionless at the floor for twenty-five minutes.

I gather all my hair into a ponytail and secure it tightly with a black silk ribbon. I pull a black terry cloth halter dress over my head and ignore the pieces of hair that fall in my face. I simultaneously slip my multi-gray sandals onto my feet and then stroll back into the kitchen. I toss an orange, a breadstick and a small jar of liquid bubbles into my sling bag, and they all land on top of the letter from Grandma Dotti.

I walk fast out the front door, and then I gradually slow down.

I don't go to the library. I really had no intention of

going there. Instead, I walk to the corner and waited for the Fenkell bus. It arrives in seven minutes and it takes me to the very edge of the city.

When I get off, I immediately take off my sandals and walk the remaining five miles to the cemetery to visit Grandma Dotti and Grandpa Kip.

It was a quiet walk. I was alone for most of it, with very few of the Fenkell businesses open. I got tired around the four-mile mark, but persevered. And as cloudy as my brain was the day of the funeral, when I walk through the stone archway of the cemetery, I found Grandma Dotti's resting spot right away. It was exceedingly peaceful - no cars or people anywhere in sight, which made me think that I was the only one there.

"Hi, Grandpa Kip. Grandma...Dotti," my voice breaks.

I sit down between Grandpa Kip and the freshly dug dirt that covers Grandma Dotti. I reach into my bag and pull out my orange. I immediately stick my thumb nail into its skin and start to peel off its layer.

"You know, Grandma, your favorite weatherman is retiring, which I find ironic now that his number one fan...is gone."

I rearrange the dirt with my feet. "Also, they canceled *The Gong Show*."

I tell her all about the classes I got for tenth-grade and how I'm nervous for physics, but she would be happy that I got French for language class.

"I know you think that it's such a beautiful language."

"All my *Rona Barrett* magazines are starting to pile

up at home because I just can't seem to read them just yet." Mad at myself, I'm thinking I should have brought some here today to read to her. "Next time I come, I'll bring 'em with me," I promise her.

My eyes fill with tears as I bite into a juicy orange slice.

"My heart brought me here today because it's still connected to you. I still need you."

I gather my orange peels into a pile for the squirrels that live nearby. I take out the bottle of liquid bubbles, remove the wand inside, and blow bubbles into the air.

"I remember you told me it's okay to be emotional and cry through the good and bad parts of life, and really, that's all I did this summer," I tell her as I continue to blow bubbles. "I cried every day, all different kinds of tears. I really doubt that they will ever stop. I already know that I'll be a grown woman and I'll think about you, and... I'll cry because I know...I'll still miss you."

I reach into my sling bag and pull out her letter. I rearrange her wilted flowers, and my bare feet flatten out the dirt that covers her. I look up at the cloudless morning sky.

"Wesley is leaving today. He's going home to be with his mom. She's better. And that's good. You know, I couldn't say goodbye to him either. It's because, like you, I know he will always remain in my heart."

I poke my right index finger into the back of the sealed envelope and cautiously tear open Grandma Dotti's letter. I slide it out and slowly unfold it.

Ruby,

In life, your heart fills up with everything you love the most. When your life is over, the most important thing is all that your heart is made of. You, Ruby, have always had a permanent spot in the very middle of it. Thank you for the greatest gift in life - your love.

I know your heart is hurting, but remember - most people are afraid to die, but more are afraid to live. Live Ruby, Live your life in happiness, not in sadness, because that is what I have always wanted the most for you.

Life will continue to hurt you, and when it does, place you hand over your heart, feel it beating, and remember all that you have. I will be there, tucked inside, beating with you.

You are forever loved, Grandma Dotti

I place my hand over my heart and feel it beat.
"I will be happy. For you. I will do that for you. Living without you in my life will be the hardest thing... I'll ever have to do, and...I don't know how to do it... but...I know that in everything you have taught me, the answer has to be there somewhere."

It's a little before 1:00 when I dust myself off, blow a

kiss to Grandma Dotti and Grandpa Kip and start my walk to catch the Fenkell bus home.

I walk down Fenkell and I think about Wesley. I'm sure he's left by now. I start to sing to myself, The Supremes' *Come See About Me* and just like Diana Ross says, come back or not, I'm gonna love you anyway.

I'm sleepy when I step off the bus at the corner of Fenkell and Kentfield. My night of no sleep has finally hit every part of my body. My eyes are so heavy, that I fight to keep them open. My saunter down my street resembles Louie, the neighborhood drunk. As I force myself up the three porch steps into my house, I am barely able to swing open the screen door. I'm exhausted and have immediate plans to take a nap in my unmade bed, but Mom and Ian look up from their bowl of scotch broth soup as the screen door slams behind me.

"Did you see Wesley?" Mom asks right away.

My heart sinks to the bottom of my stomach. "No. Why?"

"He was here, and then at the library looking for you. A couple of times. I thought you'd run into him," my mom says, looking confused.

"I guess... I missed him."

*I don't have to look at the kitchen clock. I know he's long gone.*

"Ruby, are you okay?"

"Yeah, I'm fine, Mom. Just really tired."

I know my mom likes to give me the, "I used to be a teenage girl once" story, and most of the time I love and need her advice, but not now. I feel horrible inside, and I don't really think that my mom loved

322

somebody this much, at my age, as much as I love Wesley.

"After Ian and I finish up here, we'll go to Livonia Mall. There are a lot of Back-to-School sales, okay?"

"Sure. I'll be in the back yard until then," I tell her, as I grab my usual backyard supplies - radio, a pen and notebook, and an apple, as I head out the backdoor.

My head is down, looking at my neglected toenails, as my brain repetitively tells me to *not* look in the direction of Bonnie's house. But, of course, I immediately do.

Bonnie's house is still. There are no cars in the driveway, the back entry door is shut (which I've hardly ever seen before), and it's quiet. Unusually quiet.

He's gone.

I irritably drop my things on the ground and ignore my apple as it rolls away. I wiggle myself into my usual spot under the sycamore tree, but today it seems very uncomfortable. A piece of bark protruding from the tree softly stabs my lower back. My hair gets instantly tangled into another piece, and I immediately fight with it. As I pull away, my eyes catch a carving on the stump.

I smile and gently rub the perfect heart that Wesley had carved into the tree. I turn my radio up to listen to the perfect song, at the perfect time - *Everlasting Love.*

This summer I kept thinking that I would eventually run out of tears. That at some point, I wouldn't have any left, and my body would physically not be able to produce them. But once again, tears fill my eyes and fall onto my lap.

I sing along with Carl Carlton and cry heavily into my hands. My grandma and Wesley left me when I needed them the most, but I know that there will never be a day that I will be denied the feeling of love, because the love that we shared - is everlasting.

I look over to Bonnie's house. I look up to the room that Wesley and I spent many nights this summer, and as I watch a butterfly flutter its delicate wings and sit beside me, I bite my lip and smile.

I don't know if, and when, Wesley will come back. Maybe he'll be back tomorrow, maybe tonight, maybe Tuesday morning for the first day of school, maybe not for a couple of weeks, or maybe not for a couple of months. Maybe he won't be back until next summer. Maybe I'll never see him again. Maybe he, and all his good intentions, will fade away, and he will, unintentionally, break his promise that he once thought he'd keep. That happens all the time in love.

I don't know. I'm not certain, but I am certain that I have to hold on to hope. Because everything attached to your heart should be connected to hope, which is something else my grandma taught me.

I start to scribble some notes down, and I think about all the things that I learned this summer - things that no "summer goal list" could ever prepare me for. Really nothing in this world could prepare me for what life had in store for me the summer of 1978. My average teenage goals turned out to be adverse challenges that just about threw me into adulthood.

This summer my heart found an extraordinary love, but it also lost an extraordinary love. I learned that love makes you feel a lot of things. Irresponsible, trustworthy and devoted. Weak, strong and beautiful. Anguished, impatient and secure. Courageous, euphoric and dangerous.

No circumstance, or age, ever mattered to Wesley and me. We fell into genuine and sincere love right when we both needed to, so that can never be wrong.

I think most people disregard young love and label it as immature, but this summer was the most mature I've ever felt.

I also learned this summer that love will pull you through anything, because it is always there inside of you. Out of all the things Wesley taught me - boxing, poker, basketball - love will always be the most crucial one.

My old clothes don't seem to fit me anymore, and I feel completely different inside. And even though I endured two months of watching my grandma die, and two months of feeling a sweet and innocent love grow inside me, I grew up overnight. Sometimes you grow up slowly, and sometimes you grow up fast, but both have lessons attached.

In these last two months my heart did what all healthy hearts do. It got hurt by love, and saved by love. I learned that you just have to keep your heart open. My heart was open, I lived insightfully this summer, and I grew through the pain. I grew this summer more than I set out to do.

The memories of the people in my life are like the songs I have in my heart. No matter how long it's been since I've seen the person, or have heard the song, they will mentally take me back to the best part of my life - which is the best thing for my heart.

Every song that I sang this summer will now sound different to me. They will take me back to my house, Bonnie's house, Newsted Hospital, Stoepel Park or even Harding Middle School. At first I'll feel sad, and then I will feel happy, knowing that love surrounded me in all of them.

Trying my best to say goodbye to my friends at graduation just two months ago, to a school that educated and sheltered me, to Grandma Dotti, and to Wesley, were not only life-altering changes, but incredible and frightening changes. Grandma Dotti's was frightening, Wesley's was incredible.

"Ruby! Ready to go?" Mom calls out from behind the screen door.

I dab my face with my palm and look down at my piece of tattered paper that consists of just two purple doodle hearts. Two hearts that tell me exactly what I should write about. Love.

Grandma Dotti once told me that the very best thing to write about is love, and everyone has a story to tell about it. This summer I lived two love stories at the same time, and my heart took a lot of notes. I will tell my story not by writing songs, but by writing a book.

The love Wesley and I shared this summer is crucial to a love story about heartbreak, because I now know that true love is the only thing that can heal a heart that seems too broken to fix. And my grandma, well, she deserves a book written about her. Her beautiful heart, and her beautiful life, should not go unnoticed.

First I need a title. Hmmm, what should it be?

## A NOTE FROM ME, WITH LOVE

A very special thank you to my family and friends for their unwavering support. My Dad, Fran, Cheryl, Eve, Karen, Tom, Jade, Sage, Kenny, and Joe. Thanks for believing in me and letting me hide from the world and do my thing ♥

Thank you to The Lapeer, North Branch, and all Detroit Public Libraries (especially the Burt Road and Fenkell branch) for being such a huge part of my life ♥

Love and gratitude to my Grandpa Henry who told me to write my story. I did it for you and grandma. And to my favorite uncle, Dick O'Connor, who never, ever, doubted that I couldn't do anything I really wanted to do. I just wish you were all here to see all I've done ♥

The biggest and sincerest thanks to all that truly made this book possible. Christina DeBusk, Jade Strayhorn, Diane Haber, Kendall Strayhorn, Caleb Reamer, Yasmin Ladha and Sage Strayhorn. Thank you, from the bottom of my heart, for taking the time to help me put the final touches on my biggest dream. You helped make it come true, and I'm forever grateful ♥

♥ I love you all ♥

There is no such thing as too much love in your heart, so overuse the word love and love who your heart tells you to love...and always listen to The Rolling Stones.

327

Made in the USA
Lexington, KY
27 August 2019